LOST
SONS

LOST SONS

JUDY CLEMENS

Herald Press
Scottdale, Pennsylvania
Waterloo, Ontario

Library of Congress Cataloging-in-Publication Data

Clemens, Judy.
  Lost sons / Judy Clemens.
    p. cm.
  ISBN-13: 978-0-8361-9429-6 (pbk. : alk. paper)
  1. Fathers and sons—Fiction. I. Title.
  PS3603.L4579L67 2008
  813'.6—dc22

                                                    2007049465

Except where noted, Bible text is from the *New Revised Standard Version Bible*, Copyright © 1989, by the Division of Christian Education of the National Council of the Churches of Christ in the USA, and is used by permission. *The King James (Authorized) Version of the Holy Bible* is also briefly quoted.

Quotes from *When Apples Are Ripe* are Copyright © 1971 by Herald Press, Scottdale, Pa., and are used by permission.

The quotation from *The Mennonite Encyclopedia* is Copyright © 1957 by Mennonite Publishing House, Scottdale, Pa., and is used by permission.

LOST SONS
Copyright © 2008 by Herald Press, Scottdale, Pa. 15683
  Published simultaneously in Canada by Herald Press,
  Waterloo, Ont. N2L 6H7. All rights reserved
Library of Congress Catalog Card Number: 2007049465
International Standard Book Number: 978-0-8361-9429-6
Printed in the United States of America
Book design by Joshua Byler
Cover by Greg Yoder

13 12 11 10 09 08   10 9 8 7 6 5 4 3 2 1

To order or request information please call 1-800-245-7894
or visit www.heraldpress.com.

For all who strive to do God's will.

PREFACE

A good life is spent building bridges.

Growing up Mennonite and a pacifist, I knew few—if any—military people. I spent my formative years in Mennonite communities, except for my elementary school, where I was the weird kid who "didn't believe in war," kept quiet during the Pledge of Allegiance, and never sang the national anthem.

Fast-forward about thirty years to 2005, when Marilyn Borgman contacted me to say that her book club was reading my first mystery novel, *Till the Cows Come Home*. She invited me to join the group for the evening, and I did, making the six-hour trip to Fox Lake, Illinois, where she and her husband, Jim, welcomed me into their home. We immediately formed a friendship built on mutual respect, love for our families, and the desire to do God's will. The funny thing is, Jim Borgman is not "just" Jim Borgman. He is also Senior Chief Petty Officer Jimmie J. Borgman, United States Naval Reserve (Retired). Through our continuing friendship and the Borgmans sharing the details of their military life—including a tour of Naval

Station Great Lakes—I came to have a deeper understanding of those who give their lives in service to our country. I thank the Borgmans for their love, friendship, and the time they have given to this book.

Adjutant Joseph Brown of the Goshen Police Department has given me many hours of tours, conversations, emails, and manuscript critiquing. He has been an invaluable source for delving into the mind of a police officer, and he has helped me to see at least a portion of what that life is like. A lot of Stan Windemere's experiences come from anecdotes Joe shared with me. Joe's wife, Debra, also read the manuscript with enthusiasm, and I thank her.

Many others have helped in the creation of *Lost Sons*, and the book wouldn't have been possible without them. I thank Sylvia Miller, Clayton Kratz's great-niece, and her husband, Virgil, for reading the manuscript and giving it their blessing. I also thank Pat Frazier, Jennifer Rupp, and Stanley Kropf of Mennonite Central Committee (MCC) Great Lakes; Kristal Hepner of MCC Canada, Winnipeg; Leora Gerber, who shared information about Daniel Gerber, a missing MCC volunteer; Lorraine Bartlett and Sharon Wildwind, fellow authors who read and critiqued the manuscript; Jeanette Weaver and Raul Tadeo for help with Spanish translations; John L. Ruth, Mennonite historian; Jim Harder, for permission to use excerpts from *When Apples Are Ripe*, written by his mother, Geraldine Gross Harder; John R. Smucker, my father-in-law, for reminding me of the Clayton Kratz story and loaning me the Goshen College yearbooks that put me on the track of research; Philip and Nancy Clemens, my parents, for a first-draft reading of the manuscript (and all their support); and Steve, Tristan, and Sophia, for allowing me the time to steal away to my office to write.

And a special thanks to Dennis Stoesz of the Mennonite Church USA Archives; Paul Toews, Mennonite historian;

and Jim Smucker, friend of Edith Miller, for agreeing to be characters in the book. Your information and helpfulness is greatly appreciated.

—Judy Clemens

I feel it my duty and privilege to help
the suffering, because this great world catastrophe
has not caused me any inconvenience.
—Clayton Kratz, when asked why he was applying
to join the Mennonite Relief Commission for War
Sufferers, August 1920

Religion that is pure and undefiled before God, the Father,
is this: to care for orphans and widows in their distress,
and to keep oneself unstained by the world.
—James 1:27

Those who love me, I will deliver;
I will protect those who know my name.
When they call to me, I will answer them;
I will be with them in trouble,
I will rescue them and honor them.
With long life I will satisfy them,
and show them my salvation.
—Psalm 91:14-16

All he could think about was the cold. So cold. He tucked his hands into his armpits and tried to ignore the stinging of his toes inside his boots. At least his feet still had feeling. He burrowed further into the straw, as deep as he could go before his legs met the wooden planks beneath him.

The horses pulling the cart lunged forward, smacking his head against the back rail. He closed his eyes, dizziness clouding his head and sending his stomach roiling.

Hands were on him now, pushing him forward, tossing a coat around his shoulders. He squinted up into the eyes of a man trotting alongside the cart.

"Are you all right?" the man asked.

"Yes," he said. "I am."

The cart pulled away, leaving the coat-giver and everything familiar behind.

Chapter 1
MONDAY

"Today I meet the Mennonites," Stan Windemere said.

His wife held her fork mid-air, syrup dripping back onto her pancake.

"It's for that job. You know. The security guard position."

Rose laid her fork carefully on her plate. "I don't know why you want to work for those people. They hate Jamie. They think what he's doing is evil."

"They don't even know Jamie."

"But they're pacifists." As if that explained everything.

Stan sighed and rubbed his forehead before looking at his wife. "It's only for a couple of weeks. I'll be working at night. I won't even see most of the people. I'll be in and out, and no one will know the difference."

She had no response, except to pick up her napkin and dab at the corners of her mouth.

"We can use the money."

But that wasn't it. Not really. It was the job itself Stan needed. Something to do. Something to keep him from thinking.

Rose stacked her silverware on top of her half-eaten breakfast and took it over to the sink, where she carefully rinsed her plate. Stan watched as she opened the door to the dishwasher and gently placed the plate in the rack, easing her silverware—one piece at a time—into the little bin. No clashing of metal against metal for his Rose.

"You shouldn't go," she said.

But Stan went anyway.

$\sim$

As Stan negotiated the numbered streets of Goshen, Indiana, the little burg where he and Rose had grown up, married, and raised their children, he tried not to think. Instead, he paid close attention to the shapes of the budding trees, the *thump, thump, thump* of the bricks that made up Fifth Street, and the children out at recess in the playground of Chandler Elementary.

But that brought memories of Jamie.

More distractions. The beauty of the city's courthouse, its tan bricks newly power washed. The bank that had so recently been burglarized, the director stolen from his home to let the robbers into the vault. The cedar-sided house on the corner by the stoplight. . . .

Now the thoughts came rushing in. Attacking. Jamie, fourteen years old. His principal, Mr. Albert, calling Stan at work, demanding that Stan come to school *immediately* to deal with a discipline problem.

"I can't drop everything and run to your office," Stan had told him. "I'm in the middle of my shift, on the way to a car accident on thirty-three. Whatever your issue is will have to wait."

No use in calling Rose. She would've flown to the school, clucking over Jamie like a mother hen. Only this hen had teeth, ready to be bared at anyone threatening her chick.

Finally, at the end of the day, coming home to Jamie's

sheepish expression. Being told over mashed potatoes and pot roast that Jamie had joined his friends in vandalizing the principal's home over the weekend.

"It wasn't vandalism, Dad," Jamie said.

"Well, thank goodness for that. What would you call it, exactly?"

Jamie wiggled in his chair. "We were just having fun."

"And to have fun one needs eggs, soap, and toilet paper?"

Andrea, Jamie's little sister, who would've been eight at the time, giggled, and Stan shot her a warning look.

"It was just . . ." Jamie bit a thumbnail. "We knew he was gone. Memorial Day, right? So we thought—"

"You *thought*? I am absolutely astounded to hear that. To imagine you thought and *still* decided this was a good idea."

Jamie's head dipped. "I'm sorry, Dad."

"I expect so. I also expect you've heard what happened over the weekend? With the things you decided to leave at Mr. Albert's house?"

Jamie's face screwed up with confusion. "What? They wouldn't tell me anything at school."

"I was told plenty when I stopped by the office this afternoon to talk with your principal. Seems while he was traveling, his Sunday school took care of cleaning up the property. It also seems that soap and eggs don't do anything good for cedar siding."

Jamie paled.

"I offered to have you restain the siding, seeing how you've done some painting here at home, but Mr. Albert doesn't want you touching his house. Can't imagine why. Mr. Albert also said he won't be calling the police about this—although bringing me into it kind of constitutes that—if you pay damages. I figure you have enough in your savings account to cover it."

"But, Dad, I wasn't the only one."

"You'll be paying your share. The others will pay theirs."

Jamie sat back in his chair and let out a sigh of relief. "So that's it, then?"

Stan laughed. "You'd like that, wouldn't you? Unfortunately, I have other plans." He handed his son a sheet of paper.

"Here are the addresses of all of the people who cleaned up Mr. Albert's house. You will go apologize to all of them. Tonight."

Jamie glanced at Stan's plate, still full of food. "After you're done?"

Stan raised his eyebrows. "Oh, I'm not taking you. You're riding your bike."

"But these houses are all over town! I'll never make it before dark!"

Stan picked up his fork and knife. "Well, then, I guess you'd better get going."

And Jamie went.

He really had made it to each house before dark, and the next day neither of them said a word about it. Mr. Albert had never been keen on Jamie after that, but that was all right. Jamie had stayed out of trouble the rest of his high school career.

Stan had thought the Navy would keep him out of trouble once he'd left high school and the attempt at college. Jamie had always wanted to join. Get out in the world. Make a difference.

It hadn't exactly turned out that way.

The bumps as Stan drove over the railroad tracks brought him back to the present, to the Old Bag Factory, where local artisans and other creative folks had set up shop. An adjoining building, The Depot—named this, of course, as it was one of the town's old train stations—housed several non-profits, including the Mennonite Central Committee office. Stan pulled into a parking spot.

A few cars down, a group of Hispanic teenagers lounged around a Grand Am. They were Mexican, probably. Lots of

Spanish-speaking folks in Goshen. These guys were young. Maybe out of school. Maybe playing hooky. Didn't look like trouble, but you never know. As Stan stepped out onto the sidewalk, their conversation stopped. He nodded to them, raising his hand. They checked him out, hands in pockets as they leaned against their car.

One of them smiled, elbowing his friend. "*Hey, mire ese viejo hechandonos una mirada.*"

His friend waved him off. "*Él no es viejo. Gringo justo.*"

"*Espere.*" The first one stepped away from the car, squinting toward Stan. "*¿No es ese el policia que aresto a David?*"

All four boys turned to look at him with renewed interest. "*Pienso que usted tiene razón,*" one said. "*¡Si es! ¿Qué esta haciendo el aqui?*"

"*Comprando algunos regalos para su vieja en la tienda de descuentos.*"

Three of the four found this discussion hilarious. Stan couldn't understand anything except the words *policia*, meaning cop, *gringo*, and the name David, so he didn't know if he'd find it funny or not. He assumed not.

The fourth guy, standing against the car, his arms crossed, gave a little smile, but didn't put energy into actual laughter. His eyes met Stan's, and he returned Stan's nod with a subtle tilt of his chin.

Pushing open the door of the building, Stan left them behind.

Inside The Depot, Stan paused to look around. He'd never been called to this place, so it was all new to him. By the time the businesses had moved in, he'd changed out of police uniform to his plain clothes, which meant no routine calls or stops at local merchants. He was strictly an emergency man, meeting people only when the worst had happened.

To his right was something called The Whistle Stop. Looked like a thrift store of some kind. And to his left The Switch Yard, the same sort of shop, only for larger merchandise—washers, dryers, and such. He walked past a few other storefronts— Choice Books, Ten Thousand Villages, Africa Inter-Mennonite Mission—and found himself at the doorway of Mennonite Central Committee, Great Lakes. It didn't look like a place where he'd find hatred, as Rose had predicted. Rather, it looked bright and cheerful and friendly. He stepped in.

"Good morning." The receptionist gave him a brilliant smile. "May I help you?"

She looked about thirteen, but Stan supposed that was her wholesome, milk-fed appearance. He assumed she was at least eighteen if she was working a desk. The nameplate said Sheila Yoder.

"Name's Stan Windemere. I have an appointment with someone this morning. About the security job?"

"Of course. Mr. Brenneman is on a conference call right now, but he should be ready in a minute. Please make yourself at home here in the waiting area."

Stan glanced at the surroundings. Decorated eggs in a glass case, children's books and cookbooks on a stand, a quote painted on the wall in big letters, proclaiming, "If you want to go fast, go alone. If you want to go far, go together." An African proverb, it said. And an entire wall covered with a map of the world.

"Thanks," Stan told the girl.

She kept smiling. "I'm Sheila. The receptionist, if you haven't guessed." Her laugh was light and high, like the wind chimes Stan had hung on his back porch. Rose hadn't really wanted them there, had complained about the noise, but he'd done it anyway. She'd let it go.

"You're welcome to have a seat on our sofa over there," Sheila said. "Or browse through our displays."

The phone rang.

"Excuse me." Sheila picked up the receiver. "Good morning, Mennonite Central Committee, Great Lakes." Her face lit up. "*Señor Ramos! El número que usted me dio para Sr. Gonzalez era corecto. Muchas gracias. Fue de mucha ayuda.*"

Stan stared at her. Was she speaking *Spanish?* He thought Mennonites spoke German. Or that Pennsylvania Dutch used by the Amish folks with the coverings and dark blue pants. Those Mexican kids in the parking lot—they were the ones who were supposed to speak Spanish.

"Mr. Windemere?"

Stan looked away from Sheila the Spanish-speaker to see a man, about his age, mid-forties or so, standing beside him with his hand out.

"Jerry Brenneman," the man said. "Thanks for coming."

Stan nodded.

"Sheila introducing the place to you?"

"A bit."

"Good, good. I suppose you figured out this is the welcoming area. You saw our books, our display case here." He indicated the stand. "This has the brochures, which explain our projects around the world."

Stan looked, but kept his hands at his sides. Lots of pamphlets, calendars, bookmarks. Pictures of people with all shades of skin, from the darkest of what he assumed was Africa, to the white of any Caucasian. Children. Adults. Groups. Individuals.

Jerry took a few steps to the side and gestured toward the wall. "This is our world map, which shows where volunteers from the Great Lakes region are working."

Photos of families, smiling broadly, tacked to the wall in their spot of the world. South America, China, Mozambique. There were no photos on the area designating Russia. Stan averted his eyes.

"Over here," Jerry said, "is our work area, copier, fax machine, and such. And also our resource library."

Stan glanced over the shelves of books and videos. DVDs too.

"But this can all wait. Why don't you come on back to my office, and we can talk?"

He led Stan a couple of feet further into a small room, two sides taken up with windows looking out into the greater office. On the other two walls stood shelves filled with papers, books, and prominently displayed photos.

"My family," Jerry said, seeing the direction of Stan's gaze. "My wife, Jenny, and my sons, Chad and Brent. Chad's a senior at Goshen College. Music major. Brent fled the nest and went all the way to Virginia, where he's into computers. Eastern Mennonite University. You have children?"

Stan looked at the man. "Two. One of each. Boy and girl."

Jerry waited expectantly, but Stan was done with family talk. "You have a job for me?"

"We do." Jerry sank into his chair and indicated the cushioned one in front of the desk, where Stan sat. "A security job. I spoke with your chief and he recommended you for the position. I understand you're taking some time off? A sabbatical?"

Something like that. Stan nodded.

"We have a big warehouse," Jerry said. "I'll show you in a minute. We often store large quantities of provisions there, which get sent all over the world. Food, blankets, school supplies. The thrift stores use it, too. In the big picture, not a huge financial investment in materials, but we do our best to keep them safe on our own."

"Something's changed?" But Stan suspected the answer. Or part of it, anyway.

"You know there's been trouble in this part of town. Theft, breaking and entering. We suspect the local gangs have something to do with it, but there's no way to be sure. We've done our best to lock things up, and we really haven't had too much trouble. A few things missing here and there.

"But we have an especially large shipment coming this

week. Tons of supplies meant for the earthquake that struck Pakistan last month. Clothing, food, blankets, toiletries. Five-gallon buckets stuffed with goods." He waved his hand. "After the tsunami in Asia, MCC requested twenty-two thousand relief kits from the churches. We got them all. Plus donations of more than twelve million dollars."

A vision shot through Stan's mind. Photos from *Newsweek* of the tragedy in that country. Wide-eyed children, orphaned, homeless, starving. Brown skin, brown eyes, black hair. All afraid, hungry. But some strangely hopeful.

"Five days ago," Jerry was saying, "another local charity, La Casa, was cleaned out during the night. Everything worth taking and light enough to carry, gone in only a few hours."

Stan grunted. Nodded. He'd heard about the incident, just two days after he'd walked out of the police station, his life altered.

"So we'd like to have a security presence," Jerry continued. "Someone to keep an eye on things, make sure nothing . . . unusual happens. And as I said, your chief thought you might be interested."

Stan glanced again at the man's family photo. His wife, cheerful and composed, his boys happy. Healthy. Safe.

"I might be," Stan said.

Jerry slapped his hands on the arms of his chair. "Great. Let me show you around."

They took a short walk down the hallway, Jerry pointing out desks, cubicles, a kitchenette. More quotes painted on the walls. Artwork with a worldwide flair.

Through a conference room into the warehouse. Ceilings reaching high, space filled with bins of colorful relief kits, baled blankets on flats, white buckets with the MCC's dove logo. A forklift resting quietly in the corner.

Jerry held out his hands. "It's really a multi-use space, as I said. Health kits, thrift-store merchandise, used clothing. Over here are extra supplies to fill in what might be missing in any of the packs sent by church members.

"Our material resource coordinator uses this office." He poked his head into a concrete-walled room. "Guess she's not here right now. She oversees volunteer groups, as well as the organization of the warehouse."

"Has she noticed anything missing? Any broken door locks or other signs of vandalism?"

Jerry gestured toward the far side of the room. "The back door's lock was messed up several days ago. All we could report missing were some canned goods and other food items. We weren't sure how we were going to disperse them, anyway, so we hope they went to someone who could use them. We've had blankets go missing. Clothes sometimes. Once a lamp shaped like a zebra." He smiled. "Like I said, not a lot of great financial value needs protecting here. But with the extra-large shipment we'll be storing, partnered with the increased local crime . . ." He shrugged.

"Hours?" Stan asked.

"We can negotiate. But I was thinking twelve-hour shifts. Seven in the evening to seven a.m. Sundays off. The job will only be for three weeks or so, until the last of the supplies are sent out."

Stan pursed his lips and nodded, his thumb hooked into his belt. "Why not just use an alarm? The cops would be notified if someone broke in."

"We talked about that, and if we can't find someone to take the job, we'll go that route. It's just . . . we prefer a presence here. Someone to be a face for the building, rather than a blinking box on the wall."

Stan nodded. Made sense. Sometimes it was that one person who could make the difference. Make a robbery seem not worth the effort.

"And Sunday nights? What would you do then?"

"We'd find someone. Or take turns. It should only be three Sundays, if things go as planned. We can work that out."

Sounded reasonable. And Stan couldn't work every night. Not if he wanted to stay alert.

Jerry caught his eye. "We will, of course, ask that you leave your gun at home."

Stan's head stopped mid-nod, and he felt automatically for his weapon. The Glock 40 that had become just another part of his body. The weight against his hip. The security it brought.

"I can't do that."

Jerry tilted his chin toward the gun. "And we can't do *that*."

"I've never used it. I've never even taken it out of the holster except to clean or store it."

It was the truth. Real-life police work wasn't like TV, where the young handsome or shapely cops—along with the token grizzled, cynical veterans—were constantly yanking out their guns and pointing them at people. Every real police officer knew that if you took your gun out of its holster you had to fill out a report. And they had way too many of those as it was.

Jerry smiled grimly. "I understand and appreciate that you feel more comfortable with your gun. But we have nothing here that would come close to equaling the value of a human life. We'd rather someone left with everything than be killed in the process."

What about my life? Stan wondered. *Is it worth my life to protect a warehouse full of used furniture and already-worn clothing? Or a stack of plastic-wrapped blankets?*

"I'm sorry, then. I guess we've both wasted our time this morning. Because I won't do a security job without my weapon."

"I'm sorry, too." Jerry held out his hand. "But I appreciate your coming by. I hope you find a job you feel comfortable with until you're ready to go back to the police department."

Stan stared at him. What exactly had the chief told him? What secrets had he spilled to this unyielding pacifist?

"Thank you," Stan said. "I hope you can keep your shipment safe." *And good luck with that.*

Jerry led him back out through the conference room, past the maze of cubicles, the kitchenette and work area. The wall-sized map of the world. The smiling, Spanish-speaking, adolescent-looking receptionist.

"Goodbye, Mr. Windemere," Jerry said.

"Goodbye."

As Stan left the office, his gun securely at his hip, his decision hung over him like a dense cloud of doubt. When he looked back, Jerry Brenneman stood watching him, his face a kind mixture of understanding and disappointment.

Stan turned and walked away.

At least Rose would be happy.

∾

The dam was in fine form, water crashing over the peak, cascading to the rocks and foam below, before rushing down the Elkhart River, on the way to its next destination. Stan walked along the path, hands in his pockets, trying not to think.

He stopped at a bench, a metal one alongside the packed dirt, its legs rusting at the joints. It sat pretty comfortably, he decided. As comfortable as an old metal bench could sit, anyway.

The phone on his belt had been silent. No chimes, no *arabesque*, no vibrations. Not that he was surprised. Only a few people had the number. Rose. Their daughter. The U.S. Navy.

The phone at their house had been overused. Relatives. The media. Neighbors. Church folks. Stan had finally asked them all to stop calling. Stop asking questions. Stop insisting on showing their care by dialing the number. They'd all eventually listened.

Now the phone hardly ever rang. Hardly ever filled their house with its strident tones, making their hearts flutter. His cell phone rang even less. Rang never.

Stan took a deep breath, held it, and let it out, his cheeks expanding with the effort. He watched a man, standing along the other side of the river, casting his fishing line into the water as his face reflected the hope that something would finally bite. That this time, he'd feel the tug. Stan hoped so too, for the man's sake.

Jerry Brenneman had that kind of hope in his eyes. Hope and generosity. None of the hatred Rose had predicted. None of the judgment.

But then, Jerry Brenneman didn't know about Jamie.

Stan remembered standing along that very riverbank with his son, demonstrating the proper way to wind a worm around the hook so it wouldn't squirm off. Jamie had flinched when confronted with the yellowish insides of the night crawler, not having thought about how he'd be hurting the bait, bait he himself had hunted the night before with the red-parchment-paper-covered flashlight.

And he had cried the first time he caught a fish. A tear slid down his cheek at the sight of the hook piercing the side of the fish's mouth. Jamie, Stan's son, claiming the little Sunny's eyes were begging for release. He'd thrown it back, the cool creature unable to escape Jamie's hands soon enough. They'd stayed a while longer, Stan hoping Jamie would come around and enjoy the outing. But he'd never taken to fishing like his sister had. He didn't have the heart.

A young mother pedaled her bike past Stan, pulling a small mesh-and-metal trailer. A child, probably five years old, rode in front of her, Barbie bike flashing with tassels and patches of shiny silver paint. About thirty feet further along they stopped. Parked their bikes. The mother unzipped the trailer and two toddlers tumbled out. Twin boys, it looked like.

All four of the family fresh-faced, cheeks rosy from the morning air.

Stan wondered if they were Mennonite. Easily could be. Goshen was full of them, and he'd been reminded this morning how they look like anybody else. Anybody Lutheran, Catholic, Presbyterian. Non-denominational, even. He allowed himself a quiet chuckle.

The mother pulled a loaf of bread from a separate section of the trailer and handed each child a slice to feed the already encroaching ducks. Shrieking with delight, the toddlers shredded their bread, flinging it toward the birds, who more often than not had to leave the water to waddle up the bank and snatch their prize. The five-year-old tore hers with deliberation, wadding the pieces between her fingers, throwing them to specific members of the flock.

"You go away, nasty bird!" she said firmly. "You let her have it!" Throwing yeasty missiles toward the water.

Rose had never taken the kids to feed bread to the ducks. Waste of good food, she'd said. When asked what use stale bread would be, she'd announced that she never let bread get that old. She bought bread to feed her family. Not the neighborhood fowl.

Stan had taken the kids himself, claiming it would be a simple bike ride, then stopping at the local grocery for a cheap loaf of Wonder Bread. It was their secret. His, Jamie's, and Andrea's. Their Duck Missions, they'd called them. Behind Rose's back. It hadn't hurt her. Although it might if she ever found out. Stan had always figured her protests to be more of principle than actual belief. The idea of feeding fat birds while somewhere little children were starving.

The young mother trotted after one of the twins, who'd seen a pretty duck further down the path. The other stayed with his sister, venturing closer and closer to the water. Stan watched, the older child intent on her feeding of the ducks, the boy focused on nothing but edging nearer to the river.

Stan twitched, alert. He placed his hands on the edge of the bench, ready to propel himself to the water, should the child continue on his path. Three feet he went. Then five.

"Brendan!" the mother called sharply. She hustled back, the other boy horizontal under her arm, complaining, kicking his feet.

The toddler by the water looked up, fear registering on his face.

"Brendan, come away from the water, honey. Right now."

She dumped the other twin unceremoniously beside his sister and took firm strides toward the other. "You stay up here with us, sweetheart. It's okay. No need to cry."

But he did. Tears of grief and anger, brought on by the pull from danger.

"Here," the mother said. "Here's another slice. Tear it up, honey. Go on."

The tears subsided as quickly as they'd begun. A fresh piece of bread, smashed in the sticky fingers, thrown like a baseball into the feathery crowd.

Jamie liked baseball. Liked playing it as a child, but even more when assisting the coach in the local Little League. Stan could still see him, standing behind the boy in center field, that little face filled with apprehension as the ball sailed skyward, then down toward the grass. Jamie helped position the would-be outfielder and held the boy's ten-inch glove steady as the ball smacked into the leather. The fear on the boy's face turned to wonder. And joy.

Jamie had always yearned to change fear to joy.

The supplies in that MCC warehouse would accomplish that. Children with no money would have brand-new crayons and notebooks and rulers. Pink erasers that hadn't seen a spot of lead or been chewed by a classmate. Children, victims of the earthquake, would have blankets and food and clothes to wear.

But those children wouldn't receive the goods if someone here got to them first.

Stan thought about the piles of supplies, the local gangs—Caucasian or Hispanic in make-up—the gun at his hip. He thought about Jerry Brenneman and the friendly front-desk girl—Sheila?—and the quotes on the walls. And he thought about Jamie, his uniform pressed, shoes shining, as he took his leave of home and traveled halfway around the world.

The mother held her depleted bread bag over the river-bank and shook it, crumbs floating downward toward the still-squawking birds. She crumpled the plastic and pushed it into a compartment in the trailer. "Okay, let's go, guys!"

Five minutes later she'd cajoled, pleaded, and demanded, to no avail. The twin boys ignored their mother and alternately examined the ground by the path and ran circles away from the trailer. Their sister, watching with interest, picked up a stone from the sidewalk and dropped it onto the seat of the child-carrier.

"Tommy, look!" And she dropped in another one.

The twins scrambled to examine their prizes, and the mother, wonder and relief washing over her face, jumped to belt them in.

Ah, the wisdom of the young.

Stan watched them go, the daughter pedaling double-time, the boys chattering from their enclosed, protective car. Off to home, lunch, naps. Their lives simple.

Or so Stan thought, anyway.

But then, he knew he thought too much.

∽

"You want to take the job?" Chief Gardener said.

Stan shrugged quickly, a jerk of his shoulders. He looked around the chief's office at the plants, the plaques, the book about forensics. He blinked and his eyes fell on his friend. Roy, the chief of police.

"I want to. I kind of think I need to."

Roy nodded, harrumphed, leaned back in his chair. "You've only been off a week."

Stan blinked slowly. A week. A long, ulcer-inducing week. So many images—

"You think you're ready? You can handle it?"

Stan took a breath through his nose. Let it out. "No deduction would be necessary, Chief. Security only. A presence in the place. No thinking expected." He allowed himself a small smile. Felt his friend studying his face, the new lines, the gray bags under his eyes.

"The gun thing," Roy said. "It's an issue."

"I know. *I know.*" Stan pushed himself off the chair and stood facing the window, hands in his pockets, watching the street outside. Not many cars this time of day. Before lunch. The lull.

"How's Andrea?" Roy asked, his voice piercing the silence. "Heard from her lately?"

"Last week. She called. Said she might come home this weekend. Do her laundry. Sleep in her own bed. I don't know."

Notre Dame wasn't far. An hour, at the most. But it could've been a couple of states over, as much as he and Rose had seen their daughter. During first semester, at least. Freshman year. He'd encouraged her to make her own way. Find herself without their hovering. Rose wanted to hover. Would've hovered, if Andrea hadn't thrown a fit the third time Rose showed up at her dorm room unannounced.

The only times Rose had been back to campus were for Andrea's softball games. And then only to the athletic complex. Nowhere near the residence halls.

"She's a good girl," Roy said.

Stan sighed, jingling the change in his pocket. "Yeah. I know."

They fell silent, each waiting for something. Not sure what. The chief's chair creaked, and he wandered over to stare out the window with Stan, their shoulders almost touching. "Mr. Brenneman thinks it's the gangs," he said. "The ones breaking in places."

Stan nodded.

"You think so?" Roy asked.

"Probably. Who else would it be?"

The chief didn't answer.

"But I can't see gangs wanting to steal that stuff," Stan said. "I mean, what are the Votos Locos or Dirty White Boys going to do with a truckload of towels? Detergent? That's not going to buy them much in the way of drugs. In the way of *any*thing."

Roy didn't reply, keeping his eyes on the building across the street. Or maybe on the silver maple that had now outgrown the municipal building itself.

"I guess it could be regular people who need help," Stan said. "Folks who've lost their jobs because of the immigration laws."

The chief's lips twitched. "Suppose it could be. We've got a lot of them."

A lot of them living in houses meant for four, squeezed in four to a room. Mothers and fathers and in-laws and cousins. Brothers, family friends. Children.

"If it's not the gangs," Stan said, "then the job really isn't that dangerous, is it?"

Gardener didn't bother replying. He knew, just as well as Stan, that a young parent—short on cash, long on protecting the family—was just as dangerous, just as desperate, as a drug-obsessed gangster.

A young officer parked his cruiser across the street, talked to his partner through the open door before slamming it and trotting across the street. Tall, like Jamie. But dark, rather than fair. A few years younger, maybe.

Stan recognized him as a part of the department's Honor Guard, a highly respected group of officers formed after the loss of Thomas Goodwin, their fellow officer, in 1998. This kid Stan was watching was a new member. Smart. Thorough. A graduate of the city's esteemed Honor Guard School.

The military had the same kind of officers. Keeping watch at the Tomb of the Unknown Soldier. Serving at memorials and funerals for former presidents. Military men and women who offered their services to schools, churches, and civil organizations. And, of course, participated in funerals for veterans and dignitaries. And fallen comrades.

Stan yanked his hands from his pockets, ran them through his hair. "I need the job."

The chief nodded. "Yes, my friend. I think you do."

Stan exhaled a gust of frustration. "And the gun?"

Roy turned, looked at his friend. "The Brits do it, don't they? Walk around with nothing more than a smooth, shiny stick. They're supposed to be smart, right? After all, they're the ones who came up with fish and chips."

Stan laughed. Not much, but a little.

It was a start.

⌁

The phone at the MCC office was answered by the cheerful Sheila. Stan hoped she wouldn't break into Spanish.

"Mr. Windemere! Mr. Brenneman's here. Let me put you through."

A quick measure or two of hold music as Stan looked out his back door, watching an orange cat stalk a robin, and Jerry Brenneman was on the line.

"Mr. Windemere?" His voice was friendly. Open.

"Yes. I was wondering if I might still take on the job. I've been thinking."

"Even with our restriction on the gun?"

"Yes. Even with that. I . . . talked it over with a friend. It seems like the thing I should be doing."

"Well, that's wonderful." No hesitation. "How soon would you be willing to start?"

"Tonight."

Jerry laughed. "How about tomorrow? Give us a chance to get the paperwork together. And we still have a day or two before the shipments begin coming in."

"Okay. Tomorrow."

"Five-o'clock okay? Five-thirty? You won't normally need to come that early, but I could give you the run-down on more details. Introduce you around."

"I'll be there. Five-o'clock."

"Super. I'll look forward to seeing you then. And Mr. Windemere? I'm so glad you called back."

"Yes. All right. Goodbye."

Stan hung up the phone. He was glad, too. He hoped he would remain so.

Turning, he stopped short at the sight of Rose in the doorway to the kitchen. She stared at him with wide, wet eyes, her mouth tight.

"Rose . . . "

She shook her head and held up a hand, closing her eyes. She opened them, let her hand drop. And walked back into the house, away from the husband who felt he had betrayed her in some unforgivable way.

≈

Jamie's room hadn't changed much since he went to college. Baseball trophies on the shelves, Beatles posters, a hand-knotted comforter of blue and white. Jamie's high school diploma, on his desk, slanted against the wall. The table lamp he'd inherited from his grandpa, Rose's father.

Stan sat on the bed, its springs squeaking quietly, a sound he'd heard every night when he'd perched there to tell his son goodnight. A prayer. A story. A kiss when Jamie was still young enough to accept one.

The cots at the recruit training command had no such thing as a soft, lovingly stitched comforter or the extra-fluffy pillow Jamie had hugged as he'd fallen asleep each night. He was lucky he had a pillow at all, and the standard blanket was anything but luxurious. At least everything was clean. Antiseptically clean. In that one thing Jamie had consistency between home and boot camp.

The day they'd left him there in Great Lakes, Illinois, had been gray and rainy. Cold. But still they'd seen the groups of recruits jogging, their matching sweat pants with NAVY down the legs wet from the puddles. Jamie hadn't been fazed at all. Seemed eager to get started. Eager to go out there and save the world.

Rose overflowed with enthusiasm, smiling widely and enjoying conversation with Jamie's soon-to-be commanders. She was glad Jamie had found a career, glad he seemed happy, glad he'd escaped the clutches of that girl he'd been dating. What was her name? Tammy? Tara? Stan shook his head, the name eluding him, as did the girl's face. A dark-headed girl from Jamie's high-school, if he remembered right. Not that it mattered. She was out of Jamie's life, like everything else Goshen-oriented.

Sure, Jamie had written, emailed, called. Visited on the rare holiday. But even at the first home stay he'd been different. Older. More certain of himself and every move he'd made.

A man.

Stan hadn't been as celebratory that day at the training facility. He was proud of his son, no doubt about that, but he couldn't help wishing Jamie had chosen the route he himself had taken so many years ago. There were lots of children to be saved in Goshen itself. There was no need to go stomping off somewhere foreign to find people in need.

But Stan had done his duty, listening, shaking hands, scribbling notes in his notebook. He knew most of it would seep from his brain by the next morning if he didn't write it down. Jamie's teachers, his classes, his classmates. It was all new.

Andrea had been along that day, hadn't she? A bored teenager, snapping her gum, arms crossed over her chest. Bored, or frightened. Not wanting her brother to see how much she would miss him. She'd be the only kid at home with the embarrassing parents. Not that Stan and Rose gave her cause to be embarrassed, at least not that Stan could think of. It was just that normal phase of constant irritation. Stan tried to ignore it. Rose couldn't quite manage that.

Stan rose from Jamie's bed and walked over to the dresser, where he pulled open the top drawer. A collage of mismatched items. An old wallet, stale gum, keys that fit who-knew-what. Jamie's varsity letter, never having made it to a jacket, a deck of cards, a photograph folder. Stan opened it with a finger. Jamie's senior prom. The girl had been dark-haired. Sweet, too, Stan had always thought. Rose had had some complaint about her. He couldn't remember what, exactly. Rose always had complaints about the girls Jamie dated. But something about this one had been special, and Stan wondered if Rose had, with some discomfort, seen herself in the girl's emerging womanhood.

He pushed the drawer shut and turned around, studying the arrangement of signed baseballs on a shelf. Ryne Sandberg, Frank Thomas, Nomar Garciaparra. Stan and Jamie had traveled to Chicago—Wrigley or U.S. Cellular Field—whenever an interesting team came to town. Good days for the two of them. The three of them, when Andrea got old enough. She was as big a fan as the two guys in the family, which had showed up in her softball career. Rose, of course, would rather be any place other than a steep stadium with sticky seats, beer spilling around her. That was fine. It was good not to have to worry about her those days. To give her a day alone every once in a while. She deserved it after all her years of staying home with the children.

The men that had come to the door two months ago

could've been baseball players. Well-dressed and lean, with strong jaws. When Stan opened the door and saw them, it was as if one of them had swung a bat and connected with his mid-section. He could remember clutching the doorjamb, a hand to his chest.

Glimpses of information told him they weren't the usual messengers for reporting a death. No chaplain, with a cross on his collar. No high-ranking Naval officer in his dress uniform, his hat in his hands.

Instead, two men from the Naval Investigative Service, in uniform, their faces grave, asking if they could come in. Senior Chief Petty Officer Borgman, the older agent's pin said. The gold bar on his chest. Stan zeroed in on it, his eyes caught by the shine. The younger man, a Lieutenant Miller, cleared his throat, bringing Stan's eyes to his uniform's shining buttons.

Rose, clutching Stan's sleeve and pulling him sideways, played the hostess, ushering the men into the living room. Sitting them on the sofa while she hovered, kneading her hands together against her stomach.

Stan stood frozen, the door still open to the outside, figuring somehow that if he didn't acknowledge their presence their news couldn't possibly be true. If they couldn't tell him, if he didn't hear it, it wasn't real.

But they were good at waiting, and when the silence became too much to bear, Rose joined Stan in the foyer and stared at him until he was forced to move. He went as far as the entrance to the living room, where he stopped, his feet refusing to move him closer to the men. Rose shut the front door, the click piercing Stan's ears like a shot.

The agents broke the news as respectfully and gently as they could. Jamie wasn't confirmed dead. For that they should be thankful, the lieutenant said. *Thankful.*

Jamie and his older partner, Chief Petty Officer Robert Lyndberg, had disembarked their ship, the USS *Mount Whitney*, under the blanket of night to deliver some papers—

state department materials—to some undercover defense intelligence agents. They'd stepped off the boat in Vladivostok in the dark, and when roll call was conducted the next morning, there was no reply at the sound of their names.

No reply. And no answers.

The Navy had searched for them for two days, intelligence agents and others scattering throughout the area, questioning possible witnesses, reconnoitering the haunts of suspected enemies, checking in with Friendlies. The *Mount Whitney* was scheduled for departure after those two days, and no matter the crew's concern for Jamie and his partner, they had to move on to their next destination. That didn't mean they'd stop looking. It only meant logistics had changed. They'd been hoping for news before contacting the families, but weren't sure how long to wait. It was a rough call. A tough call. They'd wanted to offer some hope, if there was some to be found.

Stan stood in the doorway, his body tingling and shaky, as if he'd been awakened from dream sleep and had only regained a half-conscious state. He knew what the officers weren't saying. What they avoided putting into words. It was the statement every sailor's parents feared. Any military parent. Any parent at all, really, military or not.

When a military man disappears there is very little hope—no matter what the officers said—of recovering him. A sailor in intelligence would not be kept as a hostage. He would be milked for whatever he knew. And disposed of.

Time was of the essence. And two days were gone.

The military was taking steps, the Navy men assured him. *Small steps*, Stan thought. Small steps, trying to find the footprints of his son in that frozen terrain of Russia.

That stomach-crunching blow, the tingling of his body, had been the last sensation Stan recalled since that day. He'd lost sleep, lost trains of thought, lost track. Lost his ability to feel. Anything.

He'd watched Rose vacillate between high emotion and low. Anger, resentment, worry, terror. But from what he could see, she functioned mostly on simmering fury, held in by the thinnest strand of social standards. It wouldn't do to have the mother of a missing sailor freaking out in the supermarket. She'd put on the strained smile of faith and steered herself through every variety of situation.

Someday, Stan feared, the string holding her back would snap, and she would forever punish herself for lack of inner strength. Lack of trust in God's plan. Lack of the ability to keep that constant mother's optimism that everything would turn out all right.

Stan pushed himself from Jamie's dresser and stepped to the doorway. A last glance at the room, a held breath. But it was the same as every other visit to the room. Each attempt to jumpstart his heart beating within him. To connect with his elder child, somewhere in the air.

Somehow it never seemed to happen.

∾

The computer crouched in the darkness. Silent. Cold. Still. Not even a hum to make it seem, if just for a moment, an ally.

Stan stood behind the chair, staring at the blank screen, the dim light from the hallway reflecting sharply off the monitor, showing a mirror image of his hands gripping the chair's back. Easing the chair sideways, the wheels skidding on the plastic mat, Stan lowered himself to the seat. Faced the beast.

As soon as he punched the button, the computer sprang to life. Humming, brightening, beeping. Stan winced at the barrage of sensations. He had never really taken to computers. Never wanted to bring work home with him. Never felt the urge to surf the web. Rose was the same. But the kids were appalled that their parents weren't communicating with the broader world.

Forget the phone. Forget actual letters. If they wanted to be in touch with their kids at college or the naval station, they needed to start using their computer. So they did. It wasn't a fancy one. Not one with all the bells and whistles—although with the noise it was making, Stan figured it had plenty of them.

When Jamie had first gone missing, the computer was a ray of hope. What if Jamie made his way to a computer and wrote to them? An email could come at any moment. Any second. They'd bought DSL and a second phone line for just that possibility, so they could stay online twenty-four hours a day without risking a missed telephone call from the Navy, saying Jamie had been found.

But as days turned into weeks, that spark of hope had turned to dread. What if he never emailed? What if the computer, unceasingly vigilant, never produced anything more from their son? It started to feel as if they were challenging fate, asking for the impossible.

So they began turning off the computer between email checks. Morning, midmorning, noon, midafternoon. . . . But soon those checks became less frequent. Morning. Noon. Afternoon. Evening. And now . . . now Stan could barely even turn on the computer without feeling an urge to throw up. Or have an aneurysm.

But what if . . .

Stan pointed the arrow toward the email folder. Clicked it.

There were no messages from Jamie.

They came for him that day, rough men, with strong hands and hard hearts. "You are to appear at once before the authorities!"

They took him, striking his face before he could reply, knocking him to the dirt path in front of the house. After speaking gruffly to him in Russian, they arrested him and took him away.

The last glimpse he had of his new friends' faces revealed their fear and helplessness. They reached out to him, but there was nothing they could do.

He soon found himself in the custody of the Twenty-Second Division.

He might as well have been in hell.

Chapter 2
TUESDAY

The day began as it had ended. Rose, silent, carrying Stan's dishes to the sink, Stan putting away the jam, the salt and pepper. Rose's mouth remained tight, her eyes avoiding Stan's for the full twenty or so hours since he'd phoned the MCC office and taken the job, that harsh glare of disbelief her last communication.

"I'm going out to work on the lawnmower," Stan said. "A belt broke the last time I used it."

Rose shut the dishwasher and left the kitchen.

Stan fixed the aging push mower and cut the grass, taking the time to rake up the piles and dump them in the back. He'd even gotten out the weed whacker and trimmed around the flowerbeds and the trees. When he'd finished, he'd stood on the sidewalk and admired a job well done.

Rose hadn't.

He showered, and changed from his gardening clothes to comfortable jeans and walking shoes. There was just enough time

before lunch—sure to be another distant, uncomfortable affair—
for his usual walk. He called out to Rose and told her where he
was going. He received no response but assumed she'd heard.

Walking out the back door and around the house, he
stopped at the sight of Rose on the front porch. He could see
her taking in the yard, her shoulders rising as she breathed in
the smell of the newly cut grass. He stepped back when she
turned, but not so quickly that he'd missed the pleased expression on her face. A measure of warmth seeped into his chest,
and he walked back in the back door.

"Rose?"

She appeared in the kitchen archway.

"I'm going to take a quick walk."

Her eyebrows lifted, and she nodded briefly before turning toward the hallway and disappearing into it.

Stan went back outside and walked east, his feet leading,
taking him on a detour from his normal route. He found himself looking at a church. Eighth Street Mennonite. He'd always
known it was there. Never thought about it much. Hadn't ever
answered a call for police help at that location. But he looked at
it now, curious about what it held in its walls. Probably nothing
too different from his own place of worship, the New Apostolic
Church in South Bend. People, hymnals, Bibles. The usual.

Until his meeting with Jerry Brenneman he'd had no direct
contact with Mennonites—at least none that he'd realized—
since his uniform days. Quite a while ago, now. And those situ-
ations had gone from a severe clashing of worlds to a respectful
collaboration.

He remembered the first call he'd taken that dealt with
Goshen College, the Mennonite institution on the east side of
town, the school where Jerry Brenneman's older son was receiving his education. It was the heart of the seventies. A party in
progress, underage drinking, loud music, the usual college scene.
Apparently not so usual for GC.

Stan and his partner had shown up at the off-campus house to deal with the disturbance in the normal way—arrests, citations—only to be confronted five minutes later with a cadre of college professors. Irate, unsmiling. Wanting to deal with the students in their own way, without the cooperation of local law enforcement. It was too late for that, Stan had explained. If they wanted to deal with their problems themselves, they'd better get to them before they disturbed the neighbors.

An eye-opening experience.

Since those years, with changes of college leadership, the relationship between the school and the police department had healed, becoming one of shared responsibility. They'd been called in for the gamut of incidents: theft, manufacturing fake IDs, domestic disturbances when the married student trailer court had still been in existence. Stan had even been called in once to take care of an incident in a dorm shower. It seemed someone had drilled a hole into the women's bathroom and was spying on the coeds as they'd taken their daily plunge. Stan and the resident director had ended up chuckling over that one. Not funny, really, he guessed, but no harm had been done that they'd discovered. High drama for a day or so, before everyone forgot about it.

"Can I help you with something, sir?"

Stan shuddered out of his reminiscences and turned toward a woman, eying him from a few feet down the sidewalk. Her voice was quiet, but firm. "Are you in need of something?"

"What? Oh. No, I'm sorry. Just took a walk and got to thinking."

"Well," she said, her suspicion turning to laughter, "you're certainly welcome to that." She held out her hand. "I'm Mary Yoder, one of the pastors here. Feel free to come inside if you like. Look around."

"Thanks. I'm fine, really. Just thinking, like I said."

"Okay, then. I'll leave you to it. I'm going on my lunch

break, but our secretary, Emma, and my co-pastor Kevin are still inside, if you need anything. Have a good day." She turned to go.

"One thing," Stan said. "Does Jerry Brenneman go here?"

Her forehead crinkled. "No, but that name does sound familiar."

"Director at the local MCC office."

"Ah, yes." Her face lightened. "I believe he goes to Prairie Street. If I'm remembering right. We have so many Mennonite churches to choose from around here."

"Right. Thanks."

He watched her step into an older-model Toyota, rust teasing the gas cap and the lock on the trunk. She waved as she drove away.

Seeing her go reminded him of his lunch date with his wife. He wasn't sure Rose was always glad to have him home these days, since he'd been encouraged to take his extended leave, but he didn't want to pay the consequences of not showing up for lunch.

Poor Rose. So wrapped up in worry and guilt.

The walk home took less time than the walk out, his feet leading him on a more direct route. As he approached his house he paused briefly, recognizing the car by the curb. The cute little red Honda Prelude. Late eighties model.

Which led him to the figure on the porch. She didn't see him yet, her eyes fixed on something in her lap. Textbook, probably.

Andrea's hair shined in the noonday light, the auburn bright against the gray porch wall. She'd inherited her coloring from her grandmother, and sometimes the matching temper showed up for a brief stint. Mostly, though, she was a thoughtful, intelligent girl. Young woman, now, Stan had to admit. She'd proven her prowess on the softball field, too, as strong an athlete—if not stronger—than Jamie. Pitching the ball with a force and aim that sent many a batter back to the dugout in frustration.

Stan took a deep breath and walked up the porch steps. Andrea stopped the porch swing with her foot so he could sit down. She closed her textbook, saving her place by clipping a highlighter to the page.

"Let me guess," Stan said. "You're here to talk me out of consorting with the enemy."

Andrea laughed. "Something like that."

"Are you going to try?"

"Do you want me to?"

Stan raised his face to the sun, watching as it flickered through the new leaves of their ancient maple, dappling the sidewalk and the porch steps in front of them. "I don't believe I do."

Andrea rested her head on his shoulder. "Then let's just tell Mom I tried, but didn't succeed."

He patted her knee. "Let's do that."

It wasn't unusual to see Andrea anymore. After that first fight with Rose about the surprise dorm appearance, it had been a month or two before their daughter had come home. But the visits began again just before Christmas, twice a month, three times. Multiplying after that visit from the NIS agents in February. A connection with home meant a connection with Jamie. Andrea needed that. They all needed it.

The first time Jamie had gone away was to church camp when he was eight. A whole week with Andrea asking where her brother had disappeared to. Daily postcards scrawled in her oversized print, the stamps crooked, more than adequately licked for sticking. Email hadn't been common yet. The regular postal service had to do. Andrea didn't understand why there weren't letters from her brother every morning and evening, or for reading at lunch. She'd been a mess the entire week, until his eventual return on Saturday. She'd then ignored him the rest of the weekend, like a cat angry with its owner for going on vacation.

Stan glanced at his watch and spoke into his daughter's hair. "You hanging out for lunch?"

She looked up at him. "If that's okay."

"Of course it's okay. I just wondered if you had time. Your practice is at what? Three-o'clock today?"

"Three-thirty. I've got plenty of time."

"Good. I'm looking forward to your game tomorrow."

"You're coming?"

"Wouldn't miss it. Your mother, either."

She grunted a laugh. "Right."

"Andi, you know she's proud of you. It's just . . . With everything . . ."

"I know, Dad." She sighed heavily. "I know."

Stan breathed in the fresh air, filling his lungs. He let it out. "You think lunch is ready?"

Andrea groaned. "Could we just wait till she comes to get us?"

"Well," Stan said, "I guess we could."

They got up, and went inside.

∽

The nap idea wasn't working. Stan lay on his bed, staring at the ceiling. He could hear Rose puttering around in the house. Opening and closing closets, stacking plates in the kitchen cabinets, pushing buttons to cause the dryer's steady hum. He'd closed their bedroom curtains, but light still penetrated the middle crack, the fabric not entirely meeting for the length of the window.

It wasn't like sleep was a friend. It had been weeks since he'd had a true night's rest. He blamed the NIS agents who had shown up at his door, as if they somehow arrived each night to keep his mind from shutting down. To remind him, in his half-sleeping state, that his son was lost in Russia, somewhere in the midst of that frozen tundra, and he could do nothing to change it.

Stan closed his eyes and concentrated on his daughter. Andrea, who got straight A's, captained the softball team her senior year of high school and went through boyfriends like Donald Trump went through money.

Jamie was a saver. Money gifts at birthdays, tickets from baseball games, junk mail from universities. Box after organized box of unsolicited college information he'd never even opened—and probably never would.

Stan rolled over and fiddled with the switch on their white-noise machine. Woods? Ocean? Rain? How about that heartbeat, meant to calm screaming babies? He pushed the generic white-noise button, the one that sounded like radio static.

Did Jamie have a radio? If he tried to contact his ship, would they hear anything other than the hiss of a lost connection?

Stan turned off the machine and got out of bed.

∾

The parking lot at The Depot was emptying. Most of the stores probably closed at five, so shoppers and workers were headed home. No group of young Hispanic males, leaning on their cars, to welcome Stan this time.

Sheila, the young receptionist, was shutting down her computer. "Hi, Mr. Windemere! Mr. Brenneman giving you the lowdown?"

That smile, so bright and cheerful.

"The lowdown," Stan said.

"Great. I'm outta here for today, but if you think of anything you need, just leave a note on my desk, and I'll get to it tomorrow, okay?"

"Okay. Thanks."

She left in a whirlwind of flashing teeth and billowing hair, her eyes shining.

"Mr. Windemere?"

Jerry Brenneman welcomed him again with an outstretched hand. Stan took it. Jerry didn't even glance to see if Stan was wearing his gun. At least not that Stan noticed.

"A few folks left, but some are still here," Jerry said. "I'll introduce you around. You have anything you need to put in the fridge?"

Stan held up a small cooler, with a lunch he'd packed with leftovers. Rose, in her state of pique over this job, had left him to fend for himself. Which was fine. He'd made plenty of lunches in his day—his own and the kids' once Rose had gone back to work during their later school days. "Should be all right in this."

Jerry led him to the kitchenette. "You can leave it on the counter if you want. And use whatever you like in here. There's a coffeemaker if you need a pick-me-up during the night. A few pops in the fridge if you prefer that. A microwave, and . . ." He lifted foil off of a plate on the counter. "Marilyn, one of our peace and justice advocates, brought in homemade monster cookies. There are a few left. They're all yours."

Stan leaned over to peek at the plate. He'd have one later. Maybe two.

"Jerry?" A young woman with Asian features stood at the entrance to the kitchenette. "I need to head out in a few minutes."

"Ah, yes. Mr. Windemere, this is Wendy Ngyung. Our human resources and communications director."

"A pleasure to meet you, Mr. Windemere. Thank you for taking on the security job. If you could come over to my desk, I'll have you fill out some paperwork."

Stan set his lunchbox on the counter and followed the woman. Partway there, he paused as a conversation in Spanish floated toward him. He looked toward the speakers, only to see the serious young man from yesterday's parking lot scenario sitting beside a desk, his back slouched, ankles crossed casually out in front. He laughed at something the man at the desk said and, glancing up, caught Stan's eye. He stopped laughing, but not smiling, and nodded briefly to Stan. The same chin raise he'd offered the day before.

"Mr. Windemere?" Wendy said.

"Sorry." He took his eyes off the young man and followed her to the corner cubicle.

"Please, have a seat." She gestured to a padded metal chair. "Here's a pen, and here are the papers." She explained each one, which was good, since it had been twenty years since Stan had filled out a job application.

"I guess we're doing this a bit backward," Wendy said, laughing. "Since we already gave you the job."

Stan took the pen and jotted down the essentials: name, address, emergency contacts.

He felt a presence behind him and glanced up to see a blond man, the one who'd been laughing with the Spanish kid, peeking around Wendy's wall.

"Wendy, I've got someone on the phone who speaks Vietnamese and not much English. Can you take her?"

"Sure," she said. "Line two?"

She picked up the phone and began talking in a running stream of tones and sing-song. Stan found himself staring. *Does no one around here speak German?*

Wendy caught his look and smiled, which jolted him back to his paperwork. By the time she hung up, he was finished.

"Sorry about that," she said. "We all do our part with whatever language we speak."

Stan nodded, feeling stupid, English being his only tongue. Unless you counted pig Latin. He'd had to become an expert in that years ago, when the kids figured he was too dumb to catch on. He'd let them think he was. *A-way Umb-day.*

Jamie and Andrea had always been close. Very close as little children, Jamie helping to "take care" of Andrea, as he was six when she was born. That turned, unsurprisingly, to the fighting all young siblings do, but often they'd end up snuggling on the couch, having forgotten the preceding spouting off of "Dad, she mixed up all my Legos!" or "Mom, he said my ponytail looks like a horse's butt!"

They'd traversed a few lean years as pre-adolescents, when Jamie was in middle school and Andrea just starting kindergarten. But they'd bonded again as adolescents, as all teenagers must when dealing with their lame parents. Once Jamie had gone into the Navy and Andrea entered ninth grade, they'd only gotten closer, from what Stan had observed. That email program the kids had forced on their parents really worked for Jamie and Andrea. Something about typing things made sharing simpler, somehow.

Stan thought about the last email Jamie had sent his sister. Upbeat. Full of vitality. Bulging with the self-confidence of a man out to save the world.

The NIS had scoured it for hints of his disappearance. Studied every bit of communication their family had had with Jamie since he'd been deployed. Stan couldn't imagine they'd found anything helpful. How could Jamie's brotherly advice, insisting Andrea dump that creepy guy from her first-year biology class, help them find him somewhere in Russia? Or Jamie's news to his mother, assuring her that his sock supply was lasting just fine? Would that send them running? *A-ha! We've found him, from the clue he left in the toe of a dark blue dress sock!*

Stan wondered how often Andrea checked her email now. Or her phone, thinking that maybe, just maybe, this time, there would be a message. There would be a note saying he'd made it. He was safe. If only he could find a phone. A computer. A friendly face.

"Mr. Windemere?"

His head snapped up.

"Is there a problem?"

He looked at Wendy's earnest face. He relaxed his features from what must've been a dour expression. "No. No problem."

"Great." She took the papers and glanced through them. "Everything looks good. Do you have any questions?"

He shook his head.

"Then thank you again for helping us out here. I feel much better knowing you'll be keeping an eye on things for the next few weeks."

Stan nodded again.

Wendy looked over his shoulder. "We're done here, Jerry. He's all yours."

Stan rose and turned to follow his new boss. He glanced sideways to see if the young Hispanic kid was still in the chair, but it was empty, as was the place at the desk. The tabletop lamp and computer were also turned off.

"Everyone lights out at five?" Stan asked. He followed Jerry toward the warehouse.

"Pretty much. By five-fifteen, at least. I was hoping to introduce you to more people, but I guess that will have to wait. Here." He reached into his pocket and came out with a key hooked onto a purple and white Goshen College key chain shaped like a maple leaf. "Most nights, since you'll be coming at seven, the office will be empty. There are other folks in the building for a while after we leave, so there's no need for you to come sooner. But I'm afraid you'll be alone a good part of the time, if not entirely."

He'd expected it. That's what happened with night watches.

"This key opens the back and front doors," Jerry said. "If you come in the back, you don't have to go through the building's front lobby at all. I'll show you where the light switches are."

They walked through the conference room to the warehouse, where Jerry led him to the side wall and an outside door. He opened it and they stepped outside.

"There are a couple of parking spaces out here, so feel free to put your car right by the door. That'll help discourage folks from breaking in too, I hope. I'll put this outside light on for you, so you can see the lock."

Stan nodded. "You're still opposed to an alarm system?"

Jerry raised his hands. "We've never needed one before, although we might consider it if things keep on the way they're going once your temporary employment is over. We'll have to see."

They went back into the building. "The door locks automatically," Jerry said. "So make sure you have your key when you leave."

Back in the warehouse, a young woman stepped out of the corner office.

"Oh, Becky," Jerry said. "Didn't know you were still here. This is Stan Windemere, who will be our night security for the next few weeks. Stan, this is Becky Weaver, our material resource coordinator. The one I told you about who organizes all the volunteer groups, keeps kit supplies up, makes sure the warehouse doesn't descend into chaos."

Becky laughed. "I do my best." She turned to Stan, her eyes narrowing as she studied him. "I told Jerry I'd be happy to keep a watch on stuff as it comes in, but he thought we needed someone else."

Stan forced himself not to look at Jerry. "Working around the clock would be tough. Couldn't do it for long."

"I said I'd sleep here. At least be a presence."

Jerry cleared his throat. "And I said that wasn't what we were looking for. We needed someone *awake*."

Becky sniffed. Looked at her fingernails. "This will work out okay, I guess. You've had experience?"

Now Stan did look at Jerry, who rolled his eyes. Stan

turned back to Becky. "I'm a detective for the Goshen Police Department."

"Oh. Then why are you doing this? Aren't you the one working around the clock?"

"I'm on leave right now. So I'll be all right."

"How come?"

"How come what? I'm on leave?"

"Yeah."

"Becky." Jerry intervened with an awkward chuckle.

Stan filled his cheeks with air. Let it out.

"Well," Becky said. "Whatever. Thanks, I guess. For watching the stuff."

Stan smiled. Or tried to, at least. "Glad to help out."

Becky gestured toward the office door and said grudgingly, "Want me to leave this open for you? There's a heater, since it still gets kinda cool at night. You can hang out in there, if you like."

"Oh. Thanks. That would be great."

"No problem."

She left them with a wave, and Jerry gave Stan a half-hearted grin. "Sorry about that."

Stan shook his head. "Don't worry about it. She obviously feels protective of her domain."

"Yeah. I guess that's it."

Jerry took Stan back into the main office. "Do you have questions? Is there anything you need?"

Stan put his hands in his pockets and shrugged. "Can't think of anything right now."

Jerry glanced at a clock on the wall. "You're getting started a little early tonight. You're welcome to leave and come back at seven."

"Nah. Thanks, though."

"All right. Feel free to go earlier than seven tomorrow morning if folks start showing up at the building before then. We've got a lot of early risers."

Stan nodded. He'd be ready to go by then, he was sure. Back to the loving arms of his wife. A sad laugh stuck in his throat. How that thought had made him smile a mere two months before. At the end of a long shift, a messy crime, returning to her concern, her touch, her comfort.

Jerry retrieved his briefcase, closed his office door, and smiled once more at Stan before leaving through the front door, which he also closed securely.

So, Stan thought. *Here I am. In the Land of the Mennonites.*

He stood there for several minutes, hands still in his pockets as he took in the atmosphere. The silence. But not silence—he could hear the refrigerator buzzing in the kitchenette. The cubicles, personalized around him, with ticking clocks, one computer still on, humming quietly.

He hadn't done his daily check for emails from Jamie. He'd forgotten. Or, more accurately, he'd chosen to forget. He just couldn't take that thrust to his heart before coming to a new job. And he wouldn't check the phone on his hip. Not again. He wouldn't make sure it was on, that the battery was charged. He wouldn't. He wouldn't.

Glancing up, he saw another painted quote he hadn't taken time to read before. Martin Luther King Jr. It filled the wall above the desk:

> As you press on for justice, be sure to move with dignity and discipline using only the weapon of love. Let no man pull you so low as to hate him. Always avoid violence. . . .

Stan gazed at it for a while, at the orange and brown, the deliberate painting, done by a steady hand. *The weapon of love.*

After a while, he walked through the office and exited the front door—making sure his key was in his pocket—into the lobby of the main building.

Lights were off in most of the stores. The thrift shops, Ten

Thousand Villages, the church-related offices across from MCC. The only store still lit, ironically, was Michiana Oak, which proclaimed to be the maker of fine Amish-crafted furniture. Oak. Cherry. Maple. He supposed the Amish folks' ban on electricity didn't extend to a business in the wider culture. Maybe he'd ask Jerry.

The building's front doors were shut and locked now, and only two cars dotted the parking lot. Probably employees of the furniture store. Jerry glanced at his watch. About six. So he could expect those cars to remain another hour, if Jerry's predictions were correct.

He walked back to the MCC office, opening the door with his key and shutting it behind him. The lights were still on, and he flipped them off as he walked through, checking the locks on the windows. He was left in a dark cocoon of an office, the light from outside sneaking in to reflect off of computer screens and Jerry's office windows. A security lamp high on the wall was still unlit, probably waiting to turn on until the daylight had dimmed.

Back in the conference room, Stan turned off every light but one, so he'd have illumination for walking through. He then stepped into the warehouse and stood quietly gazing about.

He had taken one step forward to begin a round of the warehouse when the handle on the back door creaked up and down. A rattle. A thump.

Stan felt automatically for the gun on his hip and was jolted to reality when his hand came away empty. He looked around for something he could use as a weapon and was reaching for an old cane on the thrift store's pile when he heard what sounded like a key in the lock. The door swung open and a man stood there, staring at Stan and the cane with surprise.

"Help you?" Stan said.

The man frowned. "I was about to ask you the same thing."

They stood still, studying each other. The man was probably in his thirties, Stan thought. Had that beard Stan associated with the Amish, down the sides of his face, around the tip of his chin, no mustache. Blue shirt. Dark blue pants.

"Name's Stan Windemere," Stan said. "Working security for MCC."

The man's face relaxed at once. "Ah, yes. I heard you were coming. My name's Matthew Schwartzentruber. I work at Michiana Oak and was just coming back to get something I forgot. I was fortunate to remember before I got too far out of town. I'm sorry if I startled you."

"Same here." Stan dropped the cane back onto the pile of used goods. "Any idea how many people have keys to that door?"

The man thought about it, a blank look on his face. "No. Pretty many, probably. Those who work in these stores, certainly."

"Is it usually locked?"

"Almost always. Except when someone's working in the summer and it gets hot. Then we might prop it open."

Stan nodded. "Thanks."

"You're welcome." Schwartzentruber stepped forward, his hand out. "I'm glad to meet you. I hope you find your time working here to be productive and without problems."

The Amishman's hand was strong, and Stan returned the firm clasp. "Thank you."

Schwartzentruber went through the door to his shop, using his key. Stan waited until the door had shut before going to the back and peeking through the door into the parking lot. Sure enough. There was a horse and buggy, tied to a post, the animal waiting patiently for the return of its master.

I guess Schwartzentruber should try to remember his belongings, Stan thought. Once he got home there'd be no coming back till the next morning.

Stan meandered into the warehouse office, left open for him by the prickly young woman. What was her name? Betty?

He shrugged and let his gaze wander across papers on the desk. Becky Weaver, a paper said. That's right. Becky.

Stan sat in her chair and stretched out his feet. Becky's desk was messy. Papers, photos, computer disks. Andrea's desk always looked like that. Her entire room, really. When Rose would finally demand that she straighten up and put her laundry in the hamper, Andrea would simply shove things into the closet or under her bed. It at least gave the room the appearance of neatness. Rose pretended she didn't notice. Stan supposed she would've gone nuts otherwise.

Jamie's room was always as neat as Andrea's was messy. Already training for the military life, Stan supposed, even if he hadn't known it. Papers aligned, bed made, laundry in the washroom. Jamie had always been able to survive on much less than Andrea. Probably because he knew where to find it.

Stan shoved himself out of the chair. He needed to walk.

He turned on the lights and paced the office, the warehouse, the lobby every once in a while. Rocked back and forth on his feet, hands in his pockets, staring at the map of the world on the wall.

Finally his stomach growled, and when he glanced at the clock he realized it was almost eleven-thirty. At least eight hours since he'd eaten a light supper of salad and a turkey sandwich. He got his lunchbox from the kitchenette and went to Sheila's reception desk, knowing there wouldn't be an open space on the warehouse manager's. He spread his fare out in front of him—two hard-boiled eggs, some chips, and the blueberry yogurt he'd packed himself—and said grace. A simple prayer, good enough only to give thanks for the food.

Andrea's prayers were always short, of the "God's neat, let's eat" variety. She figured God would understand that they wouldn't want the food to get cold.

Jamie's prayers were the opposite. Long, thoughtful, well spoken. Enough to drive his little sister to distraction. His par-

ents too, sometimes, as they imagined the steam and heat evap-
orating from the dishes of food. Jamie excelled at prayers.

Stan forced his food down, not really enjoying it, but
knowing he'd need it to stay focused the rest of the night. He
packed up his trash and placed his lunchbox back in the kitchenette.

One more round through the warehouse, through the office,
ending up again by the huge world map in the front. Amateur
photos of missionary families, tacked up all over the globe. Stan
wondered what would induce a family to pack up their children
and head to the far side of the world. Not money. Not glamour.

Jamie headed out into the world to help people as well as
he could, to a part of the world where none of these good Mennonites seemed to go, seeing as the Russian section was devoid
of any family pictures. Why weren't they there? In Russia. Why
weren't they there helping the people Jamie was there to help?

Stan turned away from the map and his eyes fell on a
stack of bumper stickers. *God Bless the Whole World—No
Exceptions.*

He grunted. From the way the map looked, even the
MCCers didn't seem too big on Russia.

But then, neither was he.

Why Jamie had wanted to go there . . .

Stan sighed and closed his eyes. Perhaps this job wasn't going
to help, after all.

His partner was gone, sent to fulfill another part of their mission. Back to Alexandrovsk.

Now he gazed out the window at the gathering dusk, his mind racing with impossible options and an unfamiliar kernel of fear.

"You should go," his hostess said, "before something happens to you. I wish you would."

He'd already been taken once, and released. A miracle. To expect another miracle seemed selfish. And foolish. But he had his job to do.

"I am not doing anything wrong," he said. "No one should want to harm me."

His friend nodded, put a hand on his shoulder. "Then may God be with you. And with us all."

Chapter 3
WEDNESDAY

Rose set the bowl of oatmeal in front of Stan and stood looking down at him, arms crossed. Stan didn't know if she wanted to make sure he ate or if she was expecting some sort of rehashing of the night's events, as he used to supply when he'd come home after a night's work for the PD. He spooned brown sugar onto his cereal and stirred it in, watching as it melted into graceful swirls. Rose didn't move.

"Something you need?" Stan asked, eyes on his bowl.

Rose made a clicking sound with her tongue and turned toward the sink, where she caused a ruckus by accidentally clanking a spoon against the faucet. Stan watched her tight shoulders for a few moments before resting his head on his fist, saying a short prayer of thanks, and reaching for the milk.

He was halfway through the cereal—which Rose had surprised him with, really, since she had been so adamant about him packing his own lunch for the night—when she came back to the table. This time she stood by her own chair, her hands gripping its back.

"I'm going out today," she said. "I have to get groceries and pick up some dry-cleaning. Your suits. Andrea needs a new fall jacket, so I'm going to Kohl's to see if I can find one, because I received one of those percentage-off cards in the mail. Twenty percent this time. Usually it's just fifteen. She probably won't like what I pick out, because she never does, but I can take it back as long as I keep the receipt and return it within thirty days. I checked your dresser drawers, and it looks like you could use some new socks and underwear. And maybe a new white dress shirt. I'll see if I can find anything your size. I don't need anything for myself, so today's a shopping-for-the-family day, unless I see something really on sale, you know, like they do, saying I can take 40 percent more off the sale price. And that's not including my card for 20 percent. It's almost like getting things free sometimes."

Stan blinked, his mouth open slightly, and tried to take in the torrent of words. Rose hadn't said this much since Jamie had left for Russia. The last time she'd put more than two sentences together was on the way to the airport, when she was chattering to Jamie about his belongings, his ship, his need to remember his multivitamin. It was on the way home, after leaving him in the hands of his commanders—and the U.S. government—that words had failed her. Almost as if she'd known she had just sent her only son off to . . . wherever he'd gone off to. She'd spoken even less in the last two months.

Stan watched his wife now, her mouth moving, her knuckles white against the black chair back. Her eyes darted around the room, not resting on anything—especially him—for more than a moment. But those words. The voice.

When they were first married, Rose had talked constantly. About this, about that. But Stan hadn't minded. In fact, it was one of the things he'd loved most about her. She knew so much about so many things—gardening, music, cooking, the political climate. . . . He had been happy just to sit and listen as she dissected a situation or story or person, her eyes alight with animation, her voice a lilting stream of song. Bringing forth from him a laugh or question or even a simple pique of interest. Her words hadn't been this nervous drivel launched at him over cooling oatmeal.

"Stan?" she said now.

He blinked again, returning to the present.

Her hands left the chair, were tucked as fists under her arms. "Did you hear a word I said?"

He swallowed. Smiled briefly. "Yes, dear, I did. I heard every one."

"Well, that's good, then. I'll be back in time to go to Andrea's game." She nodded curtly, grabbed her purse off the counter, and left, car keys jingling in her fingers.

Stan pushed his food away, its appeal gone. He sat, swiveling his head from side to side, seeing the spotless kitchen, the calendar with its empty squares of days, and the cookie jar. The cookie jar that had sat empty now for weeks. The first place Jamie would check when he came home from anywhere.

Stan stood, pushed in his chair, and took his bowl to the sink, where he rinsed it and placed it in the dishwasher.

Then he went to bed and tried to sleep.

It didn't go well.

∾

The softball game was a blowout, the Fighting Irish whupping their opponents by eight. Andrea struck out seven, walking only one, and allowed only one hit. Stan couldn't have been prouder.

"Supper?" he asked after she came running, jumping into his arms.

"Can't tonight, Pop. Got recruits for next year here at the game, and we're eating with them. Next time, though."

"Sure."

Andrea turned to Rose, her smile tentative.

Rose lifted her arms, gave her daughter a stiff embrace. "Good job. Good game." Patted her back.

Andrea stepped away, her face closed. Empty. "So I guess I'll see you guys soon."

"Maybe tomorrow?" Stan asked. "Are you coming home?"

A twitch of her shoulder. "Maybe. We'll see."

Stan thought ahead. "Is your next game on Saturday?"

"Yeah. A doubleheader. But it's in Indianapolis. You don't have to come."

He grimaced. "Probably can't, with my new work schedule."

Rose grunted, clutched her purse under her arm.

"That's okay, Dad. We'll beat 'em bad, anyway. It would be boring." An attempted smile.

"Sure, hon. I'll want to hear about it."

Her already-forced smile faltered, and Stan regretted his words. That had been Jamie's job. Calling after the game. Finding out what had happened.

"Andrea!"

Her friends waited, duffel bags over their shoulders, gloves dangling from their fingers. Hats backward, uniform shirts untucked.

Andrea tried out another smile. Turned to her teammates.

Left Stan and Rose standing on the first-base line, Rose's hand outstretched, fingers reaching toward her daughter.

∼

The horse and buggy were gone by the time Stan parked in the back of The Depot. His was the only vehicle of any kind in the lot. Out front he had seen a couple of cars. Probably those Michiana Oak folks. No young Hispanic men leaning on their trunks. He'd been slightly disappointed, wondering where the one had gone—and who exactly he was—that he'd seen the day before. And why something about him triggered an itch of recognition.

His key worked smoothly in the building's back door, and he flipped on the overhead lights in the warehouse. Nothing new. No shipment of goods. Just the stacks of used clothes, garage-sale rejects, and extra supplies for filling school kits.

Stan made a round of the space, sticking his head into the warehouse manager's office to make sure nobody lurked there. Nope. No one there but Becky's computer. He turned his back on it, having been snubbed by his own computer once again, the listing of emails consisting of everything but what he wanted. He'd gotten plenty of the other messages—advertisements, announcements, loving emails from relatives. . . . They figured if he and Rose didn't want them to call, they'd use the computer. Stan never hit the Reply button. Or even opened the letters to read their full contents.

His key worked again on the door to the inner office. Nightlights spread shadows around the cubicles, and Stan quickly turned on the ceiling lights, not knowing the space well enough yet to feel comfortable in only the dim illumination of the security lamps. Especially without the familiar weight on his hip. He walked the length of the office, checking windows, corners, and Jerry's office door. He left his lunch in the kitchenette's refrigerator and smiled when he saw a note taped to something wrapped in plastic: *Mr. Windemere— We had some whoopie pies left over today. Thought you might enjoy one. Sheila.*

These Mennonites sure liked their desserts. Not that he was complaining.

He stepped out the front door into the lobby of the building and found all quiet. The two cars were now gone from the parking lot. He was alone.

He stood for a while gazing into the window of the Ten Thousand Villages store. Handmade items from around the world. Decorative items, such as statues, candles, wall-hangings. But also toys, jewelry, instruments. Rose might like that bracelet.

The one made of shiny silver squares. He hadn't bought her jewelry for a long time. Any kind of present, actually.

A quote, painted on an inner wall, as in the MCC office, jumped out at him, illuminated under the store's security light.

> With each product you buy there is one more tortilla
> for our families.
> Baltazar Fuentes, El Salvador

Stan wondered where all of the items came from. El Salvador, he surmised, among other countries. He wondered who had made them and what kind of wage they actually earned. He couldn't imagine the Mennonites backing sweatshops, but you never knew about people.

Using his key, he went back into the MCC office, only to be confronted with the map of The World. *Not tonight,* he told himself.

His hands in his pockets, Stan wandered into the resource area and glanced over the books and videos. Materials for Sunday school classes for parents, young adults, and children. Biographies, introductions to different parts of the world, and a section entirely in Spanish. Some items looked ancient, some brand new. Nothing that promised a gripping tale for a Saturday night. Or even a Wednesday night, when guarding a quiet, low-value property.

He left the library and traveled from cubicle to cubicle, studying the desktops and their personal effects. Family photos, clocks, mugs ("*#1 Aunt,*" "*Goshen College,*" "*I'd rather be PEACE-MAKING*"), even a pencil with feathers instead of an eraser on the top. Memos, stacks of statistics, Rolodexes, highlighters. Pictures of pets—dogs, cats, one guinea pig—a globe bank, and a poster of South America, with push pins in designated areas.

He stopped at a familiar desk, Wendy Ngyung's, the human resources woman who'd helped him with his paperwork. It looked like she had a husband, two adorable children—preschoolers, he decided—and a dachshund named Sweetie. Her mug was floral, no words, and held a used tea bag and a spoon. He sniffed it. Mint.

The desk was full, but not messy like Andrea's, like Becky's, the girl in the warehouse office. Another photo sat to the side. One of those small double frames, hinged in the middle. Black and white photos. Two men. One from long ago, Stan's grandparents' time, he thought, judging from the hair and style of dress. The other man looking more modern—from Stan's parents' era, maybe. The thick black glasses. The short, buzzed hair. Relatives? Stan wondered. Interesting to have them on her desk. Especially since these guys had the generic Caucasian look. Not the rich olive skin or dark eyes like Wendy. Had she been adopted? But then where did she get the fluent Vietnamese? Or the name Ngyung? Her husband, he supposed, for the name. School, for the language?

He was probably all wrong. About everything. Being a detective didn't count for much when you had no worthwhile information.

He continued on, making a study of each desk, playing a game each time of seeing how much he could learn about the employees.

Wouldn't they be surprised?

He'd hoped to find something at the blond man's desk pertaining to the Hispanic kids. Especially the one who'd been lounging in the chair beside the man, laughing and talking with him in Spanish. But there was nothing Stan could see. At least not without opening drawers, and he certainly wasn't going to do that.

Jerry's office was open, and Stan stood for a while in front of the bookshelf, reading the spines of the books, studying the faces of his family. Nice boys, from the looks of them. Nice, like Jamie. Except these boys wouldn't be joining the Navy, or any other branch of the military. These were Mennonite kids. Pacifists, as Rose had reminded him. Not sailors, lost, halfway around the world.

Jerry had no idea.

Stan left the office and wandered around some more, flipping through brochures and studying those decorated eggs, willing himself not to check his phone every two minutes. Not to hope for a call. For a message. He soon found himself back at Wendy's desk, picking up the frame with the two black-and-white photos. Who were these guys?

Stan figured they were Mennonite, from their dress and the fact that they were here, on the desk of a Mennonite woman in a church agency. But there was nothing else. No names. No dates. He set them down again, looked at them for a few more moments, then turned to make a pass through the warehouse. Not much longer and he could eat his lunch.

Then do it all over again.

The devastation was almost more than he could bear. Blood-soaked fields, where battles had raged. Children, their protruding stomachs and bony knees unable to hide behind scraps of dirty clothes. Men with deadened eyes. Raped women. Raped land.

He stood gazing at a slain horse, one of a multitude, a once-regal animal distorted, defiled by death.

Was he, one man, enough to turn away evil? To bring some hope to this formerly vibrant land?

With God's help, maybe.

Only then.

Chapter 4
THURSDAY

Stan was in the warehouse, headed to the back door and home, when the handle jiggled and the door swung open.

"Stan!" Jerry Brenneman said.

"Morning."

"Part of the shipment comes in today. I wanted to make sure things were ready to go. Becky here yet?"

Stan glanced at the manager's office, although he knew she had yet to arrive. "Nope."

"She should be here any minute." Jerry let the door slam shut behind him. "Everything went all right here last night, I take it?"

Stan considered the hours spent fighting off thought. "Everything went fine."

"Good. Good. Any questions about anything?"

Stan thought about those photos. The ones on Wendy's desk. But decided he wasn't ready to share that he'd been snooping, no matter how innocent it had been.

"That Ten Thousand Villages store. Where do the items come from?"

Jerry waved an arm. "All over the world. Peru. Brazil. Thailand. India."

El Salvador. "And the people who make them?"

"Native artists."

"Adults?"

Jerry's brow furrowed. "Well, sure."

"And they can make a living doing that?"

Jerry's face cleared. "You're concerned about the workers? Don't be. They're paid a good wage. A living wage. That's why the items might seem a bit pricey sometimes. They're made by people who do a good job and get paid fairly for it."

Stan nodded. That was good. If it was true. "I saw some things my wife might like."

Jerry smiled. "It's a good store for presents. I should know. My family's gotten lots of things from there. Including all of our Christmas decorations."

Stan felt a yawn coming and tried to suppress it. He wasn't successful.

"Guess you'd better get going," Jerry said. "You'll be okay driving home?"

Stan nodded. "Not the first time I've worked nights."

"No, I guess not." Jerry turned to go, then stopped. "This warehouse will look different tonight. Fuller."

"The reason I'm here," Stan said, and left through the back door.

$\sim$

Rose was still asleep when Stan got home, sprawled across their bed, her face pushed far into her pillow. Gone were the days when they'd get up at the same time, eat breakfast together, go to their respective jobs. He to serve and protect, she to dye and highlight. Or at least point ladies toward the beauticians. She'd been good at that job. Professional, friendly, well put-together. Once Chief Borgman and Lieutenant Miller, the agents from the NIS, had come to their door, she'd had no energy for it. No sympathy for women whose sole need was a trim.

Stan turned and walked down the hallway toward Jamie's room. The bed was made, clean sheets ready for Jamie's return. Stan took one look, then angled right and entered Andrea's room instead. He shut the door behind him, undressed, and crawled under the red-and-white comforter, given to Andrea by Rose's mother. It smelled like his daughter.

When he awoke, having successfully and surprisingly slept into the afternoon, he searched the house for his wife, but didn't find her. A peek into the front and back yards was also in vain, but when he reached for the refrigerator he found a note stuck to the freezer portion, stating that Rose had left a plate of food in the fridge for when he woke up.

Nothing about what he could take for the night's supper. Nothing about sustenance for his time conspiring with those she considered the enemy.

The plate of cold spaghetti confronted him with its congealing twist of noodles. The peas, now dried up bits of green, threatened to roll off the plate, and the breadstick had toughened during its time in the refrigerator. Stan microwaved the whole lot of it long enough for the cheese to melt into the vegetables, and he did what he could to choke it down.

As he ate, he couldn't help but remember the days of lovingly created meals of stuffed chicken or spicy chili, but he was forced to the realization that once the kids were gone, the heart had gone out of the cooking. Like it was no longer worth the effort for just the two of them. Stan sighed and shook an extra helping of parmesan onto the spaghetti. It hadn't been bad, really, at first. Simple suppers, like baked potatoes with cheese and sour cream. Or even a chicken thrown into the Crock-Pot, eaten with noodles and canned corn. Those meals were still good. Still a source of sustenance and pleasure.

But once they'd been told about Jamie, well, even those simple foods seemed to tax Rose's energy. Or perhaps it was more a lack of motivation. Like if Jamie was gone, what was the point of pleasurable dining?

Stan supposed he could take up cooking, but couldn't imagine the response being anything other than hurt disbelief. That he would even *think* she wasn't doing her job. Keeping him fed.

Stan carefully rinsed his plate, watching the remains of his dinner slide down the garbage disposal. He'd have to pack an extra yogurt in case this meager meal came back to haunt him at midnight.

Plate in the dishwasher, Stan looked at the clock above the table. Four o'clock. Not even close to the time he could head out to work. He glanced out the window. A nice day. He put on his walking shoes and started around the block.

He stayed away from the Mennonite church today and avoided the dam altogether. Instead, he went downtown, past the coffee shop, the Christian bookstore, and Bridgework Theater Company. He circled the courthouse, admiring the architecture of the brick framework and the flowers blooming in the gardens. Dark-skinned laborers worked the ground, and snatches of Spanish conversation drifted toward him as he skirted their work areas. Again he thought with embarrassment of how little he knew of a language that was spoken by a good 20 percent of the city's population. Probably 30 percent if you counted those who lived in their midst undocumented. As far as he knew, they might as well have been speaking Russian.

Stan turned abruptly at the corner and headed back downtown. Past the thrift shop, past Ace Hardware, past the department store that used to be Kline's, where Rose would take the children for their back-to-school shopping. Adult clothes upstairs, kids down. Before Kohl's and TJ Maxx and Old Navy. What was the store now? He glanced up. Right. A conglomeration of shops: a chiropractor's office, Goshen Tae Kwon Do, LOTS of Sound Advice. An accountant. The Peacemaker's Academy.

He looked at that name. Wondered about it. Peacemaker as in Jamie's career, or as in the Mennonites' way? He couldn't tell, and he'd never had any cause to go there in his job with the police.

A few minutes later, he was stomping up the steps at his house, angry with himself for thinking. For taking the walk. For . . . what?

He stepped inside, slamming the screen door behind him, and dialed a number he knew by heart.

"Good afternoon, this is the Naval Investigative Service, Petty Officer Robinson speaking. How may I help you?"

The voice so chipper.

Stan gritted his teeth. "Chief Borgman, please."

"One moment, please."

Stan waited, his hand rigid on the phone, his back tight.

"Chief Borgman here."

"Chief, it's Stan Windemere."

"Ah, Detective. It's been a few days, hasn't it?"

"I've tried not to—"

"No, no, it's fine that you called. Really. It's just . . ."

Stan pushed his temple with a finger. "You don't know anything more than last time."

A pause. "I don't. I'm sorry. I wish I would. We're doing everything we can."

"Yes. I know."

Silence for several seconds.

"Detective?"

"Yes?"

"If there are any clues out there, we'll find them. I refuse to give up hope."

Stan took in a deep breath and blew it upward. What the

good chief wasn't saying was that no matter how much any of them *hoped*, it didn't change the reality. Whatever it was.

∼

Some Hispanic teens were climbing into a rusty Grand Am when Stan arrived at The Depot. He'd driven past the front parking lot just to check and was rewarded with the glimpse of the kids. The boys were unfamiliar to him, except for the dark, hooded expressions he'd viewed so many times. But was that the same boy getting into the back seat of the car? The one he'd seen before? As he drove, he craned his neck, trying to see through the reflection in the small triangular window.

A horn blared, and Stan whipped his head forward, just in time to miss the fender of a shiny Camry. Sweat sprouted on his forehead, and he avoided looking back at the car of boys. You'd think he was a new driver, rather than one who'd been policing the streets for the past twenty years. Embarrassment filled him with a bout of dizziness.

His parking spot, which he reached without further incident, was empty, but Matthew Schwartzentruber stood beside his buggy, ready to climb into the closed interior. The horse gave no sign of noticing either Stan or the slam of his car door.

"Evening," the Amishman said.

Stan nodded. "Got everything tonight?"

Schwartzentruber's brow furrowed, then cleared. "Ah. My forgetfulness the other day. This time I made sure I had all I needed. I don't want to travel back in the rain."

Stan looked up. Sure enough, the clouds had slid across the sky, covering the sun. He shook his head. His powers of observation were clearly backsliding. "Hope you beat it home."

A glint of white showed in the Amishman's face. "We'll see what Katie here has in her if the thunder starts."

Stan raised his eyebrows.

"She hates lightning."

"Well, then," Stan said. "Godspeed to you."

"I thank you."

Stan raised his hand, halting the man. "Katie stands out here all day long?"

Schwartzentruber smiled. "She could. She has. But usually I come in the van."

Stan nodded to himself. One of the many vans that transported the Amish from the country to their jobs miles from home. "So this trip today?"

"I was too late for the van. Thought I'd give the old girl some exercise. She doesn't mind waiting a few hours."

Stan smiled. Reached out to touch the soft nose of the horse. She snuffled at his fingers. "She's a fine horse."

"That she is. A hard worker."

Schwartzentruber hopped into the buggy and tipped his hat with his right hand as he grabbed the reins with his left. Katie gracefully maneuvered backward and around Stan's car, heading off at a good clip. Stan watched until the buggy had turned the corner and disappeared up the road.

A fuller warehouse greeted him, new stacks of blankets piled high against the far wall. Towers of five-gallon buckets reached to the ceiling, and Stan wondered briefly what would happen if they were to tip and fall. Not something he'd try to discover.

A wide trail led through the warehouse toward the office door, and Stan walked slowly, making side trips to corners, shadowed now by the piles of goods. Nothing was amiss, and Becky's office, lit briefly by the overhead light he switched on, was empty.

The inner office was also quiet, with only the now-familiar hums of the equipment. Very like the sound his own computer made. The computer that spit out nothing he wanted to see. He pulled his phone from his belt, made sure it was on, checked the battery life. Everything ready. Ready to field the call that never came.

Stan walked through the office and out into the main lobby of the building. Rear lights flickered as a car exited the parking lot. The Grand Am? He wasn't sure. But the car with the group of teens was gone.

Back in the office he set his lunch on the counter and investigated the inside of the refrigerator. No notes tonight. No leftover cookies or pieces of pie. Too bad.

He closed the door and turned around, recognizing the niggling in his gut. Curiosity leading him, he found himself again at Wendy's desk, looking down at that double frame with the black-and-white photos. Picking it up, he studied the faces of the two men. Serious expressions, as if to smile would be unmanly. Like all of those team photos Jamie had been in through the years. Fifteen high school baseball players, or even junior high, molding their faces into what they hoped were masculine, no-nonsense expressions. *Mess with us, we'll beat you down. We're number one. Bring it on.*

Andrea's team photos held none of the testosterone-driven awkwardness. Instead, the girls, clothed in their matching uniforms, their hair pulled back into tight ponytails, smiled brightly. *We're young. We're beautiful. We're sisters.*

Oh, the folly of man. Of young men.

The photos came out of the frame with surprising ease. Stan glanced up self-consciously, as if afraid he might be found out. Maybe these Mennonites had installed their own version of a nanny cam. A security guard cam, for those men worldly enough to want to carry a gun.

Of course there was no such surveillance, and Stan recognized his feelings for what they were: discomfort with his urge to investigate. He really had no right. But now that the pictures were out of the frame . . .

Nothing. No names. No dates. The backs completely blank.

Stan grunted with disappointment. And with annoyance. Why did he care so much, anyway?

He gently slid the photos back into the frame and set it in its place on Wendy's desk. Staring at those faces, he tried to analyze his curiosity. What was it, exactly, that drew him to these men? He shook his head, amusement overriding his curiosity. He guessed he had to admit it. He was just a nosy bugger.

Nothing else on Wendy's desk called to him. He turned and walked to the front of the office. He was not going to look at The World. He wasn't. Especially not that section to the right above his head. Where the greens and reds and purples met at the Black Sea, the borders of Romania and Bulgaria and Turkey. There, where his eyes caught on Russia and Ukraine. Where there were no pins, no smiling missionary families. No Friendlies.

He rested a hand on the wall, then used it to push away and spin around.

God Bless the Whole World—No Exceptions, the pile of bumper stickers on Sheila's desk said again.

He turned, bumping his thigh on a display table, rattling the box of pins. *Enemies—you just gotta love 'em!*

One more spin, to a poster, *Water is Life*. Ah. Relief. Water he could contemplate. Water, where Jamie spent so many hours sailing, refining his skills, learning about those enemies the Mennonites wanted to love. Water, that sea across the world. . . .

Stan lurched through the office, past the conference table, into the warehouse, out the back door. Rested his hands on the rail where Katie had been tied, her droppings still fresh in the night air. Road apples, the locals called them. Although in this case, parking lot apples. But why apples at all? Because horses ate apples?

Stan laughed without humor, leaning his head on his arms, feeling the pull in his back. Breathed in that night air, spiced with the scent of the horse.

Eventually he straightened, took a final deep breath through his mouth. Checked out his surroundings, looking for moving shadows or unidentified shapes. Nothing there, of course.

He unlocked the door and went back into the warehouse to make another round.

≈

Jerry was early again. "You okay, Stan?"

Looking up from his seat on a plastic-wrapped blanket, Stan twitched a smile at the director. "I'm fine." He stretched and rubbed his eyes. "Another shipment coming in?"

Jerry studied the stacks of goods, hands on his hips. "Mid-morning, supposedly. From Battle Creek, Michigan, area."

Stan's knees cracked as he stood. "I guess I'll be going, then."

Jerry nodded absently. "Okay, thanks again." And he was off to the inner office.

"Jerry . . ."

The director turned, distracted.

"Can I ask a question?"

Jerry's eyes focused on him. "Oh. Of course. What is it?"

"In there?" Stan gestured inside.

"Sure. Is something wrong?"

"No, no. Just curious." Taking the lead, he walked into the office, ending up beside Wendy's desk. He pointed at the double frame. "Who are those men?"

Jerry squinted with confusion, following Stan's finger, before his expression lightened. "Oh. Interesting. I've never noticed this here." He picked up the photos. "This guy, on the left, his name was Clayton Kratz. And the other is Daniel Gerber. Two of the three people who have died during their service for MCC by something other than an accident or natural causes. At least, we think so. The third person isn't pictured here. Her name was Marie Fast; she was killed in service during WWII. But these two, they actually disappeared and were never found."

Stan's heart leapt to his throat. In a moment, he said, "How'd that happen?"

"Well, Daniel Gerber, the one on the right, was a Goshen

College student, and left for MCC service in Vietnam during 1961. He was abducted by the Viet Cong in 1962 and was never heard from again. There have been 'sightings,' but none of them have ever been verified. My dad was at the college with him. Stood beside him in choir. So Gerber would be, oh, mid-sixties by now, if he were alive.

"The second man, Clayton Kratz, was another Goshen College student and one of the very first MCC workers. MCC was formed in 1920 when Kratz and two other men went to help the Mennonites suffering from the war in the Crimea."

Stan froze. "The Crimea. You mean *Russia?*"

"Yeah. He went over there to work with them and take supplies, and he never returned. The last time he was seen he was being taken away by the authorities, carried in a horse-drawn cart."

"He disappeared in *Russia?*"

"Well, yes."

Stan grabbed the cubicle wall.

"Stan? You okay?"

He swallowed. Looked at his shoes. "Sure. Sure, I'm okay." He breathed in. Out. "Is that why you don't have any workers over there? In Russia?"

"What?" Jerry looked where Stan now pointed, toward The World. "Oh. No. Not at all. Kratz really isn't an icon for MCC. I mean, no one looks at him that way. Some of us remember him, of course, but you know, life goes on. Service goes on. We're sorry we lost him, and a lot has been done through the years to find out what happened to him, and to Gerber too, but it's not something we dwell on. There's a dormitory at Goshen College named after Kratz, but I'm not sure the kids who live there even realize who he was."

Refuse to give up hope, Chief Borgman had said. Had the Mennonites given up hope?

"So why aren't there workers in Russia? Why do you ignore that part of the world?"

Jerry smiled. "We don't ignore it. That's just not the Great Lakes region's responsibility right now. I believe our MCC Winnipeg office has workers over there. You want me to find out how many are there?"

Stan blinked. "No. No, that's all right. I . . . I don't really need to know. I was just . . . " He closed his mouth, pinching his lips together. Turned to go.

"We have information about Kratz," Jerry said. "Over here." He walked toward the resource center.

Stan's feet followed.

"There are a couple of videos." Jerry ran his fingers over the boxes. "But they're out. Rats. We have some tapes that tell the whole story about him. Who he was, what we know about him. And a book . . . not here, either. Somebody must be studying him. Or the early days of MCC, anyway. Oh, here. Some Goshen College yearbooks from 1918, 1919, 1920. He'd be in those. Wow, we're getting close on a century ago now that he disappeared. You'd think we'd have some answers."

He held a yearbook out to Stan. "You want them? They'd show everything Kratz was involved in at the school, before he went into service."

"No. Thank you."

And Stan hurried outside, where his vomit landed on the pavement, the smell overtaking the odor of the hardening manure.

He wasn't as seasick as he'd feared. Rather, the motion of the boat was soothing, like a rocking chair. He was fortunate that the weather conditions were favorable.

The bunks in the officer's quarters of the USS Whipple *were fairly comfortable, as well. Cramped, but not much different from a dorm room. He sat on the edge of his assigned bunk, ducking his head away from the bed above. His few belongings took up little space in the locker that was bolted to the wall.*

He got up and made his way—hanging onto furniture—to the desk, which was also secured to the wall and floor. He pulled out a pen and paper, setting it on the wooden table.

A sudden swell sent him careening into the wall, but he steadied himself, rubbing the knee that had banged into the wooden chest of drawers, and began writing.

"I suppose by the time this letter reaches its destination, school will have opened and the different activities will be in full swing."

Chapter 5
FRIDAY

Stan sat on Jamie's bed, his head buried in his hands.

A century. One hundred years, almost, since Clayton Kratz had disappeared into the Russian landscape. All that time and his family had received no closure.

Stan pulled his head up and hung it straight back, his eyes locking on the ceiling fixture. A simple, round, translucent globe. It produced ample light and brought no attention to itself on a normal viewing of the room. It fit Jamie. Simple. Efficient. Adequate for his needs.

They'd remodeled the kids' rooms at the same time, allowing them each to choose their own paint, carpet (within reason), and light fixture. Andrea, of course, had chosen the set with the middle golden circle on which two chains hung, returned to the ceiling, and dropped again, dangling two floral globes at just above head height. With pink light bulbs. And tassels.

Jamie's was . . . just like Jamie. Not flashy. Not overkill.

There was a collection of bugs in Jamie's light now, lying shadowed against the glass. A layer of dust covered the top portion of the globe, and one of the two bulbs had burned out. Rose kept the room itself clean, dusting every week, vacuuming over the lines from the week before. Stan figured she couldn't reach the light, or she hadn't ever bothered to look up.

Stan went out to the garage and found a light bulb in the cabinet. In the mud room he got a rag, which he dampened at the bathroom sink.

Back in Jamie's room, he used his fingers to unscrew the pins holding the globe in place and gently lowered the glass. He tipped the bugs into the trash and began wiping the surface of the fixture. The dust was so thick he realized that all he was accomplishing was the transfer of dirt from one section to another. He took it into the bathroom where he rinsed it in the bathtub—the sink being too small—and dried it on the hand towel.

The light bulb rattled as he took it down, and he tossed it into the wastebasket, to keep the bugs company. He replaced it with the new one, surprised that he'd somehow managed to pick the same wattage as the one already there.

He was tightening the final screw on the globe when he heard a sound. Rose stood in the doorway, watching him.

"One of the bulbs was out," Stan said. "And I cleaned out the bugs."

"Oh. Good." She looked from him to the light, and back again. "I hope you didn't use the good towel in the bathroom."

Stan lowered his hand, an exhausted sigh threatening to break loose. He closed his eyes briefly, then opened them. "Rose . . ."

But she was gone.

Refuse to give up hope.

The weight of the screwdriver hung heavy in Stan's hand. He closed his eyes again.

Jerry had followed him outside at The Depot, only to witness him spewing all over the parking lot. Stan had blamed it on the chicken sandwich he'd made for his midnight lunch. He wasn't sure Jerry believed him, but what else could he say? Stan had taken the handkerchief the other man had offered, and driven away.

Stan yawned and reached his hand up to rub his eyes, hitting his forehead with the screwdriver. He looked at the offending tool and tossed it on the bed. Contemplating it some more, he sank down next to it, where it nestled in the crease under the front of Jamie's pillow.

Two months, it had been. Two months since Chief Borgman and the lieutenant had come to the door. Too long.

It had been close to a century, about . . . what? Eighty-some years since Clayton Kratz had disappeared in the same part of the world. Jerry said Kratz's family never knew what had happened to him. How could they go on? How could a family survive it? A marriage?

He glanced at the doorway, but Rose had not come back.

The NIS was working to find Jamie. Chief Borgman was still on the case. But after two months . . .

No one was on Clayton Kratz's case anymore. At least Stan couldn't imagine it. Who was going to reopen the case of a Mennonite kid from 1920 when there were current cases? Ones that actually had a chance of bringing someone home?

It didn't seem right. Leaving a kid out there in the cold.

His head nodded toward his chest, and he lay down, pulling his feet, shoes and all, onto the bed.

It didn't seem right.

Some time later Stan awoke. A blanket had been thrown over him, but his shoes remained on his feet. He blinked at the light now streaming through the cracks in the blinds. Looked up at the ceiling light, which sat dormant.

A century was a long time to be lost. He wouldn't accept that fate for Jamie. *Couldn't*. But there were no avenues that he, a civilian, could follow that weren't already being traveled by the NIS. Even if he was a police detective.

He could, however, follow the trail of Clayton Kratz. That road seemed to be empty.

 ～

The parking lot was clean; someone having scooped up his vomit along with the horse manure. He wondered if there was someone he should thank. If that person was Jerry. Or Matthew Schwartzentruber, the Amishman.

A quick and efficient round of the office and even fuller warehouse proved no problem. No one lurked in the corners. No boogeyman waited in the shadows.

Stan stood in front of the resource library shelves, his eyes scanning the book titles. There were the yearbooks. Old and dark against the newer volumes. He pulled them out and inhaled their musty aroma, wondering how long it had been since anyone had looked at them and why the people who had taken the videos and books had gone without them.

Carrying the books, he settled himself in Becky's warehouse office. It was a tad warmer there, and he felt better being closer to the materials he'd been hired to protect.

Laying the stack of books in front of him, he picked out the oldest. 1918. The soft cover was dark green, the spine held together by a cord woven through two holes in the side, the knot in the front the only thing keeping the book from falling into separate pages. The Goshen College logo looked much the same as the current one Stan had seen through the years on brochures or in the *Goshen News*. An oil lamp on a Bible. "Culture for Service."

He flipped to the back and grunted with irritation. No index. A statement to their worries about pride, perhaps? One thing Stan knew about the Mennonites, especially the older ones, was the stress on humility.

Back at the front of the book, he opened the cover. The yellowed pages, spotted with age, declared, "The Maple Leaf, Published by the Juniors and Seniors of Goshen College." A dedication, a foreword, the board of editors . . . Seeing that Kratz was not among them, Stan skipped a closer reading.

He paged through the photos of campus and the faculty, pausing only to notice that women graced some of these pages. Believing Mennonites to be conservative, especially back then, Stan had expected the faculty to be all men. Most of them were even mentioned by their given names, except for Mrs. Samuel H. Plank, matron of East Hall. Stan supposed she'd given the okay for that. Or her husband had.

Stan paged through the seniors. Juniors. Sophomores. No Kratz. It took a while. The photos weren't even in alphabetical order. He wasn't sure what order they were in. Nothing specific that he could find. Just a bunch of unsmiling, very serious-looking students.

The freshmen. He must be here. And there, on the second page, second row, Stan found him. A different photo from the one on Wendy's desk. A younger shot. A small smile above his tightly knotted tie and suit coat. Stan studied the boy. The young man. Innocent of what was to come.

Stan left him there and kept paging through the book, in case there were any more photos.

He found the Academy—high schoolers, he supposed. And separate departmental schools of the college: Bible, Music, Agriculture, Home Economics, Business . . . Normal? What was a Normal school? Ah, Education. Interesting title for it.

Finally, student organizations. Perhaps he'd find a picture or two of Kratz. The Cabinet of the Young People's Christian Association, Christian Workers' Band, the Foreign Volunteer Band. Stan stopped to look at that. Nothing he could see that had anything to do with Kratz or Russia. He kept going.

He stopped suddenly at the Students' War Friendship Fund. What in the world? Reading, he discovered that the students felt they had not done their part in the war effort, knowing there were people who had realized great suffering in other parts of the world. They made a financial goal of seven hundred dollars—a great amount in those days—and exceeded it quickly, ending up with over twelve hundred. This from students who were, for the most part, paying their own way through school. Interesting, again.

But then, it was likely that not many of them had gone to fight in the war, either. This was their way of offering some kind of service. A payment to appease their guilt? Perhaps.

Stan turned the page. Kept turning. Ah, there he was. The Auroras Literary Society. One group, among many such organizations, to work at public speaking. Huh.

And there he was again. Oratorical Association. Freshman team. Same photo.

No more mentions of Kratz, but interesting details, nonetheless. Athletics consisted of tennis and basketball. Complete calendars appeared with "interesting happenings" from day to day: some guy named Lantz went on a first date with Miss Meyer, the lights in the boys' dorm went out, four boys went to a taffy pulling. . . . Stan laughed to himself. The things that seemed important.

Ads for the yearbook's sponsors: dentists and printers and restaurants that had long since gone out of business. The proprietors had probably been dead many years before this night, when Stan saw their advertisements.

He laid the book aside and picked up the next—1919. Brown this time, with the tying cord broken, going only through one hole in the front. Stan opened it gingerly.

A lot of the same. Stan paged through it quickly, arriving at the sophomore class. There he was. Kratz. Another small smile in the second row. A year older. A year closer.

Again in the Auroras Literary Society. And something different—the vice president of the Library Association. Hmm. A love for books. That's good. Stan was always telling Andrea, "Find a guy who likes to read. Who loves books."

"Why?" she'd always ask. "He'll be boring with his nose stuck in a book all the time."

"He doesn't have to be a nerd. Just someone who appreciates a good story. Who has a good imagination."

She'd roll her eyes.

Jamie took several books with him when he left for Russia. His Bible—the small one he could keep in his shaving kit. *The History of Baseball*. And his favorite—James Herriott's *All Creatures Great and Small*. "You never know," he'd said with a laugh, "when you'll be camped out in a tree somewhere and need something to do."

Kratz was the secretary of the Oratorical Association this year. Taking some responsibility. Stan liked to see that. And the winner of the Interclass Oratorical Contest the year before. As a freshman, he'd beat them all out. Good man.

Stan kept going, into athletics. Baseball was first. He scanned the faces, and stopped, his mouth open. There he was. The names weren't given, but Stan was certain of it. Clayton Kratz. Smiling, a baseball cap atop his head.

Setting the book on his lap, he reached again for the earlier yearbook. He hadn't seen a baseball picture, but there it was. Spring baseball. Just a mention in the Athletics section—no team photo. And there was Kratz, third in the batting order. No telling what position he played. The last thing in the section: "Liechty was elected captain but was called to the army in the draft."

So even the Mennonites were subject to the government's will. Perhaps that money offering wasn't a guilt payment, after all.

A sound rang like a shot through the warehouse, and Stan lurched from his chair, the yearbook tumbling to the floor. He glanced at the clock with disbelief. Almost three hours had passed since he'd sat down. Heat ran through him, and he picked up the yearbook, setting it on top of the others. He glanced at his cell phone, wondering if he'd been so immersed he'd missed a call.

Of course he hadn't.

He looked up again, scanning the area around him. What had made that sound?

He was a well-lit target in Becky's office, so he quickly walked to the opposite wall and flipped the switch for the warehouse lights, turning them all on. Standing behind the wall, he peeked out the door. Nothing moved. The outside door was firmly shut.

The sound really had not been like a gunshot. More like a sharp thump of some kind. No telling if it was inside or outside, especially since he'd been lost in the yearbooks. Like an amateur.

He automatically patted his hip. Holding his hand there, on the empty space, for a moment, he took a deep breath, closed his eyes, and steadied himself. He called out, "Anyone there?"

No response. He stayed still for a minute or two, listening for another sound. Any movement.

Nothing.

Slowly, carefully, he exited the office, his eyes darting from corner to corner. Not too many shadows, with all of the overhead lights on. But still he checked every possible hiding place.

Nothing again.

The inner office was just as quiet. No movement. No one there. The door was shut and locked. He opened the door, checked the lobby. Walked it quickly, looking down the short hallway where Choice Books was located, checking behind the large planters. No one. And no one in the front parking lot.

He let himself back into the MCC office and strode through, past the desks, to the warehouse, to the back door. Steeling himself, he opened it.

No one. No movement. Nothing. Except . . . He groaned, hammering his flat hands on the hitching rail.

His poor car.

Rocks, ranging from pebbles to fist-sized chunks, lay scattered on the ground around his LeSabre. Matching dents pocked the doors, hood, and top of the wounded vehicle. The windshield displayed a crack, like a spider, across the driver's side. Long scratches ran from front to back along the side and across the hood.

Stan drooped back against the building. Looking at his feet, he noticed a good-sized rock at the base of the back door. Probably what had made the noise he'd heard. What had sent the kids—*stupid kids*—scurrying away.

He walked in a slow circle around the car, despairing of the cost to repair it. Wondering if the vandals had, indeed, totaled it.

Back at the door he let himself in and walked to Becky's office. Phoned the dispatch center.

"Police, can I help you?"

"It's Detective Windemere."

"Detective?" A woman. Alert. "I thought you were off work for a while."

"I am. But I've got some trouble. Criminal Mischief. On a car."

"Everybody okay?"

"Far as I know."

"Perpetrators there anymore?"

"Not that I can see."

"Okay, I'll send a squad. You know whose car it is?"

"Yeah," he said, sighing. "Mine."

~

The cops—as he suspected, from his own experience—had no leads. No other reports of vandalism that night. Just stupid kids out doing stupid things, and his car was in the wrong place at the wrong time. No graffiti pointed toward any one group or gang. No cigarettes, candy wrappers, beer cans. No fingerprints left behind. At least he figured there weren't any. Unless they were on the rocks. He hated to spend man hours on something that was probably just dumb kids out too late on a Friday night. Where were their parents, anyway?

If he had been anyone else on the force, he would've endured some major razzing from the officers. If the event had been a year ago, even two months ago, they would've sympathized with him, then begun some ribbing that wouldn't have ended for a long time. As it was, three squad cars showed up to make sure he was okay, but the officers tiptoed around him, not sure how he was going to respond. Asking very respectful, very gentle questions. He understood. It was really rather sweet. If one could say that about cops.

The squads left about an hour later, after helping him clean up the broken glass and sweep the rocks to the side of the lot. He didn't want Jerry cleaning up after him two nights in a row.

One of the officers promised to come by and get him at seven, give him a ride home. How he looked forward to that. Explaining to Rose.

He watched the cars disappear, heading out to their respective patrols. Closed his eyes. Went back inside. Wrote a note to Jerry, explaining what happened and that he'd have the car picked up in the morning. Taped it to Jerry's office door.

He knew he couldn't look at the yearbooks anymore that night. He already felt guilty. And stupid.

A round through the warehouse and inner office revealed nothing unusual. Nothing out of place.

Stan ended up at The World, looking at the shape of the country where two young men had disappeared. He reached up, placed a hand over the area. Rested his forehead on the wall.

Couldn't find any words to pray.

Postcard to Mr. Abram Clemmer, Franconia, Penna, U.S.A.
Oct. 1, '20
Dear Bro.
We are in Const. And expect to sail for Russia tomorrow. Everything has gone favorably so far. God willing we will be at our destination by next week. The Russians are in a bad condition.
C. H. Kratz

Chapter 6
SATURDAY

"It was the Mennonites," Rose said. "They vandalized your car."

"Rose." He was too tired to say anything else. He took a bite of egg and chewed it slowly.

Rose sniffed, hands tight in her lap, her food ignored. "They hate Jamie, just like they hate anyone else involved in the military."

"They don't hate anybody."

"They couldn't discriminate by not hiring you, so now they're trying to run you off. All because you have a brave son. Braver than theirs."

"Rose." He rested his fist on the table, the tines of his fork raised to the ceiling. "They don't even know about Jamie. How could they hate him? Or me?"

She stared at him. "You didn't *tell them* about Jamie?"

He sighed. "No, Rose. I didn't."

"And why not? Aren't you proud of your son?"

"Rose—"

"Are you afraid of what they'll think of you?"

He set his fork down, lining it up with his knife. "What would you have me tell them, Rose? 'Yes, Mr. Brenneman, I have a son. Named Jamie. He's serving his country in the military. The Navy. Something you don't believe in. Would rather die than be a part of. And, by the way, he's missing. Has been for two months. There's a good chance he's not even alive anymore, since it's been that long. Most military personnel who are kidnapped are questioned and killed. That's the reality of it. I've tried not to lose hope, but it's getting harder every day. That's why I'm not working at the police department anymore. Remember how Chief Gardener told you I was on leave? Well, I was asked to stop working. Because I was losing it.'"

He cleared his throat. Picked up his fork. "There, Rose. Is that what you want? Is that what you wanted me to say?"

Rose's eyes had widened. Glittered. Her nostrils twitched. She picked her napkin up off of her lap and threw it at Stan. Then she left the room.

Stan took a deep breath. And let it out.

∼

Five hours of restless sleep seemed to take many more, and Stan finally left his bed. He thought about seeking out his wife, apologizing for whatever it was that had happened at breakfast, but decided he wasn't sure if he was up to it. Anyway, there was a good chance she wanted him to steer clear of her for the day. Way clear.

That was enough thought about delaying the inevitable. For the moment.

Acknowledging his cowardice, Stan settled himself in the den, the 1919 Goshen College yearbook on his lap. Not wanting to spend any more time on the books while at the MCC office, he'd brought them home, where he seemed to have more than enough time to fill these days when he couldn't sleep. He lifted a hand to open the cover, but, reconsidering, got up first to set the alarm on the desk clock. He didn't want to lose track again and forget to go to work.

Back on the chair, he opened the book to the page with the baseball team's photo. His eyes went immediately to Kratz, but soon strayed to the other young men. Young men who all smiled, every one of them, with a youthful exuberance and joy. Stan shook his head, wondering at the difference between a team photo then and a current one. Jamie's friends with the stolid expressions.

Leafing through the shiny pages, he studied each layout for Kratz, scrutinizing the pictures and names. The next mention of him was on the Students' Council as a sophomore representative and an officer for the year. Impressive.

Stan kept going, but halted when the pages arrived with the "happenings" on each day. He read about someone named Weber telling an "original" joke, the War Work Drive, and Shoup losing his diary. He paused at the mention of the Freshmen-Sophomore Boys' Debate, where "The hatchet is buried." Kratz would've been a part of that.

No more mentions of Kratz, but Stan had to chuckle at the advertisement for the Goshen Lightning Rod Co. A business that still existed—and looked from the outside like it probably hadn't changed a whole lot since 1919.

Shifting in his seat, Stan set the yearbook on the floor and picked up the one marked 1920. He paused, his stomach fluttering. 1920. The year Kratz had disappeared.

The first thing Stan noticed upon opening the yearbook was Kratz's name on the list of the yearbook staff.

Business Manager . . . Clayton H. Kratz . . . '21.

The pit in his stomach deepened at the sight of that number, the year Kratz would have graduated. He turned the page to a familiar sight. The dam, as seen in 1920. The same place he and Jamie had taken their unsuccessful fishing expedition.

Where both of his kids had followed him to secretly fling bread to the well-fed but seemingly starving ducks. Where he had sat just the other day.

"What are you looking at?" Rose stood in the doorway, her expression one of muted interest.

He placed a hand over the page. "Photo of the dam."

She took a step closer. "But what is it? That book?"

Stan gritted his teeth, but held up the yearbook, the cover toward his wife. "Just something I borrowed from . . . Well, from work."

"The *Maple Leaf?*" Her furrowed brow cleared, and her eyes iced over. "You're reading Goshen College's propaganda now?"

"It's not . . . It's just an old yearbook."

"'In and out,' you said. No one would see you. It was just a job."

"It's only—"

"And now you're bringing it home?"

Stan looked away, out the window.

"I told you not to take that job. I *told* you."

"Rose." He kept his eyes on the cloud visible through the top pane. The pane with the Windex streaks, Rose only tall enough to give good attention to the lower one, the desk proving too formidable an obstacle to scale.

There in the den. Stan's room, really.

"Rose, what have the Mennonites ever done to you?"

But she didn't answer. When he turned around, she was gone.

≈

Stan spent the rest of the afternoon digging in the front flowerbeds, pulling up the creeping vines that seemed to penetrate the entire plot. The fire had gone out of his quest to scour the yearbook. The idea of Rose skulking in the hallway, her darkened aura hovering at the threshold of the room, was enough to drive him outside, where the fresh air could dissipate some of the tension.

But he could feel the pull of the book. Those pages that held the details—the public ones, at least—of Clayton Kratz's last year. His last year at the college, anyway. There could've been more years of his life. Just not years anyone knew about.

He glanced at his watch. A little after three-thirty. It was Saturday, and the first game of Andrea's doubleheader would be over. Maybe she was even into the second. He wished he were there. Cheering her on. Supporting her.

A rustling at the end of the flowerbed brought his head around, and he paused in his work. He watched as the leaves of the daffodils parted, and two amber eyes stared out at him. He leaned back on his haunches.

"Well, hello. Where did you come from?"

The eyes remained unblinking, but an orange tail swatted at the foliage. Ah, the cat he had seen out the back window. He wondered if it had successfully hunted the robin.

"Come here, kitty." Stan held out a hand. "Here kitty, kitty—"

"Cleaning out your flowerbed?"

A shadow stole over the daffodils, and the cat darted away, back from where it had come. Stan groaned inwardly. He leaned forward to ease another root from the ground and rested on his knees, tossing the vine toward the wheelbarrow.

"I was thinking I'd see you out here sooner," the woman said, "since you're off work and all. Thought you'd need something to do to pass the time until you hear some news. News about Jamie, I mean."

Stan bit his lips and gently set his shovel on the ground. He stood up slowly, back protesting. "Hello, Dorcas."

He forced his eyes to the woman's face. Inquisitive, eager, annoying as all get-out. Just seeing the force of her smile made his teeth ache.

"You folks doing okay for food? Casseroles holding out? The cookies I brought?"

"We're doing just fine food-wise, Dorcas. Thank you."

"You need any more of my cooking, you just holler."

Stan's stomach recoiled at the suggestion, and he put a hand over his midsection. Dorcas's eyes dropped to the movement, and he patted his stomach, hoping she'd misread his motions. "Rose is keeping me fed. Don't you worry."

"Well . . ." The shadows in her well-lined face deepened. "I see how she looks these days. Like a light wind would blow her into Elkhart. No color to her. She eating okay?"

"She's eating fine." Except for that day. And the day before . . .

Dorcas pursed her lips, studying his face. "I'd hear if there was any news? You'd tell me?"

"You'd hear."

Her mouth twitched, and she fluttered her hands to where they landed on her bony hips. "I'd hate to hear from someone else what my own neighbor wouldn't say."

"You'd *hear*, Dorcas."

"Well. Okay." She turned to go, her gait crooked across the lawn.

Stan knelt back down beside the flowerbed, the blooms blurring, doubling as he tried to focus.

"I do see you, you know," Dorcas said, calling across the grass.

Stan lifted his head. "What?"

"Going out at night. Leaving her alone. It's a shame when a man can't solve his problems in his own home. With his own wife."

A few more stomps and she was inside her house, the screen door slapping shut behind her.

～

Stan left the yearbooks at home. He didn't trust himself to

study them at work. The trick was finding a place to put them where Rose couldn't find and confiscate them. He waited until she was locked in the bathroom before stealing into Jamie's room and placing them under his mattress. Rose might clean Jamie's room periodically, but she had no reason to change his sheets.

She would be home. He'd have her car. Of course, she'd be sleeping most of the time he was gone, but he still felt guilty about leaving her trapped there. In their closed house, with Dorcas next door watching, waiting for any sign of movement.

Stan couldn't help but glance over at his neighbor's windows when he left, looking for a tell-tale sign, a glint of light on her glasses, a twitching curtain. A frown of disapproval.

The time at work was Saturday Night Quiet, a different feel from the previous workdays. The staff had been out for the day, and tomorrow, being Sunday, would be at church, home, and wherever else their time off took them. Where did Jerry go after church? Stan wondered. Home to a pot roast? To Das Essenhaus for a good Mennonite buffet? Pizza Hut? He just couldn't see him standing in line at McDonald's or KFC. At least not for Sunday dinner.

The mountains of supplies hunkered silently in the warehouse, waiting for their trip across the globe, and Stan studied them, hands in his pockets. How would they reach their final destination? By ship? By plane? Jerry had never said.

Stan made his routine check of the office and lobby before allowing himself to check the resource library for the videos about Clayton Kratz. Of course he didn't find them, or that little book Jerry had mentioned. The office hadn't even been open, so who would've checked them in? He grunted at himself with annoyance. He'd have to make do with the yearbooks until at least next week.

A quick search of Sheila's middle drawer revealed Post-its and pens. Stan scribbled a note, asking if she knew when the materials would be returned so he could look at them. He regarded his handwriting, curious about what she would think of his request. He wondered if she was even familiar with the materials he was asking about.

A song with a Latin beat rang out from Stan's belt, and his heart leapt to his throat. He scrabbled for his phone, yanked it from his waist, dropped it, and picked it up to frantically search caller ID. The NIS? Rose?

Andrea.

Stan placed a hand over his heart. Counted to five. "Hello, sweetheart. How did things go?"

"Like I expected. We creamed 'em."

"Good for you. Pitching go okay?"

"Fine. Struck out eight."

Stan laughed. "That's all?"

"That's enough. They weren't any too happy."

"I guess not."

The airwaves crackled between them.

"You at work? At the Mennonite place?"

"I'm here."

"I called home first. Mom said you were gone already. 'Off to help the peace-lovers.'"

Stan winced, imagining the conversation. "Sorry."

"S'okay. It's just Mom."

Mom now, anyway. Not Mom a year ago. Three months ago.

"So I just wanted to let you know how the games went."

"I'm glad you did. I wish I could've been there."

"Really, Dad. It's okay. Hardly any parents showed up."

"All right. I'll be at the next one."

"Next home game's not for a week. The two weekday ones are far away. Michigan and Illinois."

"I don't know—"

"Just come Saturday."

"I will. We will."

"Sure. Okay."

"I love you, Andi."

"Bye, Dad."

The rest of the night went by like honey through a rust-clogged sieve. Stan marched through the warehouse, the office, the lobby, checking windows, checking doors, checking to make sure Rose's car hadn't suffered the same fate as his. Extending his midnight lunch, chewing slowly, one item at a time. Minute by slow minute. Hour by hour.

All the while drawn to Wendy's desk, to the dark eyes and solemn face of a boy—a man—whose path had led him to Russia. To die among strangers.

This card gives you some idea of how Constantinople looks, the water in which you see the boats is the Golden Hoan, and that in the distance is the Bosphorous. The part of the city in the foreground is called Pera, and across the Hoan, Stainboul. We are staying in Pera.

There is quite a mixture of people here—I never saw so many races and colors before. Some of the streets are very narrow and crooked and dirty.

Our ship stopped near Athens and we saw Mars Hill (where Paul preached. Acts 17). We also visited Rome while we were waiting in Italy, and saw the catacombs there, and the Coliseum, where the martyrs lost their lives.

Chapter 7
SUNDAY

The house smelled of pancakes and sausage. No matter the chaos of the rest of the week, Sunday mornings never wavered. Pancakes and sausages, orange juice, coffee, and some kind of breakfast cake. If Stan was frustrated with the food the remainder of the time, he could always close his eyes and remember Sunday morning.

This morning Rose was already in her church clothes, her back to him as she stood at the stove.

Stan cleared his throat lightly. "Should I shower before or after I eat?"

Rose slid two pancakes onto a plate and placed a sausage next to them. The plate made almost no sound as it touched the table, but Stan heard it like a dinner gong. He sat down.

"For what we are about to eat," he intoned when Rose was seated across from him, "we are grateful. Amen."

The syrup was warm, the pancakes hot—blueberries gooey—and the coffee's steam rose in graceful wisps. Stan really was grateful.

Rose sat motionless, hands on her lap as she stared at the pancake on her plate. No sausage. No syrup. No coffee. Her breath hitched, and she seemed almost ready to speak. To engage him. But the moment passed, and Stan finally picked up his fork.

"I guess I'll get changed," he said ten minutes later. His plate empty, his stomach full, but protesting. It hadn't been the most stress-free of breakfasts.

Rose's plate still held its pancake.

Stan soon sat at the wheel of the car. Rose's car. Showered, changed, Bible in the middle of the seat, a wall between him and his wife. The silence lasted to Route 19 and well onto the bypass.

"The Crums asked us out for dinner," Rose said to the passenger-side window.

"That's nice."

"I said no."

"Okay."

Andrea used to love those Sundays out. The Country Buffet with the Crums, the Blakes, the Joneses. Sitting beside the Crums's youngest boy, eating off his plate, while he scavenged from hers. Until they got too old. Too old for innocent friendship, and it turned to avoidance of touch and sidelong glances, shot across the table. Andrea stopped filling her plate to the brim. The boy went back for seconds. Thirds.

Jamie ate his fill, like any growing boy. Steak, potatoes, design-your-own-stir-fry. He'd fill his plate once, twice. All the time wishing his mother had just put a roast in the oven before church. She had sometimes. But more often than not they ended up with friends, standing in line with the others who'd neglected to plan ahead.

Now Andrea ate at school. Cafeteria food. Or, for all Stan knew, patronizing the local Greek, Italian, or Mexican places, run by families. Families who didn't get to go to church because they prepared food for those who did.

"You're wondering what we'll eat," Rose said.

"No."

"Well, I didn't . . . I haven't thought about it."

"All right. We'll figure something out."

The parking lot was full. Stan drove to the front of it to drop Rose off at the door of the church, then found a spot in the far corner to leave the car. He checked his phone, made sure it was on vibrate, and got out, locking the door behind him. Not that he should have to worry about it at the church.

"Morning, Stan."

A man stood waiting, standing at the back of Stan's car.

"Tim," Stan said.

They walked toward the church.

Tim cleared his throat. "Beautiful day."

"It is."

Almost to the church, Tim stopped, a hand on Stan's sleeve. Stan waited, knowing what was coming.

"I'm sorry, Stan. I'm . . . I don't really know what to say. But if I can help in any way . . ."

Tim's face was a study of frustration. Stan knew what was going on in his head. Not knowing the words to say, what service to offer. If he should've just kept his mouth shut to begin with. Stan had felt it enough times himself, dealing with victims' families, other parents who had lost children.

"Thanks, Tim. I appreciate it."

Tim nodded, his hand jerking upward, then down. A gesture of futility. They walked into the church.

Stan found Rose, a statue in the corner, and together they approached the sanctuary.

"Hello, Mr. Windemere. Mrs. Windemere." The usher, a young man—just had his first child, Stan believed—greeted them with a wide smile. "Any seating preference today?"

Stan glanced at Rose, her face a rock.

Stan shrugged. "Somewhere in the middle."

Rose made a low sound in her throat.

"Toward the back," Stan said.

They sat behind an elderly couple, the woman already with the pew's hearing enhancer in her ear.

The choir stood. Began a song. Something soothing. Bach? Stan thought so. He closed his eyes. Opened them fifteen minutes later when the organ played the introduction to the first hymn.

> May the Lord depend on you?
> Loyalty is but His due;
> Say, O spirit brave and true,
> That He may depend on You!

Stan did his part. He sang. He stood. He sat. He said amen. Stood again. Recited the Lord's Prayer ("forgive our debts as we forgive our debtors"). Sang the amens. Wanted to sit. Stayed standing till the end.

The old couple leaned on each other for support as they readied to leave their row. She set the ear piece in its holder and turned to lift her purse. The husband held her elbow as she leaned to pick up a crumpled hankie from the pew, her hands trembling as she plucked at the square of fabric. Finally she succeeded, tucking the material up the sleeve of her flowered dress.

Rose didn't wear flowers. She preferred tailored suits of solid colors. Sometimes a brooch or a necklace. A white shirt with a pointed collar. Definitely no swatch of damp hankie up her sleeve.

Rose coughed. He turned to check on her, and she tipped her head toward the elderly pair. He looked and found two sets of eyes studying his face.

He cleared his throat. "Pardon me. Did I miss something?"

"Hiram just said hello," the woman told him, her smile bright in her wrinkled face.

"Of course. I'm sorry."

"You looked a thousand miles away," Hiram said, chuckling.
Stan's temple throbbed.

"It's good to see you here," the woman said. "We've been
praying for you."

Rose stiffened.

"Thank you." Stan breathed in through his nose. "We appreciate any prayers you send our way."

Rose stepped out of their pew into the aisle and stood waiting, hand on her purse strap, eyes toward the back of the room.

"Thank you," Stan said again.

The woman smiled gently. "God bless you."

"Ryan Hiebert's grandparents," Rose said.

"What?"

"The elderly couple. That's who they were. Remember
Ryan? He was a year ahead of Jamie."

Ah, yes. The Ryan who had been Jamie's friend for quite
some time. Who had gotten on Rose's bad side somewhere along
the line. Perhaps it was the time—

"I wonder what's ever become of *him*. He's never at
church."

"He went to college somewhere. Got married, I think."

"Hmphf."

Road kill. That's what it had been. A night after a youth
group event. Jamie, Ryan, and a couple of other guys had gone
around finding road kill and hanging it on signs. The only reason
Stan and Rose had found out was that they heard Andrea mention it to Jamie —in the backseat, quietly, but not so quiet as
she'd imagined. Stan had thought Rose was going to explode.

Stan had had a hard time not laughing. Out loud.

"What kind of girl would marry a boy like that?" Rose dug
in her purse for her compact and took it out, examining something around her eye.

Stan didn't defend Jamie's old friend. Boys—young men—do a lot of dumb things. Soap houses, hang dead animals on road signs, go off to foreign countries to die—

Stan swerved to miss a squirrel, and Rose clutched the dashboard, her compact flying to the floor. She picked it up gingerly and sat back, tucking the mirror into her purse.

"He probably ended up in advertising," she said a minute later.

Stan gave a bark of laughter. It was possible. The boy had already shown his creativity with billboards.

A smile hinted at the corners of Rose's mouth, and Stan chuckled again, settling a little further down in his seat. His heart thudded against his chest, and he tried to push down the unfamiliar sensation creeping up his throat. What was it, exactly? Something . . .

He glanced at his wife. "Lunch?"

As Rose had mentioned, there had been no Crock-Pot on the counter when they'd left for church. No roast in the oven.

"I . . . I didn't get to it."

"That's fine. But what would you like to do? For lunch?"

She inhaled a loud breath through her nose and let it out in a slow sigh. The smile—if that's what it had been—had vanished. "Whatever you want is fine."

Stan did his best to rekindle the feeling in his chest. That tingling. "You feel like a sit-down restaurant? Fast food? Leftovers?"

She wiggled her shoulders, looking out the passenger side.

Stan's fingers whitened on the steering wheel, and he pushed the cruise button. Cops were notorious for nabbing people on the bypass. He'd be given a courtesy pass when they saw his badge, but he didn't want the fuss. Or the ribbing it would get him back at the department. He was already dreading the backlash from the car incident, once the officers felt comfortable around him again.

Stan negotiated his way to U.S. 33, where the restaurants kept popping up like litters of rabbits. Litters? Did you call a group of baby rabbits a litter? He didn't know. He liked the sound of it, though. A litter of restaurants.

He picked one and pulled into the drive-thru lane, where service would be quick and easy. And impersonal.

∽

"You didn't hear a word I said."

Stan's chair shook, and he whipped his head up to see Rose pushing at the headrest. The Cubs were actually beating the Phillies, and Stan had been watching them. The young men with multimillion-dollar salaries. "Sorry. What?"

"I said, I'm running out to get something."

"Something you need help with?"

"No. But you won't have a car."

He let his head fall back onto the chair. "Don't need one. It's my day off, remember?"

She remembered.

"I might take a nap. Game's almost over."

It was she who didn't hear this time. The door smacked shut in the kitchen, and Stan listened as she backed out the car and drove away. He got up and went into Jamie's room, shutting the door. The yearbook was right where he'd left it. The yearbook with Clayton Kratz's name as business manager.

Sitting at Jamie's desk, Stan quickly found the photos of the dam—where he'd been when Rose had interrupted—and paged forward. He was soon rewarded with Kratz's photo, staring out at him. The same photo from Wendy's desk. Probably the last formal photo ever taken of him.

Stan thought of the portrait on the mantel above their fireplace. Jamie in his dress uniform, the United States flag at his back. Mouth unsmiling, eyes thoughtful. Penetrating.

Student Assistant for Agriculture, this photo caption said.

Agriculture? He was a business manager and in ag? Stan guessed it made sense. Jamie and Andrea had been involved in multiple clubs and interests. That's what school was for—to figure out where you excel. What you enjoy most.

Stan kept going, through the seniors, to the juniors. Kratz's class that year. Stan sat back, blinking.

C. H. Kratz   Blooming Glen, PA.
                        President

President? He was the class president? That was the office for the political kids. Or the popular, superficial frat boys. Wasn't it?

Debater, orator, athlete and social star—a many-sided man is our president, Mr. Kratz. His earnestness and ambition coupled with determination and a genial nature make him a leader in all these fields of activity.

Stan stared at the wall, his hands folded on the book in front of him. But not for long.

The School of Agriculture, as in the previous yearbooks, had its own section. Stan, interested now, read the first paragraph:

One of the great problems before the world today, as a result of the recent war, is the production of food. The very existence of life depends upon an adequate supply and this supply is obtained thru the time-old industry of agriculture.

Yes. Agriculture and business do mix. Especially in a time of need.

Stan kept going, his fingers pushing aside page after page, his eyes flying through the photos, the names, the text. Kratz had been pictured in the previous yearbooks a handful of times. But now he was everywhere: The Young Men's religious cabinet, president of the Christian Workers' Band, again in the

Auroras, the Student Lecture Band, the Book Committee of the Library Association.

He was now vice president of the Oratorical Association, on the Junior Debate team, and the Affirmative Intercollegiate Team, "clashing with Manchester's Negative Team."

The center fielder of the baseball team, in the middle of the front row, holding a bat and a smile.

A photo of him with the *Maple Leaf* staff, a tablet and pen in hand, as if writing down business items as they occurred.

And here. Stan let go with a laugh. Kratz was voted "the most handsome fellow" by the campus girls.

Who was this paragon? Could he possibly have been for real?

Stan stood up and paced, hands on the top of his head. He felt antsy, like . . . like . . . like he was going to meet this guy and he wouldn't know what to say.

Ridiculous.

The Observatory was next. The day-to-day agenda, where they mentioned those little things that seemed so important to these college students. With Kratz's new visibility, Stan expected to see some occurrences. C. W. Band meeting. Baseball game. First junior class party. Kratz would've been at all of these things.

Peace Conference. Nothing more said about that.

Junior-Senior debate—

Wait. There. Thursday, November 27. In bold print:

Ede, Orpha, Kratz, and Dave seen leaving Dorm with traveling bag.

Stan ground his teeth. These stupid comments had no depth. No background. Who in the world were Ede, Orpha, and Dave? He kept going. Another one:

Monday, December 22. Fulmer and Kratz bury themselves in German.

Finally. The German Stan had expected all along from these Mennonites.

> Friday, December 26. Kratz has a bad dream—the night after the evening before.

What?

> Monday, December 29. Kratz has his sixth date with Miller during vacation.

Miller? Who's Miller?

Stan flipped back to the juniors. The only Miller there was a David. The vice president. Perhaps the "Dave" seen on November 27?

Sophomores had a Maude Miller. A Nellie. A Bertha Miller graced the freshman page.

But no Orpha Miller. No Ede.

Back to the days.

> Sunday, January 18. Kratz juggles names in announcing a new member to the Christian Workers' Band.

That was noteworthy? Apparently so, for an orator such as Kratz.

> Thursday, the twenty-first. Flu starts. Kratz gets it.

And—

> Friday, the twenty-third. Edith Miller sick with the flu. See January 21. Isn't it too aggravating that the flu is contagious? Kratz promptly gets worse.

So there she was. Edith Miller. Ede? Enough of an item with Kratz that the other kids are making fun of their shared flu.

Nothing more until April 18, when Kratz and Eschliman

go with the Glee Club to Yellow Creek Mennonite. Stan recalls a church with that name out toward Wakarusa.

More baseball.

Finals.

Stan paused on Thursday, June 3.

Wonderful stoicism demonstrated during exams. No one dead as yet.

As yet.

Give it a few months.

Stan sat for a moment. Then attacked the book again. Where was she? This Edith Miller?

There. Listed as a soprano in the chorus. But no picture. Again, as secretary of the Philomatheans, a literary society. But the way the names were printed under the group photo was too confusing. No telling which woman was Kratz's date. Stan growled with frustration.

"Anybody home?" Andrea's voice carried through the house and wended its way into Jamie's room.

Stan slammed the book shut and shoved it under the mattress, where he lay down. "In here!"

Footsteps sounded in the hallway. "Dad?"

"Jamie's room, honey."

The doorknob turned, and Andrea stuck her head into the room. "Sorry. Didn't mean to wake you."

"That's okay. I wasn't sleeping." The truth.

She came in and sat on the edge of the bed. "Aren't you cold? I can never take a nap without a blanket."

"I'm fine."

She tucked one foot underneath her, left the other dangling toward the floor. "Where's Mom?"

"Went out to get something. Don't know what."

She looked around the room at her brother's belongings. "How come the TV's on out there?"

Oh. "I was watching the Cubs."

"Yeah. I was, too." She grimaced.

"What?"

"You'd think with a three-run lead going into the ninth they could pull it off."

He let his head fall back onto the pillow. "They lost?"

She nodded. "Chase Utley hit in two runs, only to be followed by Ryan Howard knocking one over the center field wall. It was disgusting. You'd think they'd know to pitch around him by this time." She got up and studied one of Jamie's baseball trophies. Took it down from the shelf and blew off a speck of dust, rubbing the brass with her sleeve. "Remember how Jamie always said he was going to be the shortstop? Turn all those double plays?"

Stan grunted.

"How come he ended up playing outfield?"

Stan sat up, swinging his legs over the side of the bed. "He had a strong arm."

"So how come he wasn't a pitcher?"

Stan smiled. "Not all players are made out for the spotlight, Andrea."

She grinned and set the trophy back on the shelf. "My softball trophy's bigger, you know."

"And you never let him forget it."

The kitchen door opened, and the sound of rustling bags reached them. They stopped smiling, and Andrea ran a hand through her hair. "Guess I'll go say hi."

Stan nodded. "Sure."

His head spun, and he rubbed his forehead. He really *should've* been taking a nap.

The voices of Rose and Andrea drifted toward him through the house, quiet, rising and falling. He remembered those Sunday afternoons when the kids were younger and he'd been promoted to detective so he didn't have to work many weekends, squashed together on the couch, watching the NFL or a Cubs game. He'd be trying to doze while they watched. The kids would often have other ideas, but sometimes . . . sometimes they'd let him go, give him at least the illusion of resting. Their voices quiet as they talked or did their homework or played Monopoly. He never liked Monopoly himself, all that greed, demanding money until people were bankrupt, but the kids . . .

When Stan awoke, it was to the smell of popcorn. He opened his eyes in the slanted light coming through the blinds. Evening light.

He was covered with a blanket, like the last time he'd fallen asleep on Jamie's bed. Except this time the blanket was tucked under him, and his shoes were off. Andrea.

He rolled again to the side of the bed, his feet flat on the floor while he tried to ease the fuzziness from his head. He looked at Jamie's bedside clock, the red digital lights bright in the dimly lit room. Almost six-thirty.

He yawned, stretched, stood, joints creaking. Like an old man. Wandered out to the kitchen, where Andrea and Rose sat at the table, hunched over a big bowl of buttered popcorn. He stood in the doorway, watching, until Andrea caught him in her line of vision. Rose peered back over her shoulder.

Stan took a step in. "Enough for me?"

"Sure, Dad." Andrea pushed the bowl an inch his way. "Join us."

"No, no," Rose said. "You can have my seat. I'm done." She got up, wiped off her spot at the table, and threw her napkin in the trash. "I'm going to take my bath."

Stan and Andrea watched her leave. When she'd gone, Stan moved toward the table. "Sorry."

Andrea shrugged, her face a jumble of emotions. "It's all right. I mean, what are you gonna do? I wish she could . . ."

Stan waited.

Andrea shivered, her whole upper body quaking, then looked up at Stan.

He smiled gently. "Okay if I sit?"

She pushed the chair out further with her foot, and Stan took that as a yes.

"What were you two talking about?"

Andrea took another handful of popcorn, avoiding his eyes. "Nothing. Girl stuff."

He stood again. "Need a drink?"

"Got some Diet Coke. Thanks."

He poured himself a glass of orange juice and sat back down. "Andrea, what was the name of that girl?"

She took a swallow of Coke. "What girl?"

"The one Jamie was seeing in high school. The one your mother didn't approve of."

She laughed. "Like that helps a lot."

He smiled back. "I guess you're right."

"What year?"

"Senior, I guess. Or it could've been junior. They went to the prom. Tara? Tammy? Something with a T."

"Tonya. Senior year."

"Tonya. That's right."

"Tonya Burkholder."

Now he was remembering. "What ever happened to her?"

Andrea smiled, but it wasn't nice. "You mean with her and Jamie? Or just in general?"

"Both."

"As far as in general, I heard she got married. Lives in Middlebury with her husband and kid. Not sure about anything else. Just grapevine stuff, you know."

"Okay."

"As for the other, I suppose you can guess what happened with her and Jamie."

Stan sighed. "Rose?"

"Uh-huh. Although I guess their going to different colleges didn't help, either. One year of that long-distance stuff was enough to end it. So it wasn't entirely Mom's fault."

"Why didn't Rose like her?"

Andrea looked at him, confused. "You don't remember any of this?"

He didn't, other than vague recollections. "Sorry."

"Mom always said she was too needy. And possessive of Jamie. Of his time."

"Was she?"

"I don't know. Tonya liked Jamie. Wanted to be with him. I was just a middle-schooler. All that stuff was way over my head."

"Until the next year."

"Well, I guess."

When the boys had come calling. One after another, falling like dominoes while Andrea poked her finger at them.

"Anyway," Andrea said, "I thought she was nice. She actually talked to me like a real person. Jamie liked her too. Was able to ignore Mom at least for a while."

Stan waited.

"You really don't remember the big blowup?"

"I really don't." Although something niggled at the back of his mind.

"Her parents were okay with him at first. I mean, why wouldn't they be? He was polite, nice to Tonya. And Mom was okay with it, too. And you were. For a while." She paused.

"But?"

"But then it became a bigger issue."

"What did?"

Andrea stuck her hand in the popcorn bowl, swished it around. Then looked up at him, her eyes betraying anger and confusion—probably at his faulty memory. "That she was Mennonite, Dad."

Stan gripped his cold glass. "She was *Mennonite?*"

"You still don't remember?"

But he did. Suddenly, in a flash of mental images. Those nights of Jamie's questions. His disappointment. His anger. Wondering why his girlfriend couldn't support the one thing he'd begun to see as his calling. To join the Navy. To help others. To save the world.

Rose's anger at the girl's—Tonya's—unwillingness to see Jamie's views as the right ones. She would actually object to his beliefs and argue the finer points. The biblical points. Trying to make Jamie see that how he thought of saving the world and how she thought of it were two entirely different—and incompatible—things.

And finally, in a whirlwind of tears and frustration and sadness, the end of the romance. No more calls, no more dates, no more timid questions about what to get a teenage girl for her birthday. It had about broken Jamie's heart.

And suddenly Stan understood. Rose hadn't hated the Mennonites before, he was sure of it. She probably hadn't even really thought about them one way or another. But then this girl had made Jamie care for her, had stolen him away from his family for all those evenings and weekends, and then had disparaged the ideals Jamie had held so highly. She wouldn't change her mind, and she wouldn't budge an inch in her stance of nonresistance. She had broken up with him, claiming that if he continued in his quest to join the military then neither she nor her family would be able to welcome it—and, therefore, him—as a part of their lives.

Rose had never been able to forgive her for it. Or, apparently, the entire Mennonite church.

Stan looked at Andrea. "Jamie really loved her, didn't he?"

She nodded.

"But it wasn't enough."

Her lips tightened into a line. Relaxed. "I don't think he ever really got over her. Not entirely."

"He didn't date his sophomore year? Find someone new?" He certainly hadn't told his parents. Not that Stan could blame the boy, seeing how Rose had reacted the last time. And he was, by then, living at college, where he could come and go without their knowledge.

Andrea shook her head, tracing her glass's wet ring with a finger. "As far as I know, he never even took another girl to a movie."

Stan closed his eyes. Oh, Jamie.

There had been so many good movies to see.

∾

He finally found her late that night when he'd returned to Jamie's room. A face in the junior class of the Academy. Edith Miller. Dark hair in a bun, a slight smile. Eyes alive.

But what was the Academy? Stan had assumed it was high-schoolers. Could Clayton Kratz, a college junior, be allowed—encouraged by his friends—to date someone in high school?

He read the explanation of the Academy and came to the conclusion that it really was a high school. A feeder school for the college, perhaps. It was hard to tell.

Stan looked back at the 1919 yearbook. There she was, Academy sophomore, this time. Nowhere in the 1918 book. Maybe she was older than a traditional sophomore, because he couldn't imagine Kratz would've been allowed to date a . . . what? A fifteen-year-old? No way.

Back to 1920. No more mentions of Edith other than the chorus and her literary society, except for those in the Observatory, linking her with Kratz. Stan wondered if she had still been in his life—been his girlfriend—when he'd decided to go to Russia. If she'd seen it as a call from God or the church. If she'd discouraged it.

If she'd ever gotten over it.

~

The unplanned nap had messed up Stan's schedule. Well, kept him to it, really. For the past week he'd been awake at this hour—three a.m.—keeping watch over the Mennonites. Or their stuff, anyway. So it wasn't surprising that he lay there now, eyes wide open, studying the shadows on the ceiling.

There was no more to find in the yearbooks. He'd been through them so many times in such detail. Any more and he'd begin to memorize the trivial facts about all of those people who were surely long dead.

He'd opened Jamie's closet and found his high-school yearbooks there. The two *Arbutuses* from Indiana University. Before Jamie had decided to leave college and go for his naval career. Stan had begun paging through, but at the first photo of Jamie, a smiling shot with his buddies in the cafeteria, he'd closed the covers and gone to bed.

When Jamie first talked about leaving the university, Stan had hoped baseball would be enough to keep him there. He was all set to start varsity his junior year, left field for the Hoosiers. The coach had mapped out a strenuous off-season program for that summer: weight-training, running, mental exercise. Summer league. But when the final playoff game had been lost that spring, Jamie had hung up his glove and hat and told Stan he'd be playing for a new team now.

Stan had given his blessing. What else could he do?

Rose shifted beside him, pulling the blankets, then rolling over. She faced him now, closely, her breath teasing his neck. A shiver ran through him, and he eased his head to the side, toward his wife.

Her face was relaxed in the dim light. Calm. Serene. Her body curled into an S, fists balled at her chest. Stan lifted his hand toward her, held his palm over her side. He traced her shape, his hand in the air, several inches above the blanket.

Over her hips, her thighs, then back up along her side to her shoulder. Hovered over her face, her hair.

She mumbled something in her sleep, wiggling deeper into the covers, and Stan froze, holding his hand above her head. Her breathing steadied, her face melting back into its sleeping state.

Stan brought his hand back, rested it on his stomach. Turned his face toward the ceiling. Counted the hours until dawn would break.

Cable received Oct. 30 from Constantinople
To Mumaw, Scottdale, Pa.
. . . Left Kratz Halbstadt . . .
Miller

Chapter 8
MONDAY

The morning newspaper, left face up on the kitchen table, practically screamed the news.

BRING THEM HOME!

More than three hundred Goshen College students gathered on the lawn of the Elkhart County Courthouse last night, carrying lighted candles and banners protesting our country's military presence in Iraq. From "NO MORE WAR!" to "FIX THIS COUNTRY FIRST" the students were united in one cause: to criticize our government's actions—but to do it peacefully. The group was led by—

"Now how do you feel?" Rose glared at him from the doorway. "Want to defend your new friends *now?*"

If Stan had still been at his old job, still been an active part of the Goshen Police Department, he would've known about the peace rally. The college was good about checking in, letting the GPD know what they were planning. Applying for any necessary permits.

"Well?" Rose's face had lost the tenderness of nighttime. It was hard to remember the softness, the gentleness, he'd seen just hours before.

"I don't know anything about this." He laid a finger on the paper. "But it looks like they didn't do anything wrong."

A sound shot from her lips, a hiss of exasperation, frustration. Anger, formed in her throat. She reached up to scratch her forehead, a frantic, involuntary gesture. "I don't . . . You don't . . ."

"It's not every Mennonite's fault that Tonya Burkholder broke up with Jamie in high school, Rose."

She looked up at him, her eyes piercing. "*What?*"

The phone rang. Stan looked at it. Two rings. Three. He picked it up. "Windemere residence."

"Mr. Windemere? Garcon's Garage." The words, colored by a Spanish accent, held a premonition of bad things. "We've had a chance to look at your Buick. I can give you an estimate."

"Would it help for me to come down?"

"Not really. I can tell you—"

"I'll be there in ten minutes." He hung up. "I need to go to the garage. I'll walk, so you can have the car."

Rose's nostrils flared. Her lips worked. Her eyes closed.

Stan grabbed a light jacket and headed out the front door.

∽

The car was a total loss. Not anything grand to begin with, the early 2000s LeSabre had met the car version of the Grim Reaper.

"We're talking a few thousand to get the dents out," the older mechanic said. Older meaning twenty-five instead of his partner's twenty-three. His hair, black as night, his skin brown against his teeth. "At least. The windshield's not a big deal, but the body . . ."

The younger one tapped a knuckle on the hood. "It's not worth the time or the money. For you or us." A heavier Spanish accent. Not hard for Stan to understand after his years in the police department.

The older man held out a hand, palm up. "Sorry, man."

The two mechanics stood together, the pair of them, staring at the sad specimen, their lips tight, heads nodding. Stan gazed at them. How did they do that? Look like someone had died?

"Thanks for checking it out. What now?"

The older one hitched up his shoulder. "Call your insurance company. Find out how much they'll give you."

"Start shopping for a new car." The younger man's eyes were suddenly alight.

"I leave it here?"

Older man nodded. "Your adjustor's already stopped by. Took photos and all that. We'll have it taken away once you've cleaned it out."

So Stan got to work. First the glove compartment. Maps, flashlight, registration, pens that didn't work, written directions to places he couldn't discern. Then the door pockets. Dirty tissues, plastic straws, tire pressure gauge. Miscellaneous trash under the seats. A Kleenex box. And then the trunk. Blanket. First aid kit. Jumper cables.

He held the plastic pack zipped over the pair of cables. The first ones Jamie had ever used. Almost electrocuted the both of them. But did end up getting the car going without killing anyone.

"You want these?" The young man asked, holding out Stan's car keys.

"Just the key chain." A gold rectangle, the Ten Commandments engraved on it. A gift from one of the kids, back when they picked whatever looked shiny.

He stood up, the trunk gaping in front of him, and put the key chain in his pocket.

"Here's a bag for the rest of the stuff," the kid—the younger one—said.

Stan took the plastic sack, filled it, then stood looking vacantly down at the carpeted trunk.

"Sorry again, sir," the kid said.

The car was generic, really. A goldish-brown four-door. A Grandpa Car, Andrea had called it. She'd been embarrassed to learn to drive in it. Afraid her friends would see her. Would've rather been driving her mom's Taurus, although that wasn't much better. But the job had been Stan's. Teach the kids to drive right so they didn't kill themselves. Or anyone else.

Andrea took to it immediately. Screeching around corners, muttering to the other drivers (a running monologue), never hesitating to use the horn. Stan had been green around the gills whenever they drove anywhere. Of course she'd been fine once he finally let her get her license. She'd only gotten stopped twice—once with a warning and once with a "Do I need to tell your father?" Stan had never heard the end of it at work.

Jamie had been tentative. Hands at ten and two, steady acceleration, eyes flicking regularly to the rearview mirror. Never once complained about the then-new car. He'd gotten that tight, irritated look around his eyes when he'd tried to parallel park the beast, but he hadn't let loose with the words. His confidence grew quickly, and before Stan quite knew what had happened, his son was out by himself, licensed and legal.

Stan eased the trunk lid closed and leaned on it until he heard the click. Kept his hand on the cool metal, took a breath. He could sense the men watching him. He wrapped the handles of the bag more securely around his wrist and walked out the front of the garage.

∼

Rose was gone when he got home. No note. No leftovers in the fridge. No message that Chief Borgman had called with an update. Stan made himself a peanut butter and jelly sandwich. Washed it down with some milk.

With no yearbooks left to study, Stan felt his motivation for staying awake waning. He went into his bedroom, where Rose had already made the bed. He eased back the comforter, slipped off his shoes, and lay down. He was tired enough it only took him about forty-five minutes to fall asleep.

When he woke the house was still quiet. A search found Rose in the laundry room. He stood in the doorway.

"Car's totaled."

Rose pulled a wad of towels from the washer and plunked them into the dryer.

"I guess I'll have to use your car again tonight."

Washcloths. *Thwack.* Underwear. *Thwack.* What looked like a bra and some socks tangled together. *Thwack, thwack.*

Stan went to the kitchen and packed his lunch—another PB&J—with an apple, some chips he wasn't sure were good anymore, and some cookies he found in the freezer.

He went back to the laundry room. "We eating supper together tonight?"

Rose spun the dial, pushed the button. Began loading the darks into the washer. Paused to lean on the washer, fingers on her forehead.

"Want me to make something?"

Rose took down her hand. Checked the pockets of Stan's church slacks. "There are some hot dogs in the refrigerator. You could make them in the toaster oven."

"With mac and cheese?"

She shrugged. Dropped the pants into the washer. "Sounds all right."

Stan went to the pantry. Took the toaster oven off the shelf and placed it on the kitchen counter. Got the hot dogs going, started on the mac and cheese.

The kids used to love this meal. Jamie with his meat and

pasta separate, Andrea with chunks of hot dog stirred into the cheesy macaroni. Accompanied, of course, by strawberry Jell-O with mandarin oranges. No time to make that now. They'd have to get along with plain old applesauce.

Soon they ate. They cleaned up. And Stan left for work.

∼

The warehouse was no fuller, the incoming supplies stalled for the weekend. Stan figured there would be more, since he'd be employed another two weeks, but he didn't know for sure. He made a quick check of the corners, the shadows, the office, the lobby. Everything quiet, as usual.

Placing his lunch on the counter, he found a couple of notes, one on top of a book. The other one, just a slip of paper, was from Jerry.

> I was able to reach the administrative assistant in our Winnipeg office. It seems MCC has no volunteers living in Russia right now, though some of our workers do travel there occasionally to meet with partners who are supported by MCC. We have found it extremely difficult to place volunteers in Russia due to visa restrictions, so we base our volunteers in Ukraine. Currently we have 8 MCC volunteers living and working in Ukraine. Hope this helps.

Stan reread the note. He turned around and rested his back against the counter, breathing in and staring at the ceiling. After a few moments he rubbed his eyes, turned around, and picked up the other note. From Sheila.

> You were asking about the Clayton Kratz materials. This book was returned today. A Sunday school class had a presentation about him yesterday and had checked out this book and the videos. The videos are

still with the church members, but I thought you
might find this interesting. If you still want them, I'll
let you know when the videos come back in.

Stan clenched his fingers, let them go, and reached for the
book. *When Apples Are Ripe* by Geraldine Gross Harder. A small
hardback, mostly red, by some publisher called Herald Press. A
drawing on the front, of a couple walking somewhere. Maybe
along a stream. Or a river. Stan looked closer. The Elkhart River?
Here in Goshen? By the dam?

He opened the book to the table of contents, but just as
quickly closed it. He knew what would happen if he started
to read. He looked at it, felt the nicked-up cover with a finger.
Strode through the office, out to his car—Rose's car—and put
the book in the trunk. Out of sight.

Went back inside. Spent the night pacing.

Dear Orie:

Just a few lines about my doings since you left us so suddenly at Alexandroff. We left Alexandroff with Mr. Kopp about 11:30 on Saturday. On our way from the city we met the army coming back again, they told us that a telegram was sent from headquarters telling that the army should not withdraw from the city. We passed out from the city quietly but all of us felt a little better when we got out of gun range from the Reds. We drove all afternoon and spent the night at the same place we had spent the day before. The next morning we started out early and gathered considerable information on the way concerning the action of the Reds. We learned that about three thousand of the Red Cavalry broke thru the lines to the east of Halbstadt robbing several villages and throwing the whole region into panic. The people of Halbstadt had scarcely quieted down by the time that we arrived here Sunday forenoon. Apparently the army about Alexandroff was called over to the region east of Halbstadt but after the aeroplanes drove the Reds back the army was again ordered back to Alexandroff.

My headquarters will be here at Peters, that is, if he can get fuel for the stove. Mr. Peters assigned the front room to me, the one in which his desk is located. His will be a mighty fine room. The ladies of the house do no work here but leave that to the two maids in their service.

Mr. Peters intends to call his committee together tomorrow and see what can be done in the way of relief work. Up to this time we have no news from Alexandroff or Chartizer but the people here are of the opinion that if Chartizer does open there will be plenty of chance to help them with food supplies.

I am also sending a letter to Arthur concerning some supplies which he can probably put into my trunk.

Sincerely yours,
Kratz

Chapter 9
TUESDAY

Rose was in the shower when Stan got home, so he poured himself a bowl of Rice Chex and a glass of orange juice, and settled in at the table. After a quickly said grace, he opened the new book, *When Apples Are Ripe.*

Kratz's picture, on the title page, stared out at him. A photo he hadn't seen before. A serious shot, in suit coat and necktie, his hair parted far to his left. Stan's breath hitched as he took in the boy's expression. No smile this time, and eyes looking distant. Almost sad. One would think he knew his fate, but that was, of course, impossible. Stan turned the page to find a letter from the author:

Summer, 1970

Dear Reader,

Some people who reach out for their goal in life do not take time to look around to see the smiles that cover up tears, to see the shy person and help to draw him out, to understand how a mother

143

feels, or to play with a lonely child who wants to be noticed.

Clayton Kratz, a Pennsylvania Dutch farm boy who loved apples, reached out for his goal but he also had time to look around and care about others as he grew up. He wanted to be a farmer for as long as he could remember, but he stopped reaching for his goals for a while during his college days to notice and do something about a desperate need in the world.

This is an important year for those who know about Clayton. It was apple time in Pennsylvania when he was born and it was apple time again when he disappeared forever into a dark night exactly fifty years ago. This year is also the fiftieth anniversary of the Mennonite Central Committee, the organization that sent Clayton on a mission of service to the suffering people in Russia after the First World War. People call this organization the MCC. Clayton was one of the first three MCC workers.

What was it that inspired this young Mennonite to look at the needs around him? What was it that made him brave to the end, and how did he show his courage? How did he disappear? You will want to find out. And as you read, I think that Clayton will be sharing some of his courage and concern for others with you.

> Sincerely yours,
> Geraldine Harder

"What's that?"

Stan started, spilling milk onto the table from his spoon.

Rose exhaled sharply. "I don't want to know, do I? Something else from those people?"

Stan looked at her. At her tense face, her clenched fists. Studying her, he made himself remember why she was angry. Why she was afraid. He turned back a few pages to Kratz's photo and held it up for Rose to see. "His name was Clayton Kratz. He went on a service trip to Russia in 1920."

Rose's eyebrows lifted.

"He disappeared on that trip and was never seen again. At least, not by anyone who knew him."

Rose's lips twitched. "A Mennonite?"

"Yes." He tapped the photo with a finger. "One of the first workers MCC ever had. He was twenty-four."

A sound escaped Rose's lips. She turned abruptly and went to the back door, peering out the window onto the small porch. Her shoulders, which had been tense and straight, slumped, and she leaned her forehead against the glass.

"Rose?"

She pulled herself up, tugged on the hem of her sweater, and went outside, shutting the door quietly behind her.

Stan sat for a moment, looking at the door, mouth slightly open, then turned back to the table. He checked the copyright date—1971—skimmed the acknowledgments in the book, as well as the list of illustrations and the contents. And there was the first chapter: "Apple Time in Pennsylvania." He began to read:

> Clayton Kratz, a Pennsylvania Dutch farm boy, knew
> it was autumn because the apples were ripe. . . .

≈

Ten hours later, Stan woke up in his La-Z-Boy. He had moved to the den from the breakfast table after clearing his dishes and had settled in to read more about the young Mennonite man. He'd learned about Kratz's childhood, his siblings—twin brothers and three sisters—his days in a one-room schoolhouse, and his chores on the family farm. There was a photo of his first home, and Stan spent some time studying the stone structure.

Stan had paused briefly after reading about Clayton's brother William, who had died from diphtheria at the age of nine, when Clayton was only seven. That pause was enough to send Stan into sleep, head lolling onto the recliner's back. When he awoke, the light in the room had shifted, and he pulled the string on the reading light by the chair.

The pages of the book were fanning open, and he laid a hand on them, finding where he'd left off in chapter three, "The Stone House on the Hill." The Kratz family was having devotions soon after William's death. His father read from Psalm 91 in the King James Bible:

> He shall call upon me,
>   and I will answer him.
> I will be with him in trouble;
> I will deliver him, and honour him.
> With long life will I satisfy him.

Young Clayton asked his father, "Why didn't God answer our prayers to help William get better?"

"We don't know the answers to some questions," his father explained.

"But William never did anything bad. Why couldn't God have given him a long life?"

His father smoothed his graying hair. "I think God *is* giving William a long life. William loved Jesus and tried to be like Him. He is alive in heaven now. He is not dead, Clayton, so his life will be long as the Bible promises."

"Besides," his mother said, "we will always remember William. He will keep on living in our hearts."

Stan closed the book. He placed it on the desk. And went outside to dig in the flowerbed.

~

Dorcas left him alone this time, but the orange cat came to visit. Definitely the preferred of the two companions. Stan watched as it huddled, this time behind the irises.

"Back again, eh?"

The cat took a tentative step toward him, toward his out-stretched hand, its neck elongated, keeping its body at the maximum distance. Its nose touched Stan's finger, tickling him.

"That's right. Nothing to be afraid of."

The front door opened, and Rose appeared on the steps. Stan snatched his hand back, and the cat froze in its spot, sinking toward the ground.

Rose's eyes widened. "What in the—"

"I don't know where it came from. It just showed up. I didn't feed it or anything."

Rose blinked, grabbed at the railing. "But it's—"

"Not supposed to be here. I know."

Stan looked down at the cat, who crouched silently, watching. "Go on. Get!" He waved a hand at the cat, who raced away, through the neighbor's yard, into the alley.

"Stan!"

He looked up. "What? It's gone."

"Yes. Yes, I know."

"If it comes back we'll call someone. The pound. Whatever."

She stared at him, her face soft, her eyes pools of sorrow. Then she went back inside.

Stan rested an elbow on his knee and rubbed his face. Put away his tools. He was done.

~

The back parking lot was crowded when Stan got to work. The first person he saw in the warehouse was Jerry, along with Becky and several other people unloading a truck.

"Hey!" Jerry smiled and beckoned him over. "What do you think?"

Stan pursed his lips, surveying the space. "Not much room to move anymore, is there?"

Jerry laughed. "This should be it, except for walk-in donations. We've received the shipments from all our usual places. Michigan, Illinois, Ohio. A truckload was brought all the way up from Tennessee. This one here was from Wisconsin."

Stan whistled. "Hope that stack of buckets doesn't come down on anyone."

"It won't. It's secure."

"If you say so."

A new voice broke in. "That's it from the truck, Jerry. Anything else you need?"

Stan turned to see the young Spanish guy from his first day, stopping at Jerry's side. Stan blinked, studying the kid. For that's what he was. Seventeen. Maybe eighteen.

"Thanks, Luis." Jerry gave the boy's shoulder a pat. "Have you met Stan Windemere? He's keeping an eye on the place for us at night."

Luis jerked his chin upward in recognition.

Stan put out his hand. "We've seen each other." Luis looked at Stan's hand for a moment, then took off his work gloves and shook it. His grip was strong. Strong and competitive. Stan held back a smile.

Luis patted the gloves against his thigh. "That all you need us for?"

Stan glanced behind Luis at the group of three other young men, leaning against a stack of blankets, hands gesticulating wildly as they talked. The lilting Spanish conversation drifted toward them, and Stan wondered what they were talking about. Their evening plans? Supper? Girlfriends? Breaking into the warehouse later?

"That's all, Luis," Jerry said. "Thanks a lot. I'll be in touch when it's all getting shipped out. We'll need your help then, for sure."

Luis hitched a thumb toward his friends, a question in his eyes.

"Them too." Jerry smiled. "And anybody else you want to bring. I mean, look at all this stuff."

Luis grinned, and Stan blinked at the change it made in his face. Perhaps he wasn't as old as he'd originally thought.

Jerry made sure the door was shut behind the kids and walked with Stan into the office, waving his thanks to Becky.

"Who is he?" Stan asked.

"Who?"

"Luis. The kid."

Jerry picked up a briefcase from the chair in his office. He turned around, set it on his desk, and rested his hands on it. "Remember a couple years ago when there was that gang shooting? In the cars? Where the kid who was shot was the brother of someone in the other car? David Ramirez?"

Did Stan remember? He'd been part of the investigation. Not something he liked thinking about.

Jerry continued. "Well, they were Luis's cousins. Several years older than him, of course, when that happened."

Stan flashed back on it with a jolt of recognition. Luis's face. Younger. Wide-eyed. Peeking around the corner of a door while Stan questioned his aunt. The dead boy's mother. A house full of relatives, all grieving. All angry.

"So what's he doing here?"

"Helping out whenever he can. Trying to stay out of trouble. It's not easy."

"And the other kids? The ones here tonight?"

Jerry shrugged. "Luis vouches for them. I'm giving them a chance."

"Are they the same ones he hangs out with in the parking lot?"

"I think so."

And those boys knew who Stan was. He remembered that first day, their Spanish conversation in the parking lot. He'd heard the word for police, the word *Gringo*, and a name. David. Those kids had recognized him right off, while he just saw them as yet another group of potential troublemakers.

Stan shook his head. It was good, what Jerry was doing. Kind. But also stupid. Weren't the gangs the main thing they'd hired him to keep away? Granted, some of the gangs were white kids, but a good portion of them were Hispanic.

Jerry picked up his briefcase. Held it at his side. "It's a risk, I know. But these boys have more going against them these days than is fair. The gangs don't help things, of course. But there are some good kids. Just like in any neighborhood."

"Sure."

Jerry's lips tightened, then relaxed. "When I was a kid, there was a bully at my school. Warren Nightingale. He'd pick on anybody. For anything. He was good at it, too. Did it when the teacher's back was turned or when the parent helping at recess was dealing with something else. They could never catch him red-handed. He had an older brother. Ed. He was just as bad. Probably picked on Warren more than anybody else, though. So Warren took it out on the rest of us.

"One day little Scotty Lantz got in his way. I don't remember why. Some trivial thing. Was ahead of Warren in line, pitched the kickball too hard, who knows. But Warren wasn't having any of it. Knocked Scotty flat on his back and was heading back for more. I was pretty big for my age—I know I don't look it now, but I got my growth spurt early—so I went up to Warren, spun him around, slugged him right on the nose." He grimaced. "Of course, I got caught. Sent to the principal's office. Stayed there the whole afternoon.

"I didn't know what would happen with my folks. I knew they were going to be mad. They'd probably ground me for weeks, with no TV. But it was worse. My mom gave me the silent treatment until my dad got home. Then we sat in the living room, them on the sofa, me on the chair facing them. 'We're very disappointed,' my dad said, 'that things turned out this way. Now that this has happened, what makes you think you're any better than the bully?' 'Because I'm kind,' I said. 'Kind? How can you be kind when you hurt someone?' 'Because I was standing up for little Scotty,' I said. 'Defending someone smaller than Warren.'

"My dad nodded, considering my explanation. Then he said, 'Have you ever been kind to Warren?'"

Jerry stopped. Looked at Stan.

Stan stepped back to let Jerry out of his office.

Jerry was halfway to the door when he turned around. "Was that stuff Sheila and I found helpful? About our volunteers in Russia? And the book on Kratz?"

"Yes. Thank you."

Jerry stood looking at him, his head cocked to the side. "Anything else I can get for you?"

Stan put his hands in his pockets. Shrugged. "Just when those videos come in."

"We'll let you know."

Jerry turned around again, prepared to leave.

"My son's in Russia."

Jerry stopped. Faced Stan. "Doing what?"

You didn't tell them about Jamie? Aren't you proud of your son?

"He's in the Navy. He's stationed over there."

"Ah. No wonder you're interested in that part of the world." He smiled. *Smiled.* "I'm sure you're very proud of him."

Stan choked back an exclamation. "Yes. Yes, I am." He was. He was very proud.

And Rose was wrong about the Mennonites.

About this one, anyway.

~

Stan whiled away the rest of the night, meandering between the warehouse, the front lobby, and the main office. He'd checked multiple times to be sure the kids hadn't come back to steal what they'd unloaded. Nothing. He was probably wrong about their motives. He *hoped* he was wrong.

His sandwich had gotten crusty, and the chips were as stale as he'd feared. When his meal was half-eaten, he threw the remainder in the trash.

Kratz's photo was partially covered by a stack of papers on Wendy's desk, and Stan reached out to slide the memos to the side. There they were. Those eyes. Not as morose as the photo in the book. But not the crinkly eyed smile from the baseball pictures, either. Stan turned away.

There were some new items on the display table in the welcome area. He glanced over the brochures, bumper stickers, pins. Stopped at a credit-card-size piece of plastic. Picked it up.

> I pledge allegiance to Jesus Christ,
> And to God's kingdom for which he died—
> One Spirit-led people the world over,
> Indivisible, with love and justice for all.

Not exactly the pledge he'd grown up saying. But he couldn't find anything really wrong with it. Except that nowhere did it mention the country Jamie was working for. Fighting for. Missing for.

He set it down. He could just see Rose's reaction to such rhetoric. She'd come storming into this place for sure. Preach some fire and brimstone about loyalty and honor. Now, that would be a sight to behold.

He went back to the warehouse. Looked out the back door. The moon was bright, reflecting off the windows of Rose's car. Nothing else caught his eye. No cars. No movement. No Hispanic kids—or any others, for that matter—waiting to catch him dozing.

He shut the door and looked at the stacks of goods in the warehouse. Going to God's kingdom. Providing love for those the world over.

Jamie would approve of the pledge. He might be a member of the U.S. Navy—and as proud of that as he was loyal—but the alternative pledge really did state his dream. To find justice for all people.

He'd wanted that ever since his addiction to *Star Trek*. Those *Next Generation* reruns, especially. In those future—albeit fictional—times, the entire earth was united. No one starved. No one had wars, except with aliens, of course. And no country ruled over all. Everyone on earth worked with everyone else. All had justice. It really was "all for one, one for all."

Andrea, of course, just wanted to be Seven of Nine, the tough Borg woman from the *Voyager* series, but Rose would never dream of letting her daughter out of the house in that tight outfit. Not even for Halloween. Stan had to agree. It was definitely one of the battles worth fighting.

Stan went back into the office. Stared down at Clayton Kratz. From the little Stan knew so far, Kratz would've lived by the alternative pledge. Christian Workers' Band, the Young People's Christian Association, his church. And from all indications, he hadn't just lived for it. He'd died for it, as well.

8-27-20

To whom this may concern,

This is to certify that Clayton H. Kratz has been appointed a relief worker under the direction of the Mennonite Relief Commission for War Sufferers of Scottdale, PA., U.S.A. and is subject to the plans and policies of this Commission.

In testimony of which we have hereunto set our signatures this Twenty-seventh day of August, Nineteen Hundred and Twenty.

Chapter 10
WEDNESDAY

The book hit Stan as he walked in the front door.

"Have you read this? This . . ." Rose waved at *When Apples Are Ripe*, where it lay open and crumpled by Stan's feet. "Chapter thirteen? 'What Should a Christian Do About War?'"

Stan rubbed his shoulder where the book's corner had struck him.

Rose's eyes burned. Smoldered with anger and disgust. "Is this the new way? The way you'd like to go? Tell our children to go?"

"I haven't gotten to chapter thirteen."

"He's a draft dodger, Stan. Whoever this guy, this *Mennonite*, is. Ran home to Mommy so he wouldn't have to go to war when the other young men did. Is that what you wish Jamie would have done?"

"Jamie wasn't drafted, Rose. He enlisted."

A growl burst from Rose's throat. "You are so . . . I can't . . ." She pressed her hands to her face.

Stan picked up the book. Unbent the pages. Was it true?

Had Kratz dodged the draft? Had he escaped while others had gone to fight? "Lots of other people have dodged the draft. Including some prominent people in our government."

Fire shot from Rose's eyes. "That doesn't excuse him. Your sweet little Mennonite." She paused, her eyes darting to the book. Stan held it close against his chest.

A smile twitched at the side of her mouth. "But I guess it doesn't really matter, does it. He was born in what? The late 1800s? However you look at it, no matter what happened to him. Whether he was a coward or just some Mennonite kid who went off to find his fortune. He's still *dead*."

Stan looked at his wife. Felt the book beneath his arm. And walked back out the door.

∼

The little family wasn't at the dam this time. A bit early in the day for them, Stan supposed, although he could remember days with toddlers that began at dawn. Or sooner.

He tucked his hands under his armpits and wished he'd brought a jacket. The misty air coming from the waterfall matched the chill he already felt inside.

A quick look in the trunk revealed a blanket—the red and green plaid kind with the fringes. For spontaneous picnics or an hour spent stuck in the snow. He pulled it out of its plastic sheath and flapped it open. It smelled new.

With the blanket around his shoulders, he reached in to the passenger seat and got the book. Took it over to the bench. Sat down.

He looked at the cover. Should he go directly to chapter thirteen? Skip the earlier years of Kratz's life? Did he want to invest any more time in someone who had dodged the draft?

But he hadn't dodged service. Hadn't dodged death. He may have been a pacifist, but he had still disappeared in a war zone.

Stan turned to chapter four, "Time for Sunday Meeting." And started to read.

> On a hill looking over the neat little village of Blooming Glen stood the Mennonite meetinghouse where the Kratz family attended . . .

∼

An hour later Stan was still cold. Too cold to sit at the dam. Too cold to stay away from home out of spite. Rose would be wanting her car. And his stomach was growling.

He had learned a lot about the boy named Clayton Kratz. How he'd loved the singing at his church and wanted nothing more than to become a farmer. But when his father turned sixty-five, they sold the farm and moved to town, where Clayton enjoyed walking to school and playing baseball with his schoolmates.

Clayton was sixteen when his father died. He and his family sang a song from the *Church and Sunday School Hymnal* during devotions to remind them that they would be reunited someday.

> How pleasant thus to dwell below,
> In fellowship of love;
> And though we part, 'tis bliss to know
> The good shall meet above.
>
> Yes, happy tho't when we are free
> From earthly grief and pain,
> In heav'n we shall each other see
> And never part again.

Halfway home, Stan turned the car north on State Route 15 and made his way toward 33. Toward the car dealerships. He spent some time looking around at the used car lots, talking with the salesmen, thinking about what he wanted. When he found it, he signed the paperwork, told the guy he'd be back, and drove home.

Rose wasn't there. He grimaced. She'd be ticked at him, taking the car when she must've needed it. A pain shot through his stomach, and he pressed on his abdomen until the feeling subsided.

He put his book under Jamie's mattress to join the yearbooks, yanked a jacket from the front closet, and took off down the sidewalk.

Fifteen minutes later he was knocking on Chief Gardener's open office door.

Roy looked up. "Stan?" He slid his reading glasses off his nose and studied his friend, eyebrows raised.

"You got a half hour?"

Roy pushed a button on his phone. "Do I have a half hour?"

A chuckle came over the intercom. "Sure."

He pushed the button again. Smiled. "What you got in mind?"

In two minutes Stan was in the passenger seat of Roy's Cherokee, his head against the headrest as they drove toward the car dealership.

"So what's Rose gonna say about this purchase?" Roy asked.

Stan shrugged. Watched hazily through the windshield. "Wouldn't matter what I bought."

"Yeah, I hear ya." The chief rolled his tongue around the toothpick in his mouth. "How's the job going? The one over there at the MCC?"

Stan breathed in through his nose. Let it out. "Good, I guess. Been there a week now."

"No trouble? Other than your car, I mean."

"No. No trouble."

Silence for a few minutes. Stan's head drooped to the right and he gazed out the passenger window.

"You like the folks over there? They treating you okay?"

"They're treating me fine."

"Good."

Stan rolled his head left. Looked at his friend. "What did you tell him?"

"Who?"

"Jerry Brenneman."

"The head guy over there? You mean about why you're not working?"

Stan nodded.

"Just told him you were on family leave. Didn't say why, exactly. Said you needed some time off from the job."

"He wasn't worried about that?"

"Apparently not."

Stan laughed to himself. Him and Luis. Jerry's charity cases. Stupid moves? No. Maybe.

They pulled up in front of the dealership.

Roy watched as Stan freed himself from his seat belt and got out of the car. "You need me to stay?"

"No. Thanks. I appreciate the ride."

Roy leaned over the seat. Looked up at Stan through the open door. "I heard your stomach growling, buddy. You want to go get something to eat once you're done here?"

Stan looked at him. Looked at the sky. "Maybe another time."

"If you say so. All right, then. Stop by anytime." He stayed there, over the passenger seat, until Stan met his eyes. He nodded, and drove away.

$\sim$

"What is that?" Rose said.

Stan looked back at the driveway, through the window. "A truck."

"I can see that. But what's it doing *here*?"

He tossed the keys into the basket on the stand. "I bought it."

She stared at him. "A truck."

"Yes."

She licked her lips. Blinked. Shook her head once, sharply. Went back to whatever she was knitting.

"Okay if I grab something to eat?"

She waved a hand toward the kitchen. Didn't look up.

Stan found a bagel. Ate it toasted with cream cheese while he stood looking out the back door. There was that cat again. Stalking something under their pine tree. Stan put a hand on the doorknob. Stopped. Rose wasn't there, in the kitchen, and couldn't see the cat trespassing.

He finished his bagel and washed his hands. Went back to the living room. Watched Rose while she knit.

"I'm going to sleep," he said. "Care where I do it?"

Click, click. "Sheets are off our bed. In the wash." *Click, click.* "Sorry."

Stan rocked back on his heels. Went to Jamie's room. Read until he fell asleep.

∾

The smell of something delicious woke him. Roast beef? Soup? He rubbed his face, put the book back under the mattress, and padded out to the kitchen.

The table was set for two. Soup bowls and the oversized spoons. Linen napkins. Fresh rolls from the oven.

"Smells good."

Rose finished rinsing off the oven sheet and set it in the sink to dry. "You hungry?"

"Sure."

He glanced at the message tablet by the phone. Nothing there. No flashing light on the answering machine. No message on his cell.

Rose tipped her chin toward the refrigerator. "I put a lunch together for you to take tonight. Some egg salad. A clementine. Some cookies. Don't forget it."

Stan's eye twitched. "Rose, did something happen?"

She picked up his bowl, took it to the stove to ladle something into it. Brought back a steaming serving of beef stew. "Why would you think that?" Her eyes glinting.

He opened his mouth. Shut it. "Just making sure. No calls from Chief Borgman?"

She had her own bowl now. The soup splashed into it. She set it on the table. "No calls." She sat, hands folded under her chin. Eyes closed.

Stan watched her for a moment. Said, "We thank you, Lord, for what we are about to eat. Bless it to our bodies." He hesitated, studying his wife. "And bless the hands that prepared it. Amen."

Rose pulled apart her roll. Buttered it. Ate it. And reached for another.

∼

The truck felt good. A 2003 Chevy S-10. Red. Quick. Stan planned to park in the front this time. Under a light.

But when he got there, the parking lot wasn't empty. Three cars, filled with kids. Hanging out. Laughing. He drove by slowly. Luis and his friends? He couldn't quite tell.

The parking lot in the back was in its usual state. Dark. Free of other vehicles, including the buggy. Stan locked the truck's doors. Set the alarm. Told it not to get into any trouble. Inside the warehouse he flipped on the light for the outside, since Jerry must've forgotten. He hoped it would deter any would-be vandals.

A quick look around showed nothing new in the warehouse. He strode through the office and out to the lobby, where he stuck to the shadows. Not afraid to be seen by the kids. Not even opposed to it, really. He just wanted to get a look before he was caught spying.

The boys were still in the parking lot, leaning on their cars, talking, a few smoking cigarettes. Stan studied their faces, a little too far away for details. Mostly Hispanic kids, their clothes baggy and loose, a variety of tattoos detailing their skin. Nothing to worry about, really, except for the question of why they were hanging out there. Why in the parking lot of this Mennonite-run building?

Jerry's kindness, perhaps? A sense of approval? Or just an empty place to congregate?

Stan's eyes moved across the group, and he found himself in an eye-lock with a familiar face. Luis, sitting on the trunk of the Grand Am, his feet on the bumper, hands resting on the car. The boy didn't seem surprised to see him. Looked like he expected it, actually. Was that a nod he just gave Stan? A hint of a smile?

Luis said something to his friends and hopped off the car. They started an intricate goodbye with members of the other groups. Handshakes, gestures, words. Nothing Stan could hear, of course.

Luis's friends eased into the Grand Am, filling up the back seat, the driver scooting behind the wheel. Luis opened the passenger door, bent to get in. At the last second he paused, flicked Stan an amused expression. Then he got in the car, and they drove away, the beat from some sort of music filling the air.

It didn't take long for the other cars to follow suit, heading off in the same direction as the Grand Am.

Stan went back in, made a rigorous search around the office and warehouse. Spent the next few hours worried about his new truck, checking it every five minutes.

While he marched back and forth he considered what he'd learned from *When Apples Are Ripe* before his nap. The most interesting was that Mennonites didn't baptize babies. They expected a person to make their own decision about following Jesus and make a commitment, sealed with baptism.

Jamie and Andrea had been baptized as babies, each

watching the minister with wonder, as if they knew a holy man when they saw one. Immediately after, of course, they'd realized they were wet or cold or any number of infant complaints, and let out with ungodly wails. But for the actual ceremony they'd remained still.

As they'd grown, they'd never wavered from God. At least not that Stan knew about.

A peek outside showed the truck alone. No vandals. No stupid kids with rocks.

The Mennonites, Stan had read, had been persecuted for this belief about baptism. Hunted like animals. Tortured, killed, burned, drowned. . . . Name an awful way to die, and chances were they experienced it. All because of when one sprinkled water over a child's head.

Kratz was a full-blooded Mennonite, steeped in the traditions and convictions of the faith. He taught at the local school, proving himself as an honest and loving role model, and encouraging the children to learn all they could. But his love for farming soon pulled him to Goshen College, where he could receive training in agriculture.

Stan walked out into the lobby of the building. All was quiet. The dim lights showed the merchandise in the Ten Thousand Villages store, the display different from the week before. This time it was a showcase of baskets—large, small, colorful—handmade by women in Kenya.

He made a circuit of the storefronts before ending up back at MCC. He went in. Sat on the sofa in the welcome area. His eyelids drooped.

Before he had fallen asleep that afternoon he'd come to chapter thirteen. The chapter that had so incensed Rose she'd beaned him with the book. "What Should a Christian Do About War?" He'd read it with a mixture of dread and interest. Would he find that the boy really was a coward at heart? Had he shirked his duty?

Stan read with surprise that Clayton's brother, Jacob, had chosen to join the army. How had that happened? Had he not been a result of the same upbringing? The same pacifist teachings?

When Clayton's number came up to be called into service, he told his roommate he would be a conscientious objector and suffer any hardships that might come because of his beliefs. He could not be a soldier and kill. That he knew for sure.

He was not a coward.

But instead of having to go to prison, he went home at his mother's pleading, to work on his brother-in-law's farm. During that time, farm workers were actually considered just as important—if not more—than soldiers. But as soon as the armistice was signed in January 1919, Clayton headed back to school, where he really wanted to be.

And there he stayed, until he received the call from MCC.

A loud buzzing noise jolted Stan from his reverie. He jumped up from the couch, heart pounding. Smoke alarm? Taser? Bug zapper? He thought this last with giddy anxiety as he patted his empty hip.

It buzzed again, and Stan ran into the lobby. Nothing there. No movement. No sound. No cars in the parking lot.

He ran back through the office, into the warehouse. He flipped on the bright overhead lights. Saw nothing.

Again, the buzzer. His head snapped toward the back door. A doorbell. Of course. Again feeling for the gun that wasn't there. Picking up the cane from the stack of thrift store merchandise. Walking slowly to the door.

"Who's there?" He glanced at his watch. Almost eleven.

A voice, words indecipherable, came through. Male. Stan held the cane firmly and opened the door.

"Luis?"

A nod from the boy. Stan stepped quickly outside, assessing the situation. No other kids. No other cars. Just a bike, propped against the building. Stan let the door close behind him. Pressed the cane against his leg, kept his other hand free, at his side.

"What is it? Did you leave something?"

Luis glanced at the cane and shook his head, his expression unreadable. "I want to talk."

Talk? "About what?"

He leaned against the hitching post. Crossed his arms. "David."

"David."

His eyes flashed. "My cousin, David Ramirez. Who was shot a while ago."

"I know. I remember. You were there."

Surprise. "No, I wasn't. I was a kid."

"I don't mean in the car. I mean at the house. With the family."

Luis kicked at the pavement. Dislodged a stone. "My aunt's never gotten over it, you know. Hasn't forgiven my cousin Ivan. David's brother. Blames him." His mouth twitched, his face tight.

Stan wanted to go over, sit by him. Lean against the rail, talk to him. But electricity filled his veins. Had him looking side to side. Waiting for Luis's friends to come charging. "Ivan was in the other car."

"But he didn't *shoot* him."

"No." Stan looked again to the right. To the left. Listened for voices, rustling, footsteps. Heard only the faint hum of the outside lights.

Luis's voice was strained. "It wasn't Ivan's fault."

"Whose fault was it?"

He pushed himself from the post. "The guy who killed him. Who do you think?"

Stan nodded. "Not the driver of the car? Or the driver of David's car?"

Luis looked at him, his face contorting. "What?"

"The other kids in the cars, who were probably egging on the shooter? How about the leaders of the gangs, wherever they were? Ivan was *there*. He chose to be there. As did David."

Luis stepped up to Stan. "David didn't choose to be murdered. Shot down like a . . ."

Stan watched, waiting for the end of the sentence. "Like a what, Luis? Like a criminal?"

"He wasn't a criminal."

A staring contest. Boy against man. Very angry boy. Young man, really. Stan held on.

"Is it their mom's fault?"

Luis blinked. "My aunt? What does she have to do with it?"

"I'm just asking. Some people like to blame the parents for everything."

Luis stepped back. "Not me."

"Good. Good. That's fair."

"What do you think?" The boy regarded him, eyes narrowed.

"About whose fault it was?"

A nod.

Oh, Lord, help me.

Stan looked at the boy. The questions in his eyes. The hardness of his face as he tried to be a man. Be tough. Be strong.

Stan held out his free hand. Dropped it back to his side. "I think it's everybody's fault."

"Huh?"

"I'm a cop, right? I can't police everything, make everybody follow the law. But I do my best. I serve and protect as well as I can. The teachers, the people who try to help the Spanish-speaking kids in the classroom, they do their best."

A growl from Luis.

"All right, most of them. Parents, bosses, neighbors. Everybody does what they can to make this town work. It's not easy. We've got a lot of different kinds of people. A lot of languages. A lot of cultures."

"What does that have to do with anything?"

Stan smiled. "It has everything to do with it. With community. We all need it. We all want it. We'll do anything to have it. We find people we want to be with and do what it takes to belong. Even if we know it's not really the best thing for us."

Stan didn't look at the boy now. Looked around them, instead, at the darkness surrounding the parking lot.

He sensed Luis moving away. Heard the scrape of tires on the loosened gravel by the side of the building.

Watched as the boy pedaled quickly away.

AUG 15, 1920
RECEIVED LETTER FROM O MILLER THIS PM I
MADE DEFINITE PLANS TO BE IN SCHOOL THIS FALL
IF YOU NEED MY HELP SERIOUSLY I WOULD BE WILL-
ING TO GIVE MY SERVICE

C H KRATZ

AUG 18, 1920
NEED ANOTHER MAN SERIOUSLY IN GROUP SAIL-
ING SEPT 1ST CAN YOU GET READY IF YOU REPORT
AT SCOTTDALE THUR OR FRI THIS WEEK CAN WE
DEPEND ON YOU WIRE TODAY

LEVI MUMAW

AUG 18, 1920
WILL REPORT AT SCOTTDALE ON FRI

KRATZ

Chapter 11
THURSDAY

The day's *Goshen News* was displayed on the kitchen table, covering Stan's usual place. It was open to "Letters to the Editor." Stan picked it up and read the first submission.

Dear Goshen College students and faculty:

I couldn't believe it when I read about the so-called peace rally you held on Sunday night at the courthouse. You chanted slogans and held signs reprimanding our country and those military men and women who have pledged their lives to making our world a better, and safer, place. I would ask all of you to stop and consider what your harsh words and actions mean to a soldier or sailor in a far-off place who is reading his hometown newspaper and seeing such a painful lack of support for our troops. While you're enjoying this spring with your families, have some compassion for those of us who aren't together. We would prefer your prayers rather than your criticism. You Mennonites claim to want peace—let's see it in the way you treat other people.

Rose Windemere, proud mother of Jamie Windemere, Second Class Petty Officer, U.S. Navy

Stan dropped the paper onto the table and sank into his chair, rubbing a hand over his eyes. He remembered dinner the night before, the lunch Rose had packed, how she'd eaten her food. He rested an elbow on the table and leaned his forehead on it. *Oh, Rose.*

"Embarrassed?" Rose's voice pierced him, flung from the doorway to the living room.

Stan sighed forcefully, the gust of air sending his napkin fluttering. "I'm not embarrassed. Just . . ."

"What? Just what, Stan?"

He rolled his head side to side on his hand. "I don't know, Rose. I'm not sure anymore."

She snatched the paper from the table, blowing his napkin to the floor. "One of us has to stand up for our son. Not slink off cowering to the enemy every night."

"The Mennonites are not the enemy."

"Oh, no? Who else goes out in public, saying what Jamie's doing is wrong? They probably think he's getting what he deserves. That all military people should disappear."

"Rose!"

She hiccupped. Pursed her lips. "Well, they do."

"Rose. Honey. The Mennonites don't want Jamie to die. They don't want *anybody* to die. They just want to find some other way to make peace. Some way other than fighting."

"But . . ." Words failed her. Left her sagging, shoulders bent, head drooping. Finally, "But Stan, you're taking their side."

Stan shook his head. Placed his hands on the table. Looked at his plate. "Rose, I'm not . . ."

"What?"

He shook his head again. And again. Kept shaking it until she went away.

$\sim$

The Kratz dormitory was like any other. A brick, four-story building with symmetrical windows and entrances at either end. Nothing exciting. Nothing really to set it apart. Stan stood looking up at it, marveling that this was the memorial for a man who gave his life for others. Who perhaps never had another warm, clean room to sleep in, once he gave up school for service. Jerry had mentioned this building when Stan first asked about the black-and-white photos, and when Stan left the house today, after skipping breakfast and trying unsuccessfully to sleep, he'd found himself wandering toward Goshen College's campus.

He hadn't been to this dorm before. That shower incident from years ago had been in one of the others. Yoder? Miller?

Students milled about, talking, laughing, sleep-deprived. Racing across the train tracks at the sound of a whistle, lugging their heavy backpacks on slouching shoulders. A certain percentage of them disappeared through the Kratz doorway, their voices cut off by the closing of the glass doors. Others headed to different halls. Guys. Gals. In pairs or as individuals, wrapped up in life, college, themselves. As most college students were.

Stan stepped toward the doorway, glancing about. No one eyed him suspiciously, wondering what he was up to. No security cameras hung in high places, recording the day's events. He pushed open the door and was taken into the heart of college life.

Coffee shop, game room (with pool and Ping-Pong tables), painted cement walls. Lounges with semi-comfortable couches, young men and women draped over them, with or without laptop computers in their hands. The occasional shout, a door closing, the clunk of a pop can falling in a vending machine.

He and Rose had moved Jamie into his dorm on a hot autumn day. Indiana University. Relatively close. A state school. What Jamie had thought he wanted. His roommate turned out to be a farm kid from the southern part of the state. What was his name? Mike? Matt? He'd come with his flannel shirts, his well-worn jeans, and a wide smile. A good match for Jamie. But it hadn't been enough. The roommate left school after one year, headed home to tend the farm after his father had a heart attack, leaving Jamie to make it through one more year before deciding he'd had enough. He was ready to go *do* something. Ready to follow that dream.

A scream somewhere down the corridor made Stan jump. No one else seemed to notice the noise. The scream was followed by raucous laughter and the sound of running feet. Stan walked a little further. Stopped at the entrance to the laundry room. While multiple machines were in service, only one girl occupied the room, head bent over a textbook, brown hair hiding her face and most of the pages. No way to tell how old she was, what book she was studying, or even if she was actually awake.

Andrea hadn't gotten used to dorm life. By every prediction she'd be a natural—extroverted, people-oriented, fun-loving. But somehow it hadn't suited her. The rules, the expectations, the "girl" stuff. If she could've occupied a dormitory floor with her softball teammates, she would've been fine. Less talk about hair and clothes and romantic secrets, and more about opponents, off-season training, and how to get grass stains out of warm-ups. Stan knew the minute she was allowed she'd be moving off-campus with some other softball players. Away from the frills and potpourri and late-night girly chats.

A dryer buzzed, and the girl looked up from her book, her hair falling away from her face. She was pretty, young, preoccupied. The clothes in the finished dryer apparently weren't hers, for she returned to her book, looking up again when she realized Stan stood in the doorway. He backed out. Left her alone.

He wandered down the hallway, smelling the damp, the coffee, the . . . socks? He stopped when he found the plaque. A statement in brass, hung head height on the wall.

CLAYTON KRATZ RESIDENCE HALL
Clayton Kratz (1896-1920?)

Clayton Kratz came to Goshen College from his home in Blooming Glen, Pa. During his years as a student here (1917 to 1920), he built up a significant record of leadership and all-round achievement. In his third year, Kratz served as president of the Junior class while he was also a member of the baseball team, captain of the debating team, vice-president of the oratorical society, a student assistant in agriculture, and president of the Christian Workers' Band. In the fall of 1920, instead of returning for his senior year, Kratz accepted an invitation from the new Mennonite Central Committee to serve in its first overseas relief unit. In September 1920 he sailed for southern Russia to administer relief aid to the victims of the Russian civil war, many of whom were Mennonites. Within a month of arrival in Russia to serve struggling civilians, Kratz was arrested on suspicion of being a spy. He was released once, he was soon taken into custody again. It is suspected that he was executed, but the exact time and manner of his death remain unknown to this day.

A concise history of the man, followed by construction information: the date of the groundbreaking in 1963, the year it was first occupied (with 132 students), along with the men responsible for the plans and building. Original cost—520,000 dollars.

Stan wondered if any of the students ever noticed the plaque was there.

Or whose name adorned the place where they lived.

∾

He was awakened by the doorbell. Glancing at the clock, he saw that it was almost four. He'd been sleeping for almost five hours, ever since he'd come back from the college.

The doorbell rang again, followed by knocking, and he swung his legs out of bed and stood up, grabbing at the headboard when dizziness swept through him. But an old awareness kicked in, an awareness built from nights of sleep broken by phone calls. A sick officer needed a replacement, a shooting had occurred in town, one of his kids was going to be in past curfew and didn't want him to worry. Which, of course, caused a whole new thing to worry about.

He walked briskly to the front door and opened it. The woman had already gone down the steps, but stopped when she heard the door. Turned around. Smiled tentatively.

And Stan remembered why he'd been so sorry when she and Jamie had broken up after that first year of college.

"Tonya Burkholder."

Her smile grew. "Wenger, now. And that's Gabriel."

He hadn't seen the boy before, who'd already made it halfway down the sidewalk to the car, veering crazily, as if his chunky toddler legs couldn't steer him straight.

"Excuse me." She gave a little laugh and bounded after her son, scooping him up in her arms. He whooped joyfully, giggling.

Stan cleared his throat. "Keeps you busy."

"That he does. Say hello to Mr. Windemere, Gaby."

A shriek and swat at his mother's shoulder were his

response, and she grabbed his wrist, pinning it between his stomach and her arm.

Stan looked at the two of them. Thought about his house. Rose's house. "Want to come in?"

"Oh, thanks a lot. Really. But the baby's sleeping in the car."

His eyebrows rose. "Another one?"

"Two months old. Her name's Lily."

Another flower. Wouldn't Rose be thrilled.

Stan gestured toward the car. "May I?"

"Of course."

They strolled together down the walk to peer in the cracked-open window of the Integra.

"She's a cutie. What I can see of her." Dark hair. Dark pink lips.

Another light laugh. "Yeah. She's pretty bundled up."

Gabriel wiggled himself out of Tonya's arms and banged on the car door. Tonya grabbed him and swung him in a half-circle, away from the car. He squealed with delight.

"Here, Gaby." She reached into the open passenger window and rummaged through an oversized diaper bag, coming up with a tiny ball and a monster-truck toy. The boy grabbed the truck and roared, driving it back toward the house.

Tonya let out a breath. "Whew. Guess you're past those days now, huh?"

Way past.

"Which is why . . . Which is what . . . I saw Mrs. Windemere's letter in the paper today."

Stan flinched.

"Is Mrs. Windemere home?"

"No. She's out." At least he thought so. He hadn't seen her. Was that relief he saw in Tonya's face?

"Her letter made me think about Jamie. Not that I haven't been since . . ." She shook her head, as if irritated with her lack of words.

Stan grunted. "There hasn't been anything in the paper to remind people lately."

"I don't need a reminder. Besides, I was glad when they stopped that ridiculous count. It seemed so . . . ghoulish."

She referred to the "Days Chief Petty Officer Jamie Windemere Has Been Missing." A small photo in the paper, the number in red. What were they going to do, Stan had wondered, if Jamie never came back? Keep the count going until he would've died of old age? Until the paper went out of business? But it wouldn't come to that. Stan had seen to it. "We didn't need the reminder, either."

Tonya glanced at him. "No, I'm sure you didn't."

They stood by the car as Gabriel tore through the yard, engine racing, legs pumping. Stan winced as the boy's little feet threatened to stomp into the flowerbed, but the truck zoomed to the right and left the blooms undisturbed.

Stan looked deeper into the flowerbeds, trying to see behind the bushes. No way that orange cat would be coming around now.

"Anyway." Tonya blew her bangs out of her face. "I saw the letter today and wanted to stop by. The kids and I were in town. I . . . I still think about him. We pray for him."

We. She and her husband.

"Is he good to you?"

She blinked. "You mean my husband? Yes. Yes, he is. Greg . . . he's a very good man. He teaches at the Mennonite seminary in Elkhart."

Stan nodded. Her husband was a good man. He was glad, of course. Of course he was.

She chewed her lip. "I guess there's no news? About Jamie?"

"No. No news."

"I'm sorry."

"Me too."

They stood there a little longer, until Gabriel was back,

flinging the truck at the little ball, which bounced under the car.

"Gabe."

"I'll get it." Stan crouched down, scanning the street between the tires. There it was, halfway out, unreachable from either side. "Hang on."

He was back in a minute with a rake, which pulled the ball out in no time.

"Thank you."

He nodded. Tossed the ball in the passenger window before the boy could grab it and lose it again. "Thanks for coming by."

She guided Gabriel to the other side of the car, where she had to persuade him into the car seat with the promise of a lollipop. The belt finally clicked in. "It was nice seeing you again."

"Yes. You too."

She got in the car, put on her seatbelt.

"Tonya."

She looked at the passenger window.

"When you say you still think of Jamie . . ."

She smiled briefly. Painfully. "It wouldn't have worked, Mr. Windemere."

"No. No, I guess not."

"Goodbye."

He held up a hand as she drove away.

$$\sim$$

It was no use trying to go back to sleep. And he knew what drew him. The little book under the mattress. He pulled it out and settled himself in his den, feet up on the footrest of the La-Z-Boy.

Chapter nineteen was entitled "Two Weeks to Get Ready." Two weeks for Clayton Kratz to have vaccinations, interviews by ministers, a physical exam. A chance to see Edie Miller, now his fiancée, one more time, traveling to Maryland to see her and her family. Telling Edie she would help him in this work of service by offering prayers for strength and courage. Finally, back home, kissing his mother goodbye.

Kratz left the United States with two men, Orie Miller (no relation to Edie that Stan could find) and Arthur Slagel, on a ship bound for Russia. They made other stops along the way, such as an audience with Pope Benedict XV in Vatican City. The Roman Colosseum. The Appian Way, which the apostle Paul himself had traveled. Then on to Greece, where the Pennsylvania farm boy stood by the Acropolis and the Parthenon. And finally onward to their destination aboard a ship called the *Providence*.

They disembarked in Constantinople, where they spoke with workers at the American Embassy and the Red Cross. Kratz also was heartened by a letter, sent from his Goshen College friend and roommate, Dave.

Stan froze in his reading. He'd known, of course, that Kratz didn't stop in Constantinople. He'd known he was on to Russia. What he didn't know was that Kratz and Miller got on yet another ship to travel to Russia.

A naval destroyer.

Stan set down the book. He walked to the window and took some deep breaths.

This pacifist had boarded a ship belonging to the military. A ship that crossed the same waters the Navy crosses today. The same waters Jamie had crossed.

Stan placed his hand on the cool window, covering the Windex streaks. Took another breath. Concentrated on the feel of the pane beneath his hand. Waited until his dizziness went away.

Back in his chair he read some more. Kratz and Miller stayed in the officers' quarters of the USS *Whipple*. Slept on officers' bunks. Ate meals with the officers.

"You can do a lot of good," the Navy men told them. "The Russians need your kind of help."

Stan stared at the bookshelf across the room and considered the ironies of Kratz's trip across the Black Sea. This peaceful Mennonite, willing to suffer instead of going to war, was on a ship with weapons, officers, a command system.

He got up. Dialed the NIS. Was put through to Borgman right away.

"Detective? I haven't—"

"I know, Chief. I'm sorry to bother you. I know you'll call me when you have news. But I was wondering . . . I'm interested in deck logs from a ship in 1920. Any chance they still exist?"

Silence. "1920?"

"I know. It's crazy. But I'm doing some research on . . . on someone who was a civilian passenger on the USS *Whipple.*"

"Weren't they . . . that was a ship in Europe. The Black Sea."

"Yes."

Stan heard papers shuffling.

"All right. What was the name?"

Stan told him. Gave him Orie Miller's name, as well. Plus the dates they sailed.

"I'll see what I can do. I can't promise anything. Records that old are in the archives in Washington. Probably on microfiche. It could take a while."

"I know. But I'd appreciate the effort." A pain shot through his stomach. "As long as it doesn't keep you from—"

"Nothing will keep me from finding your son."

"Thank you. Thank you, Chief."

He hung up and went back to his chair, his head pounding. Back to Kratz's journey in a naval destroyer.

The *Whipple* docked in Sebastopol, a city in Ukraine. The two men departed the ship and found the home of Russian Mennonites, where they were to stay. They were grateful for their German, for it was the only way they could communicate with these Russian people.

Stan took a moment to study a photo on the page. A photo

of Kratz and the family he had stayed with. A picture taken by his partner, Orie. It was a small photo, so Stan lurched out of his chair to rummage through the desk drawers for a magnifying glass. When he couldn't find one, he walked to the kitchen, where he searched the drawer full of helpful, but misfit, items. There he found it.

It was a shack, really, where Kratz had stayed. Where this family had lived. Kratz wasn't smiling in this picture. But then, the rest of them weren't, either. It wasn't a happy time.

Stan sat down again, laying the magnifying glass within his reach, should he need it again.

Kratz and Miller spoke with government officials in Melitopol, both at the American consul and with General Wrangel's people—the folks who led the White army. Two days later they were given an interpreter to travel with them, by train this time, further into Russia.

So much further that they began to see the consequences of the war. People in rags, children with no shoes. Buildings with broken windows, the few scrawny horses. The Mennonites had been wealthy before the war, but now they'd been pillaged and raped, violated and left to starve.

The two men met with Mennonite leaders in the area, and it was arranged to take them to Halbstadt, where again they met with church leaders. Leaders who had been praying and hoping for help from America.

"I am well and glad that I am here," Clayton wrote to his mother.

In Halbstadt they learned to know Johann Peters, a leader in the community who took them into his home. They traveled, with Peters and the interpreter, to Alexandrovsk, where they met with even more government officials. Orie was to leave with the interpreter the next day while Kratz stayed to help in Halbstadt. But when they woke up, the armies were near. Their escapes came quickly—Orie and the interpreter to head back to Constantinople to make arrangements for supplies and Kratz and Peters back to Halbstadt. But before Orie left, Kratz quickly penned a letter to be sent from Constantinople to his friends at Goshen College. He ended his letter this way:

> I must close because in one-half hour we are leaving Alexandrovsk. The Whites are apparently evacuating the city and we already hear the cannon in the distance. Here I got my first taste of real war-fare. Within the past few hours many soldiers passed our window in retreat. I must close.
>
> Your old pal,
> Kratz
>
> P.S. My regards to all. I enjoy the work.

The work consisted of planning for the distribution of food, clothing, and other supplies whenever they would arrive from Constantinople. Kratz took his job seriously and did it well. Not that Stan was surprised, by this time.

But Johann Peters wanted Clayton to leave. The war was coming closer, and he was in danger. Kratz refused to do so. He felt it his duty to stay. To help these people. He thought that a person really lived only when he forgot about himself, serving others.

They finally persuaded him, and he was to leave in the morning, driven by the Peters's last two horses and accompanied by Peters and his teenage son. But before daylight even arrived, Kratz and Peters were arrested by the advance guard of the Reds. They were taken to an officer who freed them only when they promised that someone would come back if he were to call for them.

Back at the Peters's home, they celebrated Clayton's twenty-fourth birthday on November 5. Five days later, he was summoned to appear again before the authorities. Peters accompanied him and could only watch as the men struck Kratz, placed him under arrest, and took him away.

When Peters tried for the next few days to find out what had happened to Clayton, he was told that although they didn't really believe he was a spy, he had been arrested as one. Peters could find no one who would tell him where Kratz had been taken.

The last person to report seeing Clayton Kratz alive was a Russian Mennonite in the town of Wernersdorf. The man was able to throw a coat around Clayton's shoulders as he was hauled away in a horse-drawn wagon. He reported that Kratz appeared quiet and composed.

"Are you all right?" the man had asked.

"Yes," Clayton had answered. "I am."

∾

Jerry was waiting for Stan when he arrived at work. He stood, leaning against the hitching post, hands beside him on the wood as he watched Stan pull up and park. Stan got out and pocketed his keys.

Jerry grinned. "Nice truck."

"Thanks."

"Sorry you had to get a new vehicle."

"Not your fault."

"No?" He straightened up. "Got a few minutes?"

Stan blinked slowly. Held a hand out at Jerry. "It's your time. You can use it how you want."

"Great." He hooked his thumb over his shoulder and led Stan to his office. No one else was around. It was quiet, dimly lit, like most other evenings when Stan had arrived.

"Have a seat."

Stan scratched his neck, looking at the ceiling, then lowered himself into a chair.

Jerry had the *Goshen News*. He held it out to Stan, open to

Rose's letter. "I don't get this paper. I live in Elkhart. Get the *Elkhart Truth*. But one of the staff members brought this in today. Thought it might be a relation of yours. Spoke some concern about having you in here each night alone."

Stan looked at him. Closed his eyes. Opened them. "And you said?"

"There was nothing to be concerned about." He raised his eyebrows. "So is this your wife? You said your son is in the Navy."

Stan ran his tongue over his teeth. Wished he would've remembered to brush them. "She's my wife."

Jerry nodded. Pulled the paper back toward himself, laid it on the desk. "She's pretty angry at us. The Mennonites, I mean."

"She is."

"Do you know why? Other than the fact that we speak out against war?"

Stan laughed quietly. Sadly. "I know why."

Jerry waited, watching him. Eyes focused, forehead furrowed.

Stan stood up, walked to the corner, looked out the window facing the outer office. Turned around. "Jamie's missing. Has been for two months. Left his ship for a mission and never returned."

He stopped. Waited. Saw comprehension light Jerry's eyes.

"In Russia," Jerry said. "In late February." He closed his eyes, shook his head, a growl coming from his throat. "I *knew* his name sounded familiar." He stood up, went to stand in front of Stan. "I'm sorry. I didn't realize . . ."

Stan stepped back. Bumped the wall. Moved to the side. "I know. And I didn't tell you."

"Your wife is angry at us."

Stan grimaced. "We had a bad experience with a Mennonite girlfriend of Jamie's several years ago. Rose thought the girl was unreasonable and . . . well . . . wrong. Jamie was . . . it was a difficult thing for him." Stan lifted his shoulders. Dropped them. "And I guess . . . Rose needs to have somebody to blame for what's happened now."

Jerry nodded. "And we're likely targets. That's okay. It's not the first time we've had fingers pointed at us." He went to his desk, folded the paper, placed it in his briefcase. "I'm sorry about your son."

Stan turned around. Walked out of the office. Went back to the warehouse, but instead of going in, just leaned on the door, a hand supporting him as he breathed in and out.

"Stan?" Jerry again. "Your interest in Clayton Kratz. . . . Do you still want more material?"

Stan pushed himself up. Faced Jerry. "If you have it."

"Well, I was thinking. The Mennonite Church USA Archives at Goshen College has a collection of Clayton Kratz materials. Original papers from back then. Copies, too, of some others. If you give them a call, they'll be glad to pull things for you. Or you can just show up."

Stan looked at him. "I can go, even though I'm not Mennonite?"

Jerry smiled. "Sure. You can't take items out—no one can—but you'll be free to look all you like. They're open every weekday. Till five, I think. It's right on the college campus, along Route 15. Newcomer Center, beside the church."

Stan sighed. Leaned back against the door.

And hoped Rose never found out he was considering setting foot on that enemy territory again.

～

It was another quiet night. Stan checked on his truck only every fifteen minutes, instead of the more frequent rounds he'd made the night before. He was half hoping Luis would show up again. Offer some companionship, no matter how strained. He was beginning to see why he'd never done security previously and why he probably wouldn't choose to do so again.

It was boring.

The same desks, the same corners, the same map of The World. No added shadows, except in the warehouse, and those were still monuments to the stacks of goods surrounding him. No rowdy officers playing tricks on each other, no idle chat with the receptionist, no calls in the middle of the night. No dead bodies to identify.

He stood for a while staring at the photo of Clayton Kratz. Which was the same as the night before.

He wandered into the resource library, just in case the videos had returned and Sheila had neglected to keep them aside. Nothing he could see.

But there were more old Goshen College yearbooks. He pulled one out. 1960? Right. The other fellow in that frame with Kratz. What was his name? Garber? Gerber? Gerber. He was pretty sure. Hadn't Jerry said his father stood next to him in choir? Stan paged through, looking for the music section. Found a page with the Collegiate Chorus, searched the faces. He walked to Wendy's desk, compared her photo with those of the men in the choir. And there he was, in the back row. One of the men beside him was probably Jerry's father. Stan sighed, placing a finger on Daniel Gerber's face. Another young man lost to service.

He put that yearbook back and pulled out another one. Ah. 1921. The year after Kratz disappeared. How did he miss this the first time around? He fluttered the pages, knowing that even with the tedium of the night he shouldn't get further involved searching through the photographs. Those vandals would probably show up just to punish him.

He set the yearbook by his lunch, which he'd packed himself—again. And when he sat down to eat, it was all he could do not to crack the cover. Instead, he thought about what he might find at the archives at Goshen College. And imagined himself discovering the clue that would set Kratz's family free at last.

Sometimes in the evening at the supper table while eating Mother's good sausage cakes, mashed potatoes, pork gravy, and applesauce, Clayton took a second look at his mother. She looked older and her shoulders were not quite as straight as before. She was still beautiful. Women who are gentle and loving are beautiful.

—from "Death Is a Door That Opens," chapter 8 of *When Apples Are Ripe* by Geraldine Gross Harder

Chapter 12
FRIDAY

Rose was looking out the back door when Stan got home, her shoulders tight. She wore slacks, a sweater twin-set, and a thoroughly sprayed hairdo.

"Rose?"

She whipped around. "What? What is it?"

"Nothing. I just . . ." He gestured at her clothes. At her carefully applied makeup.

"I'm going back to work."

"At the salon?"

"Part-time. While we see how it goes."

"Oh. Well, good."

"You're glad I'll be gone?" Her voice was defensive, while her eyes shone with hurt.

"No, I . . . " Yes. "I'm glad you feel ready. I hope it goes well."

She gazed at him, her mouth soft. Vulnerable. "I'll be home by five. In time to make supper."

"Okay."

"Well." She plucked her purse off the counter and hovered for a moment before heading toward the door to the garage.

He watched her go. "Have a good day."

The door clicked shut behind her.

～

The Mennonite archives didn't open until eight, so Stan sat down to eat some breakfast, accompanied by the 1921 Goshen College yearbook.

He found only one mention of Kratz. Nothing on the pages about the Auroras, the yearbook staff, student assistants, or the Young Men's Cabinet. No picture with the debate team or silly gossip in the Observatory. No smiling face within the now somber-looking baseball team.

But on page 116 he found him with the Reconstructionists, a newly organized group formed to keep in touch with the worldwide program for peace and goodwill. Following the description and photo of the dozen or so young men in suits and ties were two full paragraphs and the portrait from Kratz's junior year.

> Mr. Clayton H. Kratz of Blooming Glen, Pa., was for three years a member of the class of 1921. We will always remember him as a cheerful and thoughtful classmate, always willing to help his class. His sacrificial spirit was shown, when in September of 1920, he gave up his college work to enter Relief Work in Russia. Shortly after entering this service the Bolsheviki forces invaded the district in which he was located and no definite official information concerning his circumstances has been obtainable since.
>
> The class of 1921 greatly regret that Mr. Kratz is not one of its members for graduation but they rejoice that he chose so noble a field of service. It is

the wish of his classmates that his efforts may bring
comfort to a people in need and it is the sincere
hope of all that he may be in safety and may again
return to his Alma Mater.

Stan could find no mention at all of Edith Miller, Kratz's
fiancée.

He closed the book. Set it aside.

Watched the minute hand on the clock until it was time
to go.

~

The archivist was a cheerful, friendly man at least half a
foot taller than Stan. Dennis Stoesz. Pronounced, he told Stan,
as "Stows." He joyfully yanked out card catalogs, scribbled
down notes, and wheeled his ladder around the caged archive
shelves, pulling boxes with a smile.

Stan soon sat amid an array of papers, containers, and
instructions. Only one other person occupied the room—a student, iPod in his ears as he scoured a stack of photos.

"If you want to copy anything, the machine's right there."
Dennis gestured to the copier. "Just keep track of how many
copies you make, and we'll settle up before you go. And if you
have any questions, my office is right down the hall. We close
at noon for an hour, but if you're coming back, you can just
leave the materials."

Stan thanked him, watched him walk away, and sat down,
taking in the array of Dennis's finds. He swallowed, trying to push
down the butterflies in his stomach. What was wrong with him?

He clenched his fists, released them, and opened the first
box. The earliest. He pulled out the top folder, marked August
1920. He opened the cover. And found himself looking at
Clayton Kratz's original application to the Mennonite Relief
Commission for War Sufferers.

Stan shoved himself back from the table and stood up, paced the room, rubbing his face as he tried to breathe, to slow the escalation of his heartbeat. Clayton Kratz had handled that paper. Written those words in that ink.

Died because of it.

Stan stood at the window, staring out at his truck, visible through the panes. Breathed in. Breathed out. In. Out. A final inhalation through his nose. Held it in his lungs. Let it out his mouth.

When he turned around, the kid at the table was staring at him, eyes lifted from his photos, shoulders raised in suspicion. When Stan's eyes met his, the boy averted his gaze and looked back down at his stack, still observing Stan with his peripheral vision.

Stan stuck his tongue into his cheek, studying the cage surrounding the archive materials. Then he sat back down.

Swooping cursive adorned the service application, with Kratz's name and address. His mother named as next of kin. Elizabeth Kratz. Questions about how soon he could be ready to leave, his previous jobs, his marital status (Single). The admission that he hadn't much experience driving a car—well, who had, in those days? A statement that he was a total abstainer from alcoholic beverages and from narcotic drugs.

Will you cheerfully acquiesce in the decision of a majority? YES.

Is your temperament and experience such that you can easily adapt yourself to the difficult and unpleasant conditions of life in a foreign land? I THINK SO.

Have you vigorous, medium or poor health? QUITE VIGOROUS.

Yes. A ballplayer. A farmer. A young man with much to offer.

Stan sat back, the paper in his hands. The very paper that had sent young Clayton Kratz on his mission to help save the world.

Jamie's Navy Enlistment Contract had been much the same. The personal questions, the references, the questions about physical aptitude. Jamie had considered every question thrown at him by the recruitment officer with his brow scrunched in concentration, fingers clenched into fists on his lap. The recruiter filled in the form with Jamie's answers—and some of Stan's and Rose's—before signing the form and giving Jamie the paper and a pen. Jamie read it over painstakingly, had Stan and Rose proofread it, and then read it again himself before signing. The whole way home he revisited all his answers, wishing he had said things differently.

He needn't have sweated over it quite so much. He was a shoo-in. Good grades, thoughtful answers, supportive references. Stan's breath hitched in a laugh. He hadn't asked Jamie's high school principal, Mr. Albert, for a reference. Not after the egg, soap, and toilet paper incident. But he hadn't needed to. There were plenty of other teachers, as well as their minister and church youth leaders, to fill in the spaces.

Stan set the paper to the side. Clasped his hands together, stopped them from shaking. Reached for the next sheet. A memo, certifying that Kratz had indeed been appointed as a relief worker and was subject to the plans and policies of the commission.

The next section, September 1920. The first thing, a copy of a memo to Elizabeth Kratz, informing her that Clayton, along with Orie Miller and Arthur Slagel, had safely reached Naples, Italy. It was signed, "Yours for the needy, MENNONITE RELIEF COMMISSION, Secretary, Charles Fowle."

Next, a copy of a letter from Levi Mumaw in Scottdale, Pa., informing the three workers of the supplies they would be receiving in Constantinople: 240 bales of used clothing, 47 bags of shoes, 35 cases of shoes, 3 cases of shoe repair material.

A copy of a financial report, listing the expenses of the three men on their trip to Russia. Haircuts, deck chairs, tips, baggage expenses. A cable sent to their superiors, a guide for Russia. Meals, train reservations, hotel bills, ink and pens.

An entire three weeks of travel for three men for 465 dollars. Amazing.

In October. Copies of letters back to Scottdale, the home office, telling of their travels and preparations. Letters to each other, updating their partners on their work. Their successes and failures.

"Mr. Windemere?"

Stan started, then looked up—way up—at Dennis Stoesz. "Yes?"

"I thought you might be interested in this." Stoesz held out a light-brown satchel. Small. One big flap with a snap to hold it down. "It was Kratz's. He had it with him on his trip, and it was sent back here after his disappearance."

Stan looked at the little bag. Held out his hand. Took it.

"I never let things leave the archives," Stoesz said, "but when the students went on their trip in 2000 they begged me for it. They wanted something of his to take with them, so I let them have it. And as you can see, they returned it."

"What students? What trip?"

Stoesz looked at him. "You don't know about the trip?"

Stan shook his head.

Stoesz pulled out a chair, sat beside him. "Four Goshen College students followed Kratz's footsteps across the ocean to Italy, Greece, and Russia. Tried to find some answers. They made a video of their voyage."

One of the two videos missing from MCC? "Do you have one?"

"Of their videos? No. But they're around."

"Yeah. I know of a copy. At least I think so. I'm just waiting for it to get turned back in."

Stoesz nodded. "It's a good video. There's an earlier one, too. Oh, you know about it?"

"Waiting for that one, too."

"Good." He stood up. Pushed in his chair. "Well, anyway, I thought you might like to see the satchel."

Stan clasped it tightly. "Thank you."

Stoesz started to walk away, but Stan stopped him. "Did they find any?"

"Who? Find what?"

"The college kids. Answers."

Stoesz shook his head. "Not really. You can read about their trip online, of course."

"Online?"

"Sure."

Stan laughed to himself. The Mennonites had all this history online? Of course they would. It had just been him, wanting to avoid that technological creature in his den.

Stoesz still stood in the doorway. "Of course there's nothing like handling the real thing. I'll take papers and material items any day over the cyber world."

Stoesz left, and Stan turned back to the table, lifting the bag, studying it. Kratz had taken it to Russia. He had held it, kept his possessions in it. But he had disappeared without it. Probably hadn't had a chance to grab it when he was arrested. Which was probably good. It most likely would've been confiscated.

Stan laid the bag to the side, keeping his left hand on it as he reached for more of the papers. His fingers felt cool against the fabric.

On to November 1920. A letter from Orie Miller at his post in Constantinople to someone named A. M. Eash, addressed to an orphanage in Jerusalem.

> We came here Oct. 28th. Five days later Kratz and I went to Russia via American Destroyer. Visited the various Mennonite colonies now within the Wrangel area, and also saw something of conditions in the purely

Russian districts. My previous experience has never shown me anything like this in the way of lack of everything that one considers necessary in life. Outside of food, the population literally have nothing. Left Kratz there with several thousand dollars, to do what he can with money, and I came back here last week.

There being Halbstadt, Stan figured. After the army came through. When Kratz was staying at the Peters's.

And then it began. Telegrams, letters, questions about Kratz's whereabouts. Memos in which someone named "C. Atechny" had been reported missing in South Russia, last seen at "Halberstandt." Confusion, with the commission having no one of that name on staff, but knowing Kratz had gone missing. Letters from Scottdale to New York City, and back again.

My dear Mr. Mumaw:

I have received yours of November 13th and note that you are unable to identify the Mr. C. Atechny mentioned in the telegram sent by the State Department to this address. I cannot conceive of having the name of any one of Mr. Miller's party so garbled as to read Atechny, and imagine that someone else must be meant.

Charles W. Fowle

Foreign Secretary

Near East Relief

Stan paged through the letters, his heart in his throat, his body responding to the ignorance and hope in the memos. All saying "it couldn't be," and that Charles Fowle's Russian friend, a Mr. Jolkowsky, "feels that there is no cause whatever for alarm as the Bolsheviki would not knowingly or willingly do him any harm, and therefore there need be no fear for his personal safety." But as for the relief supplies Kratz had in his possession, "Mr. Jolkowsky remarked with a typical smile and shrug that the Bolsheviki have doubtless 'Nationalized' these, provided they had not already been distributed to the needy people for whom they were intended."

So, Stan thought, Kratz had been sacrificed for items that most likely never reached those he'd gone to help. Perhaps the money had been in the now-empty satchel under Stan's hand. He closed his eyes, a combination of disgust and despair sweeping over him.

When he opened them again, the next page stopped him short. A copy of a letter to Elizabeth Kratz, Perkasie, Pa., Clayton's mother.

> Dear Sister,
>
> Having received an inquiry from Bro. Derstine, by telegram asking about your son Clayton in Russia, we hasten to answer by wire and this letter. We are very sorry that we do not have more definite information to give you. During the past week we have noticed newspaper reports stating that a Mennonite relief worker had been taken together with a Red Cross worker by the Bolshevists. But the name did not correspond with any that we had sent out. . . .
>
> We were still hoping that it was another and not your son Clayton, but the report given out by the North American thru the *Evening Bulletin* gives a different name. We therefore do not know which is correct.
>
> The newspaper reports given today, indicate that the community where he was working is now in the hands of the Bolshevists as it had been a number of times during the past few years. This means that we will be cut off from communication from them until the way is opened in some other way.
>
> We are hoping to get some word direct from the brethren Orie Miller and Arthur Slagel who had left

Constantinople last week but could not have been in the territory now taken. As soon as we have further news in regard to the matter, we will advise you promptly.

>   Yours very sincerely,
>   Secy. Charles W. Fowle

News that never came. News that Clayton's mother had died waiting for. Stan turned to the next page.

Two memos. Written the same day. One with the same type of encouragement from Charles Fowle: "I am glad that there apparently need be little concern for Mr. Kratz's personal safety." But the other from the Department of State, in Washington, D.C.:

> In reply the Department informs you that it has . . . been advised by its representative in Sevastopol that a Mr. Clayton H. Kratz and not Mr C. Atechny has been captured by the Bolsheviks. Steps are being taken to endeavor to procure information concerning the present whereabouts and welfare of Mr. Kratz and if possible to procure his release.

It was signed "William" something. A name Stan couldn't decipher. The director of the Consular Service for the Secretary of State.

He wrote of steps taken that never went anywhere. At least nowhere Kratz had been.

Stan continued to scour the papers. Mentions here and there of Kratz, of continuing to ask about him. Looking for him. But above and beyond all else was the commitment to the Russian people. To get them supplies—food, clothing, shelter. To relieve their suffering.

Kratz was all but forgotten in the ensuing months, as new workers and supplies were sent. Sporadic reports were given of rumors of relief workers being shot, then the gossip being proved false. News that all Americans had been safely evacuated from the Crimea. But no sign of Kratz.

Months of work. Months of hope. A memo half a year later, in April 1921, with ideas of getting in touch with Brother Kratz in South Russia, "who we hope has already organized some form of relief work there."

And in July, workers asking the commission "not to increase the dangers to the lives of those of us over here who are trying to find Kratz and open relief centers to help Mennonites and Russians."

Still looking. Still hoping. But finally afraid.

Another letter, from an A. J. Miller to Mr. Ch. G. Rakovsky, Ukrainian Socialist Soviet Republic, Charkow, Ukrania:

> Let me therefore bring to your attention the case of Clayton Kratz, an American citizen whose whereabouts in the Ukraine are not known to the American authorities or the relief organizations since the time of his arrest and disappearance in the vicinity of Militopol or Halbstadt in the Ukraine last November. . . . His passport number was 84613, dated August 25, 1920, Washington. He represented the Mennonite Relief unit, a pacifist organization whose only purpose was to perform a humanitarian service for the welfare especially of women and children.
>
> His widowed mother and his friends are suffering under the anguish of almost a year of uncertainty and suspense, hoping for some word from him, but despairing as the time drags on and no news is forthcoming. To know the truth concerning him, whatever it may be, would be relief from the strain of hoping against hope, waiting and waiting from month to month. . . . Will you not kindly give me the assurance that an investigation will be begun at once so that I may be enabled to reas-

sure our committee in America? It is very important that this be given prompt and adequate attention. It will do much to restore confidence on the part of the Americans.

And finally, simply, under the longhand scribble of "Confidential, publicity forbidden" on A. J. Miller's next memo:

No trace of Kratz.

~

Stan made copies until the college student had left, and Stoesz came to tell him it was time to close for lunch. A glance at his watch showed Stan how fast time had flown.

"Will you be coming back this afternoon?" Stoesz asked.

A sharp pang shot through Stan's head, reminding him of his lack of sleep. "No." He held up a handful of copies. "But I will take these."

"Do you know how many you made?"

Stan looked at the papers. They blurred before his eyes, and he swayed on his feet.

"Here." Stoesz took them at the same time he studied Stan's face. Once Stan sat, the archivist quickly sorted and counted the copies, quoting Stan a price.

"I have this too." Stoesz held out a stack of papers, clipped together. "It's Orie Miller's diary from 1920 and '21. They were only recently typed, and there are mentions of Kratz in it. You can have this copy for six dollars, if you want it."

Stan wanted it. He paid in cash.

"If you have any questions, please call," Stoesz said. "Or come back."

Stan nodded, scooped up his papers, and turned to leave the room.

"Mr. Windemere?"

Stan stopped. Looked at him.

Stoesz held out his hand. "I'll need that back."

Stan looked at Stoesz's hand, finger pointed, and followed it to its focus. Up to where he held Kratz's satchel tightly against his chest, his fingers clutching it like a lifeline.

≈

The phone at NIS was answered after the first ring by the same chipper, albeit professional, voice as last time, offering the same conversation.

"Good afternoon, this is the Naval Investigative Service, Petty Officer Robinson speaking. How may I help you?"

"Chief Borgman, please."

"One moment, please."

It was more than one moment. Maybe five. Six. Ten.

Finally, "This is Chief Borgman's phone, Chief Abron speaking."

Stan clenched his jaw. "This is . . . Stan Windemere here. My son, Jamie, is—"

"Of course, Detective. How may I help you?"

Stan shouldn't have been surprised. The agents in Borgman's section shared information. It only fit that this Chief Abron knew who he was.

"I'm calling . . ." No words would come. Why was he calling? Was he desperate for information on Jamie? Or was he wanting information on Kratz's voyage on the *Whipple*?

"You'd like to know if we have anything new regarding Chief Windemere, your son."

Stan swallowed, his voice having disappeared somewhere in his throat.

"Chief Borgman isn't here, but if you can hang on . . ." Abron's voice muffled a bit, as if he turned from the phone. "He's there? He's there. Great. Chief Borgman?" His voice clear again.

"I'm here. Detective Windemere? You there too?"

Stan cleared his throat, surprised at the sudden addition of Borgman to the conversation. "Here."

"I'm in Virginia," Borgman said. "But as soon as you called, Chief Abron got me patched in."

Stan's heart skipped a beat. "You've found Jamie."

Chief Borgman took a loud breath. "No. But we've found *some*thing."

A wave of static filled his head. "What is it?"

"It's not much. But it's more than we've had. A Friendly, who claims to have seen Chief Windemere in the presence of a known faction leader. He's a member of a highly secret group known as the Needle. We don't know much about them because they're pretty new in the whole scheme of things. But we're in full investigative mode now, and are finding out everything we possibly can."

"When? When was he seen?"

A pause. "Not recently. Almost two months ago."

As soon as he disappeared.

"So . . ."

"So we follow it up. And we don't quit until we know."

"You won't quit?"

"We won't quit, Detective. You have my word."

His word. Stan would depend on it.

～

When Stan woke from a fitful sleep and walked to the kitchen, the flashing light on the answering machine caught his eye. He froze. Took a deep breath to stop his pounding heart. He hadn't heard the phone. And his cell phone, always attached to his belt, had not rung. He went the final few steps into the room and pushed the button.

"Hello, Mrs. Windemere, this is Lisa Klassen from Goshen College. I'm a professor here. I saw your letter in the *Goshen News* and wondered if we might talk sometime. I'd love to hear from you about your views of our school and how we might better voice our wish for peace. If you could call me, I'd really appreciate it." She left her number.

Stan stared at the phone and its now slowly pulsing light. Not the message he'd been hoping for. Not the one he was dreading, either. But one that could have serious ramifications.

He watched the answering machine. *Blink. Blink. Blink.* Should he erase the message? Set the little red light back to a steady beam? Save Rose from the consequences of her actions?

No.

But by failing to intervene, he would also suffer the consequences: Rose's anger. Her tension. Her fear.

The door from the garage opened, and Rose was there. She looked from him to the answering machine. Her breath caught loudly. "Is that—"

"It's not . . ."

They stopped, staring at each other. Waiting.

Stan took a breath. "It's not about Jamie."

"Oh." She swallowed.

"It's for you."

She looked again at the answering machine. Again at Stan. She narrowed her eyes. Took a step in. Another. Set her purse on the counter. Left the room.

Stan could hear the closet door open. The swish of her jacket sliding onto the hanger. The click of the hanger on the pole. The door closing.

Her footsteps came back to the kitchen. She held out a finger. Pushed the button on the answering machine.

Stan watched his wife's face as she listened. The voice on the recording was kind. Gentle. Intelligent.

The message ended. Rose inhaled through her nose. Sucked her cheeks in. A less extreme version of the face the kids used to make, pretending they were fish. Saying, "Look, Daddy! What am I? What am I?" Kissing with puckered lips.

Rose's face relaxed. A brief smile fluttered across her mouth. She glanced at the floor, then looked back up, the smile not reaching her eyes. "Friend of yours?" she asked. And she went out to the garage, where she chose a pound of frozen hamburger to use for dinner.

～

Stan stayed in the kitchen while Rose cooked. While she threw the beef into the skillet, along with chopped onions. Mixed them with ketchup, mustard, and brown sugar. Sloppy joes. One of the kids' favorites, right up there with the boxed mac and cheese.

Rose stopped periodically to peer at him as he stood in the doorway, her eyes narrowed, dark. Stan's thoughts pinged from one side of his head to the other. Should he tell her about Chief Borgman's discovery? Raise her hopes? Give her nightmares about what Jamie might have suffered at the hands of Russian terrorists? Might still be suffering? Offer her cause to believe their son is alive?

He teetered one way, then the other. Yes, she had a right to know. No, it would only hurt her more than she'd already suffered.

She finally spun around toward him, meat flying off the upraised spatula. "You want me to call her? Is that it?"

"Call who?"

"That woman. The one from Goshen College."

An onion piece fell to the floor.

"No. You don't have to call her. It's up to you."

Eyes narrowed again. Nostrils flaring. A spin back to the stove.

"Rose."

Tapping the spatula on the skillet.

"Rose."

A slower turn, spatula left in the pan. Arms crossed across her chest.

The hot stove behind her. A knife on the counter.

"Nothing. Never mind."

Back to cooking.

Stan got the dishes from the cupboard. The silverware. Napkins. Pulled the buns from the bread box and opened the new bag of chips.

When they were seated and Stan had offered the prayer, he looked at his wife. "Rose, there's been a development."

Her eyes widened.

Their dinner grew cold.

～

"The supplies are scheduled to ship out next Wednesday," the note said. It was waiting for Stan in the kitchenette. "If you have any questions, let me know. Otherwise, we'll plan on your work continuing (excepting Sunday, of course) until that date."

It was signed, simply, "Jerry."

Next Wednesday. Not as long as they'd originally predicted. That was good, he supposed.

He turned around in the kitchenette, ending up looking straight at the shelves of the resource library. His eyes wandered over the spines of the books and videos, and, glancing at the clock, he decided to take a few minutes to peruse the selections.

He began at the far left. Nothing new. It was basically the same stuff he'd noticed before. Lots of books about foreign countries—usually the production of a church, a missionary, or the Mennonite conference. Videos, too. English and Spanish. The spots were still open where the Kratz tapes were missing, and he found nothing else to interest him except five big volumes making up something called the *Mennonite Encyclopedia*. Goodness, who would've imagined such a thing? He ran his fingers over the spines of the books and pulled out volume 3, encompassing I to N. He was surprised at the weight in his hands. He'd never thought there were that many Mennonite people, or places, to make up such a tome.

Resting the book on the kitchenette counter, he paged to the Ks. And there he was, among several entries. A full column on Kratz, Clayton (1896-1920). Interesting that they'd posted 1920 as his death date, seeing they had no idea if that was even correct.

Since the article was short, he decided to read it. He'd already made a full circuit of the offices, lobby, and warehouse, so he figured he could take a few minutes without too much danger.

The article began with the information Stan knew, about Kratz's time at Goshen College and his call to service. But then it went into a little more detail about his disappearance. The hairs on the back of Stan's neck prickled as he read.

> After an inspection tour Kratz was left at Halbstadt to set up a headquarters while Miller returned to Sebastopol to arrange for the transport of the supplies which Slagel was to bring from Constantinople. Before the relief program could get started the Red Army overran the Ukraine, forcing Wrangel into precipitous retreat into the Crimea. The Russian Mennonites urged Kratz to flee, but he chose to stay as long as possible, believing that American relief workers as neutrals would be safe.

And later in the article:

> G. A. Peters, who gives the only firsthand account of Kratz's disappearance reports that . . . in view of the manner of his arrest and the attitude of the officials, Kratz was not executed but probably died of some disease before being released.

And then, suddenly, there was Stan's kind of work. Police reports. Investigation.

> Endeavors of the following year by A. J. Miller, then director of the MCC relief program in Russia, to determine what happened to Kratz, which included inquiries in Kharkov and Moscow (Foreign Office), were completely fruitless. He deposited a memorandum on Oct. 10, 1921, on the case, with Foreign Minister Litvinov [the memo Stan had seen in the archives] and later a similar memorandum with Minister Rakovsky in Kharkov, but neither brought any results. Miller investigated the case thoroughly locally and speculates that the arrest may have been instigated by the highest volost official, Bagon, a Lett who had previously worked in a Halbstadt printing plant. At this time of disorganization it was impossible for the central government officials to properly control the local underlings, many of whom were of a hoodlum type and were a disgrace to the party they pretended to represent, and it is quite possible that the arrest was a purely local blood-lust matter. It is known that Kratz was struck brutally on the occasion of his final arrest.

Stan swallowed the acid that seeped up into his throat, and closed the book. Walked briskly out into the lobby to clear his head, covering the space once. Twice. After a third time, heading back into the office.

The buzzer was piercing the silence.

Stan walked through the office, into the warehouse, to the back door. "Luis?"

A muffled "Yes."

Stan opened the door. It was raining. Luis stood alone, his bicycle against the hitching post this time. Stan looked at him. Luis's wary eyes, his defensive pose.

Stan's head said, No. Send him away.

"Come on in. Bring your bike."

He held the door open as the boy walked the banged-up Schwinn into the space. Luis looked around, found a bare section of the wall. Water dripped into his eyes.

Stan walked past him. "Come on."

They sat in the welcome area a few minutes later, water heating in the kitchenette, Luis's denim jacket spread over the back of a chair to dry. Stan poured the water, found two packs of hot cocoa in the cupboard. Gave one mug to Luis. Sat in Sheila's chair to drink his.

Luis sipped at his cup. Winced. Blew on the chocolate. Stan stirred his. Spun in the chair to look at The World. "You know any of those people?"

Luis studied the wall over the rim of his mug. The photos of the missionaries. "No."

"Me neither."

They sipped some more.

"Know Sheila." Luis tipped his head toward the desk.

"Yeah. She's a cutie."

Luis's eyes lit up briefly. He took another sip.

"Knows Spanish too."

Luis laughed now. Lightly. "Yeah. Grew up a missionary kid, or something."

"Ah."

More sipping. Stirring.

"You're friends with the guy who works at that desk?" Stan hooked a thumb toward the seat where he'd seen Luis when he'd come early to fill out papers.

Luis nodded. "He goes to the Spanish Mennonite church, same as my mom."

"And Jerry?"

Eyes to his cup. "He gets me in to work sometimes. And my friends."

"Yeah." Another sip. "He's had you helping to unload the shipments. There's a lot of stuff in that warehouse. A lot that will help a lot of people."

Luis's eyes raised. Met Stan's. Moved away. He finished his drink. Stood up. "Guess I oughta get going."

"Sure."

They took their cups to the kitchenette. Washed them out. Placed them on the drying towel.

Stan grabbed a paper towel. Handed it to Luis. "For your bike seat."

Luis nodded. Took it.

When Stan looked outside he was glad to see the rain had let up. He held the door while Luis rolled his bike through and mounted it.

"You coming to help with the shipment this week?"

Luis licked the corner of his mouth. "Yeah. Wednesday, isn't it? Yeah, I'll be here."

"With your friends?"

"Them too."

"Good. Jerry's glad you're around. To help out."

Luis placed a foot on the pedal, and rode away.

The poor boy did not know yet, that nearly everybody innocent, must suffer here.
—Kate Peters, in a 1922 letter to Elizabeth H. Kratz

Chapter 13
SATURDAY

"Are you going to wait," Rose asked, "or drive over without me?"

Stan stopped inside the door. So no news about Jamie. "Over where?"

"Andrea's softball game. She has a doubleheader today, starting at eleven."

He knew that. "When do you get off work?"

"Noon. I'll be home at twelve-fifteen."

He tried to read her face. An impossible task. "Is Andrea pitching the first game?"

"She's scheduled to."

"You couldn't get off?"

Her eyes sparked. "I just went back to work yesterday."

"Oh. Right. Well, then, do you mind driving over by yourself? I'd like to see the first part of the game."

"So would I."

He waited.

"But you go on without me. I'll get there as soon as I can."

"Okay."

She sat down across from him at the table and sipped her orange juice.

He picked up the box of cereal, looked blankly at the nutritional chart. "Are you going to call back that lady from Goshen College?"

Her glass met the table with a click. "No. You'd like me to, I suppose."

"Only if you want to."

She looked at him. "Is that right?"

"Rose . . ." He opened the cereal box, unclipped the top of the inside bag. Lifted the box to pour it. Set it back down. "If you want to call her, call her. If you don't want to, don't. It might be good for you to tell her in person how you feel. You never know. She might actually listen."

An image of Jerry, the concern in his eyes as Stan told him about Jamie, hovered in his mind.

Rose still watched him. "You think so?"

Stan raised his eyes. Met his wife's. Saw the anger, the defiance. The fear.

"You never know, honey. Maybe she really does want to find out how to . . . how to get along."

Rose's eyes shined brightly as her mouth parted. She reached two fingers up. Pressed on her lips. And turned away, her face hidden from view.

∾

It was a beautiful day for a softball game. Sunny. High sixties. Not much breeze. Stan set up their lawn chairs along the first-base line. When Rose arrived from work she'd have a prime spot, not crowded in among the still-unfamiliar parents and students.

He checked his phone again. Yes, it was on. No, there weren't any messages.

Yet another technological disappointment.

Andrea, warming up along the third base side, by her

team's dugout, lay on her back, a teammate pressing her out-stretched leg toward her chest. Right leg. Left leg. Again. They switched places, Andrea pushing the girl's legs further. Further.

Andrea helped the girl up, and they separated to do a few more stretches on their own before heading onto the field, Andrea moving to the mound, her teammate behind the plate. Andrea swung her arm above her head, down. Again. She hollered something to the other girl, who was closing up the fas-teners on her protective catching gear. Soon she crouched behind home plate. Threw a ball to Andrea. A signal was passed. Andrea tossed up the ball. Caught it. Began her wind-up.

Stan's amazement at her talent never wavered. She was strong. Confident. Even with the specter of Jamie's disappear-ance hanging over the day, Andrea could focus as well as he'd seen her do the year before. Perhaps even better.

But then, Stan hadn't told her the latest news. It wouldn't have been fair. Not right before a game. Maybe afterward, if they could go out for supper. Maybe then. When the game was a memory.

Jamie was his sister's biggest fan. Well, besides Stan and Rose. Perhaps returning the fandom Andrea had shown him when he was on the high school team and she in middle school. She'd been the proud, adoring little sister, yelling, screaming on the sidelines. Cheering. Berating the ump. Painting banners, as well as her face.

During her high school career, Jamie had made it home for only a few games, but he was always there afterward, on the phone, wanting to know every detail, every pitch, every signal she and her catcher had disagreed on. Stan had started taping the games at Jamie's request, sending them to him when he could. This year he wouldn't have to do that. There was an official uni-versity tape made of each game. He could simply buy a burned CD and send it. He smiled at the thought of Jamie watching the game on his ship, his fellow officers cheering along. . . .

Stan jerked himself awake. Rubbed his eyes. Looked around for the concession stand.

The Mountain Dew was cold, straight out of the food stand's fridge. A bit different from the high school's booster club cooler, ice melting in the hot sun. Stan wiped the can across his forehead, the condensation running down, catching in his eyebrow.

The short nap he'd gotten at home hadn't been enough. Three hours. He wasn't even sure if it was better than nothing. He supposed it must've been.

The first batter was coming up to the plate. Stan stood to the side of the concession stand and popped the tab on his pop. A stream of foam fizzed over his hand, and he shook it off, wiping the remainder on his pants.

Andrea's beginning pitch sizzled past the batter, who stepped out of the batter's box. Adjusted her gloves. Her helmet. Stepped back in.

The next pitch went high, and the next inside, bringing cheers from the opposing fans.

"Focus, Andi, focus." Stan glanced around him, but no one seemed to have noticed his muttered words.

Andrea shook off the catcher's next signal. And the next. Finally stood up, whirled her arm, threw a strike. And then another.

Stan smiled. Raised his can to his daughter. The first K of the day.

Stan didn't have trouble staying awake after that. Before he knew it, they were entering the sixth inning. Andrea had given up only one run, a blooper hit falling into center field in the top of the fourth to bring in the runner on second. Fortunately, her team had answered with three of their own in the fifth.

Stan glanced at his watch. Close to one. Rose should've been there. He stood up, stretching, looking over the cars in the parking lot. No sign of her.

Rather than sit down again, Stan stood behind his chair,

easing his upper body from side to side, working out the stiffness of fatigue and of sitting in a lawn chair.

Andrea's team was coming up to bat when Stan felt a presence at his side.

He glanced at his wife, her face still. "You okay?"

"Fine."

He studied her unyielding profile.

Her jaw bunched. Relaxed. "How's the game?"

He told her, hitting a few highlights, but she gave no sign of hearing his words. Instead, her gaze traveled to left field, where it remained for a good part of the afternoon, while Andrea hurled pitches and led her team to victory.

"It is so cute, Dad!" Andrea patted the Chevy S-10, a grin on her face. "When did you get it?"

"Oh, earlier this week."

"Wednesday," Rose said.

Andrea accepted this terse statement with upraised eyebrows, her mouth in an O. She looked at Stan, a question in her eyes.

"I can't drive it," Rose said. "It's a stick."

Andrea grinned. "I'll teach you, Mom. My Prelude's a stick. I learned real quick."

Stan grunted a laugh. "And gave Jamie gray hairs doing it."

Andrea laughed, too. For a moment.

Jamie had been home for a holiday from the naval station when Andrea bought the little sports car. He'd actually gone with her to buy it, thinking his presence would keep the salesmen honest. Even wore his uniform to raise their impression of him. Stan had wanted to go along, but the kids gently dissuaded him, saying they could handle it. He let them charge ahead without him. Sibling bonding, and all that.

Once the car was home, Stan offered to give Andrea lessons driving a stick, since she'd learned on his automatic. Again he'd been rebuffed. Jamie took on the role of teacher.

When the kids had returned from their first round of driving, Jamie was a few shades paler than when they'd set out, confiding in Stan that if the gears were ground out it wasn't his fault. Stan figured he'd be drafted as the teacher after that, but Jamie's color—and courage—had returned, and he'd finished out the lessons.

Now Andrea drove like a champ. And the Prelude's transmission had yet to fall out.

"Hungry?" Stan asked her now.

She blinked. "Yeah. Guess I am."

"Me, too. What would you like?"

She looked at Rose. "Mom?"

Rose dragged her eyes from the distant outfield. "What?"

"Where do you want to eat?"

A shrug. "Wherever you like. I'm not really hungry."

Andrea's eyes went blank. Her head went back, face to the sky.

Stan watched her. Tried to read the tension in her shoulders. "How about Wendy's?"

Andrea's eyes shut. Her head came back down. "Wendy's is fine." Her voice flat.

He looked at Rose. Back at Andrea. "Want to drive the truck?"

She looked at him. Gave him a smile.

~

They could've all fit in the truck, but Rose chose to drive her own car. So after eating, Rose went on home while Stan took Andrea back to the dorm.

He stopped at the curb, the truck still running. His brain struggled with the option of telling her or not telling her about Jamie's sighting. "You coming home at all tomorrow?"

She looked out the windshield. "I don't know. I've got lots of homework."

"Sure."

She gathered up her bag, her mitt.

"You did great today, sweetheart. I'm proud of you."

A flicker of a smile danced across her lips. "Thanks, Dad."

"Your mom's proud of you too. You know that."

"Yeah. Yeah, I know." She leaned over, gave him a peck on the cheek. Scooted out the door.

"I love you," Stan said.

She stopped, her hand on the door. Looked at him across the seat. "Love you too." She slammed the door. Headed up the walk, bag across her shoulders. Glove dangling from her fingers. Went in the tinted door.

Stan drove back to Goshen. Went straight to work.

~

The night was a study of how many ways he could stay awake. Trips outside to check on his truck. Rounds of the lobby, studying the display in the Ten Thousand Villages windows. Reading the MCC brochures, the newsletter from Washington, D.C., the verse-a-day calendar on Sheila's desk. Paging through *Extending the Table: A World Community Cookbook.*

Stopping by to greet Clayton Kratz as he sat quietly on Wendy's desk. Asking him what secrets he was keeping behind that glass pane.

Checking to make sure his cell phone was on and that he hadn't missed any messages.

It wasn't until Stan's stomach rumbled that he remembered he'd failed to pack a lunch. He looked at his watch. Twelve-fifteen. Too late to order a pizza.

He went to the kitchenette to check out what might be available.

Coke. Popcorn. Peanut butter crackers.

He guessed it would have to do.

After popping the corn in the microwave, eating, and making rounds, he stood in front of the books in the resource center. He'd found the *Mennonite Encyclopedia* last time. Maybe there would be something else with information about Kratz.

There wasn't. But at least another half-hour had passed.

He walked through the office, jogged in place, did some jumping jacks. Went down to the floor, did a few push-ups. After the last one, he stayed there, his cheek against the carpet. Would it really hurt anything if he would take a nap? Just a brief one. Nothing long.

He pushed himself up one more time. Got to his feet.

How else could he research Kratz, with the videos out? *When Apples Are Ripe* and the yearbooks, their pages exhausted, lay at home. Under Jamie's mattress. He'd been to the archives. He'd seen the *Mennonite Encyclopedia*. He had Orie Miller's diary at home, waiting for him to find time to read it.

He hadn't been online. And Dennis Stoesz, at the archives, had said there would be information there.

Stan stood rooted to his spot, his heart fighting with his brain. There would certainly be something interesting online. But could he get past his revulsion of it? Sit in front of the computer and do anything but stare at the email program?

Becky's computer perched on the desk in her dark office. Waiting to be used.

Stan ran a check of the lobby. Made sure the front door was shut behind him. Walked through the office, the conference room, into the warehouse. He peeked out the back door at his truck, then made a round of the warehouse, checking all the corners.

No one. Nothing. As usual.

Becky's office, being in the warehouse, gave him a vantage

point in which he could sit at the computer and still see the warehouse through the large window above her desk. The whole wall was a window, really. He sat down, looked at the computer. Swallowed. Pushed the button.

The familiar hums and beeps assaulted his ears, and he stood up, rocking on his heels while he waited. Looking around the office, anywhere but the screen. Finally the computer stopped the random sounds and remained on the consistent hum. Stan sat down.

He hunted around the screen to find how to get online. It wasn't hard. The password filled automatically, allowing him access. He'd have to talk to Jerry about that.

He went into Firefox, and the Google bar blinked on. Easy enough. He typed in *Clayton Kratz*.

Sixty-nine thousand three hundred hits. And it looked like the entire first page really was devoted to the Clayton Kratz he was looking for. Not some other mix of names adding up to Clayton and Kratz. He clicked on the first.

It was an article written by one of the four Goshen College students who had traveled to Russia in 2000. Sidney King. The article was apparently a story in a larger collection of Mennonite writings in an anthology entitled *Gathering at the Hearth: Stories Mennonites Tell*. Stan began reading.

It covered the bases as Stan knew them. Why Kratz went to Russia, who he went with, how he disappeared with barely a trace. But there were questions too, about how Clayton dealt with his brother joining the military; how he felt when traveling on the naval destroyer, the *Whipple*, amid the guns and officers; what those foreign lands looked like to a farm boy from Pennsylvania.

And then, suddenly, news Stan had not been privy to. An excerpt from a diary, written by a man named C. E. Krehbiel, an MCC worker in Russia during 1922 and '23. Sweat sprouted on Stan's forehead as he read.

August 15, 1922

   Today a Mrs. Dyck called this afternoon and said she knew the man who [killed] Kratz. His alias at present is Grigori Saposhnikov. He has lived in her house for 11 months and wants to go to the U.S. He runs an electric plant. He is a Jew and has a wife and no children. He is supposed to be a bad man in general.

December 24, 1922

   Johann Wall made inquiry at Kharkow on Clayton Kratz and through a Jew he knows from Lodz found that records of Kharkow 3853a state that Kratz was arrested at Halbstadt by Bagon, etc. . . . the latter having accused him or charged with being an English spy of the government and that he was then brought to Bachmut, etc., and finally to Kharkow where he was turned over to the Gubernia at Alexandrowsk and the records says shot there!

Stan sat back, his fingers in his hair. A diary? With news like this? Why wasn't it broadcast? Why did no one know? Why hadn't this Krehbiel told anyone?

King addressed these questions in his article. Perhaps Krehbiel realized it was hearsay. Perhaps he didn't want to distress Kratz's waiting family and fiancée.

Perhaps . . . Perhaps . . .

He had been negligent. Thoughtless. Stupid. Stan scowled at the screen. Sure, it might've been second-hand knowledge, but often that held at least some truth. Stan should know. He'd busted a multitude of criminals because of rumor and hearsay.

Shaken, he finished reading the article, his brain fuzzy with . . . what? Excitement? Anxiety?

He went back to Google. Clicked on the next item: OurFaithDigest.org. Another article about the quest of the four college students. Mentioning that one of the students, "Kennel," carried Kratz's old passport pouch (ah, it was for his passport). The satchel Stan himself had held.

More written about the Krehbiel diary, stating where it had been found. Ruth Unrau, a volunteer at the Mennonite Library and Archives in North Newton, Kansas, had been transcribing the diary, only to stumble across this news.

Had she felt the sweat appear on her scalp? Had her heartbeat sped up? Did she realize what she had stumbled across?

Interviews with historians—John Ruth, from Pennsylvania, called a "Kratz expert." Another, Paul Toews, who had traveled to the former Soviet Union many times to research Mennonite-related holdings in archives and libraries there. Both amazed by the diary's discovery, wondering what it could mean.

What it could mean? It could mean that Kratz had been shot. That they finally had an idea what happened.

And then their questions, the same as Stan's. Why hadn't Krehbiel *told* anyone? If he had, one of them stated, those details were lost.

Lost. Stan growled with disgust.

He went back out to Google. Found lots more on Kratz. Scholarships given in his name. Business fellowships, the Goshen College dormitory, a mention of him in the history of Blooming Glen Mennonite Church, where he'd attended as a boy and teenager, where a memorial stone now sat in the graveyard.

Kratz was mentioned in an article about Daniel Gerber, the MCCer who'd disappeared in the 1960s, who resided beside Kratz in the frame on Wendy's desk. The second MCC worker to die in a war-torn land.

Stan's head ached. He closed down the search engine and stared at the screen. He could check email from here. Find his account online. Have yet another rejection from the list of senders.

He shut down the computer. Went out to make sure nothing had happened to his truck while he was online.

September 12, 1920

To the Goshen College Record

I suppose by the time this letter reaches its destination, school will have opened and the different activities will be in full swing. I am indeed sorry on the one hand that my work for the coming year will not be with my fellow students at Goshen College, but on the other hand I feel convinced that the work to which I have been called is of greater importance than the completion of my college course this year.

Kratz

Chapter 14
SUNDAY

"I'm sorry, Rose." He stood in the kitchen, eyes on his wife's back. "I can't go to church."

He'd be falling asleep in the pew. It had been a challenge just getting home from work. There was no way he could manage the trip to the church, let alone the service itself.

"I was planning on going." Her dress pressed, her high heels on. Sausage and pancakes filling the house with their fragrance.

"I can't."

She looked at him, beyond him. Her gaze missing his face by a fraction.

He held out a hand. "You don't need to stay."

The hurt in her face.

"You're welcome to, but I have to sleep."

She stacked his plate with food. Pancake after pancake. Two sausages. Three.

Left him. Came back several minutes later in soft warm-up pants and a sweatshirt. "I hate turning my phone off in church, anyway." Not meeting his eyes.

He ate most of the food, guilt stoking his appetite. Thanked his wife. Stepped toward her. Stepped away.

Went to their bedroom to sleep.

～

It took Stan a moment when he woke up to remember Chief Borgman's news. Remembered the Krehbiel diary giving a possible explanation for Kratz's disappearance.

He sat up in bed, head swimming. "Rose?"

Her voice, quiet, words indiscernible. Was she on the phone?

He walked quickly, stocking-footed, through the living room, to the kitchen. Saw her, outside the screen door, on the back stoop. Looking down. Talking.

"There you go, kitty. There you go. Now finish up. That's right. Drink your water."

Stan took a step back. Another. Waited in the hallway until the words stopped. Until the door closed. Her footsteps, soft, water running, the creak of the kitchen floor. Watched as she walked from the kitchen to the front door. Let herself out.

Stan viewed her through the window until she was settled on the porch swing. No movement. No swinging. He opened the screen door. Regretted the frightened jerk of her shoulders.

He walked out, sat beside her on the swing. "No calls?"

"I would've gotten you." Spoken to the porch railings.

He let out a breath. "I know. I know you would've."

A few seconds passed. "Feel better?"

He glanced at her. "Yes, actually. I slept hard." He looked at his wrist. No watch. It was on his nightstand. "You know what time it is?"

She wore hers. The silver one with the diamonds he'd given her for an anniversary. Their twenty-fifth. Just a couple of years before.

"Almost five."

"I slept for nine hours?"

"Just about." She tucked her watch hand under the other. "You'll never sleep tonight."

"No." He rubbed his eyes. "It won't be for long anymore." Now she looked at him.

"The supplies are supposed to ship out on Wednesday. I only have two more nights."

She studied his face. Turned back to the street.

"Want to go out for supper?" he asked.

Her clasped hands tightened. Relaxed. She looked down the block. "No, thanks. I'm not really hungry."

That was okay. He wasn't either.

∼

The phone remained silent. No calls from Chief Borgman. No updates from the NIS.

By midnight Rose lay asleep in their bed, and Stan sat on the floor in the den, copies of the archive's papers spread around him. Newspaper clippings from 1920 and from 2000, when the college students went on their trip. Memos from the '20s. Telegrams, handwritten letters, postcards, expense sheets. The articles from the various Mennonite magazines. All with the same information. All telling of Kratz's disappearance, the hope for finding him, the failure of all investigative roads.

He dove into Orie Miller's diary, hoping for something exciting. Something revealing. But the only new things he found were items that could in no way lead to finding Kratz: their rooming assignments on the ship, Kratz's second typhoid inoculation, Kratz losing to Miller in shuffleboard.

There were some interesting details to flesh out the stories Stan already knew. How they stood in line to board the ship, how they went on walks in the towns, gathering supplies.

More about the naval destroyer itself, the USS *Whipple*, its officers, and how excellent their meals were. How well-chosen the library was onboard, and a description of the ship's very own Victrola.

Stan hurried on. Found the question "Where can Kratz work most effectively during the next month?" And the simple statement about leaving the Alexandrovsk train station: "We bade Kratz goodbye." Not knowing it would be the last time he saw his friend. His colleague.

And the last mention of Kratz, on November 27. "No further news from Kratz." Nothing else, even though the diary continued through March of the next year. The work, the service, really did go on.

Stan set aside the diary. Looked at the mess surrounding him. All these papers. All the information. Nothing new. Nothing to point anyone toward what had happened to Clayton Kratz.

Except for that new Krehbiel diary excerpt. He pawed through the papers, scattering his semi-organized piles into slippery stacks. There. The article from *Our Faith*. It had been several years since the diaries had been found. Had anyone unearthed confirmation of the rumor? Had they found the Kharkow 3853a records? Had the killer been found? He couldn't imagine they had. There would've been more papers, articles, memorandums. There would've been a celebration in the Mennonite church. If they even remembered Kratz anymore.

There were a couple of historians named in the articles. Would they know? Could they help? He skimmed the article. John Ruth. Paul Toews. How could he find these guys?

He went to the kitchen and picked up the phone. Called 411. Gave the town noted as Ruth's home—Harleysville, Pennsylvania—and asked for his listing. But there were too many John Ruths for him to know which would possibly be the right one. He hadn't a clue what this John Ruth's middle initial was. So he called information again, asking for Fresno, California, and Paul Toews. The operator couldn't find any listing under that name, regardless of how Stan pronounced it. (Claves? Cloes? Rhyming with *meows*?)

He looked around at the floor. Grabbed up the *Our Faith* article. Looked again for the names of the historians, to see if there was any other information. There it was. Paul Toews worked as the director of the Center for Mennonite Brethren studies in Fresno. He picked up the phone. And put it back in its cradle.

He trudged back to the den. Regarded the computer. Looked over his shoulder, as if someone might be watching, then entered the room, picking his way through the maze of papers on the floor.

The computer booted right up, and Stan immediately went online, pulling up Google, ignoring his email program. He typed in the name of Toews's workplace. And there it was.

Three clicks later he found the staff, with an email moniker there for him to use.

> Dear Mr. Toews:
>
> I am investigating the death of Clayton H. Kratz, who went missing in Russia in 1920. I believe you are familiar with the case. I have found word of the Krehbiel diaries, which talk about a record called Kharkow 3853a. You are mentioned in regard to the find as someone who was planning to study the files in Russia. Have you been able to find anything of interest, to either confirm or deny the truthfulness of Saposhnikov's guilt? Or found out any more about why Krehbiel didn't reveal this information when he heard it?

Stan thanked the man for his time and signed the letter.

He studied his signature line for a moment before adding, "Detective, Goshen Police Department."

He might be on leave, but he hadn't lost his title.

Stan sent the email, closed out the screen, and pointed the cursor over the button that would turn off the computer. But his hand moved, leading the cursor to the online button. Clicking it. Opening the email program. Clicking *Find New Mail*.

There were several new emails. Two encouraging him to buy cheap dRuGs/pHaRmAcEuTiCaLs from Canada, one suggesting he update his information at PayPal, and one from someone named Jim Smucker. Nothing from the NIS, Jamie, or even Andrea.

Jim Smucker? He squinted at the name, trying to make a connection, then sucked in his breath at the sight of the subject line: "Clayton Kratz/Edith Miller." What? He opened the email.

> Dear Mr. Windemere,
>
> My friend Jerry Brenneman told me you are researching the life and disappearance of Clayton Kratz. I did not know Clayton, but was acquainted with his fiancée, Edith Miller, when I was a boy. Jerry asked if I might tell you what I remember, as it would add details to your findings. It is hard to recall much from then, as it was many years ago, but I'm happy to share what memories I can.
>
> I first knew Edith when I was a very small boy. She came to our house on numerous occasions. She once arrived dressed as a man and calling on our Aunt Orpha, who had lost her husband and was staying with us while taking a course at the Wooster Business College. Orpha saw through it immediately and would have none of it. I think Edith was in college at Wooster at the time along with my Aunt Gertrude, who was also staying with us.
>
> Even at that very young age I was aware of the sadness that hung over both Edith and Orpha, and I know that long after Edith married Earl Lautenschlager she

told my mother she kept "Kratzie's" picture in her drawer and looked at it every day. Her marriage to Earl Lautenschlager was a good one, but she never forgot Clayton, and never stopped loving him. The Lautenschlagers remained family friends for many years, and presumably Edith lived and died in Wooster. If you have more questions I can probably remember some more.

Peace,

Jim

Stan sat back, blinking. Someone who actually knew Edith. Not Clayton, but someone else close to the heart of the time. And why did the name Orpha ring a bell? A sudden thought came to him and he jumped up, practically running to Jamie's room. Yanking out the yearbooks from under Jamie's mattress, he paged through them frantically. And there it was, in the 1920 book: "Ede, Orpha, Kratz, and Dave seen leaving Dorm with traveling bag."

Was this the same Orpha that Jim Smucker mentioned? The same friend? It would be consistent with the sadness. The grief she felt for Clayton and for her good friend Edith.

Stan let the yearbook fall to the bed and ran his fingers roughly through his hair. Clayton Kratz had had a life. A college career, a fiancée, a family that loved him. Why? Why had he gone to a foreign land to disappear among strangers, last seen in the company of rough men and soldiers?

He pushed himself from the bed, stumbling through the house, returning to the computer. Stabbed at the button— *Find New Mail.* Jabbed it again. And again. Checked the connection. Pounded the button. *Find New Mail. Find New Mail.*

Watched, over and over, as the message came back without fail: *No New Messages. No New Messages.*

No New Messages.

We would have died, we would have starved to death. But then the Mennonites came, sent us people, and sent us food. And in this way we stayed alive.

—Russian Mennonite survivor, Katarina Suprunova

Chapter 15
MONDAY

"Stan?"

He squinted up at Rose from amid the papers. His back screeched at the movement, stiff from his position on the floor.

"Stan, what are you doing?"

He looked back at the mess in front of him. Papers upon papers, the yearbooks, the little red biography, his own notes. He opened his mouth. Closed it again.

"Is this that Mennonite again? The one who disappeared almost a century ago?"

He cleared his throat. "In Russia."

Silence.

"Our son was *sighted*, Stan. He was *seen*. And here you sit among papers for someone else's son? Someone who isn't even alive anymore? Him or his parents or even his siblings?"

The back of his neck itched, as if the computer behind him were watching things play out. Mocking him. Scanning for new messages every two minutes. Finding nothing.

"You don't have anything else to say?"

He didn't.

"Well, that's great. Just great." She walked away. Came back. "I'm leaving for work. See if you can get yourself together."

He nodded and rubbed his burning eyes. He was sure they looked as bad as they felt, stinging and blurry.

Rose hesitated in the doorway. Made a noise—half grunt, half growl—and left.

Stan looked at the clock. Close to eight. He got up, shuffled through the papers to the bathroom, where he stood under a shower that he alternated from hot to cold and back again. Scraped a razor over his face. Avoided his bloodshot eyes in the mirror.

Dressed, he went to the kitchen. Picked up the phone. Dialed the number.

"Good morning, you've reached the Naval Investigative Service, Petty Officer Cerna speaking. How may I help you?"

Finally, a different voice. More somber. But professional. Polite.

"I need to speak with Chief Borgman, please."

"One moment, please."

Waited. Hoped Borgman wasn't there. That he was out hunting down Jamie. Finding him. Bringing him home.

Waited. Hoped Borgman was there. Ready to offer good news. Positive, optimistic reports of when Jamie would be coming home.

Waiting. Hoping.

"Detective Windemere." Stan's name had come up on caller ID.

"Chief Borgman."

A pause. "I was going to call you later this morning."

Stan's heart stopped. "You found him?"

"No. But we have a few more leads. Nothing definite. We've been questioning people about the sighting. Looking into the Needle. The Russian group. We heard through informants that they're claiming to have biological weapons. Some agent which could wipe out entire towns. We don't know what kind. They're demanding the release of prisoners. They've told us the names of their comrades, but we have yet to find record of any of their people being arrested."

"Are they declaring hostages?"

Borgman hesitated. "They're claiming—now remember this is through second- and third-hand hearsay—to have something we would want in return for their demands. We don't know what it is. It could be Jamie. It could be Chief Lyndberg, Jamie's commander. It could be the biological agent itself. We just don't know. But we're looking. Believe me, we're looking."

A groan, from deep within, came from Stan's throat.

"We also," Borgman continued, "have gained some knowledge about a building where hostages could be held. We're going in as soon as the insertion team is ready—perhaps as soon as this morning or early afternoon. The Needle has supposedly used this building in the past. We don't have hard evidence that they're there now, but it's a strong possibility. Witnesses have seen some movement and it may be—"

"His captors."

"Yes."

Stan squeezed his eyes shut. Saw spots.

"I'll call as soon as I know anything more, Detective. I promise."

"I know."

"Goodbye, Detective. Keep praying."

He hung up. Stood in the kitchen. Didn't move until his legs threatened to let him fall.

≈

When the phone rang later, Stan turned his head slowly to look at it. Two rings. Three. He pushed himself up from the table.

Away from the bowl of cereal, soggy from the morning of soaking in the milk.

Picked up the phone with a shaking hand.

"Mr. Windemere?"

"Yes."

"Um, this is Sheila. From MCC. Are you all right?"

Was he? "Yes. I'm fine. Is everything okay? Did something happen?" His night off. His breath catching at the thought of those supplies.

"Everything's fine. I'm calling because those videos you wanted? About Clayton Kratz? Well, someone turned them in this morning. I thought you'd like to know. I'll leave them here on the counter in the kitchen, if that's okay."

"No."

"You don't want them anymore?"

"Yes. I do."

Her voice strained. Uncertain. Speaking her words slowly, as if to a child. Or someone she suspected of being mentally unbalanced. "All right. I can leave them somewhere else then. On my desk?"

"I mean, no, I'll come get them."

"Now?"

"If I can."

"Well, sure. That's fine. I'll have them here."

He grabbed his keys, went out to his truck. Stopped. Went back inside. Put on his shoes. Returned to his truck. Paused with his key in the ignition, closed his eyes. Rested his elbows on the steering wheel and his forehead on his hands. Lifted his head and backed the truck out of the garage to drive toward MCC.

The sky was brilliant, the pearly clouds looking fake against the blue. Like in those older movies. *Oklahoma!* Or *The Wizard of Oz*. Where Stan was convinced they put up false backgrounds. The other musicals Andrea insisted on watching. They'd watch them as a family. At least the first viewing. *The Music Man*.

Fiddler on the Roof. West Side Story (although Andrea had a headache from crying so much they never watched it a second time). *My Fair Lady. The Sound of Music* every Christmas. Jamie put up with them rather well. They tried to mix in something for him, and Andrea ended up liking the "guy" movies too. *The Man from Snowy River.* The *Star Wars* films. And of course anything to do with sports: *Miracle. Remember the Titans.* And, naturally, *Hoosiers.*

Their house had been without movies lately. It was like in high school or college when you broke up with someone and avoided the radio at all costs. All of the songs were about love— lost love, broken love, or simply being in love. Now it seemed all movies were about families—making them, loving them, losing them. It took too much of an effort to watch.

Stan found himself taking the route through Goshen that led past the police department. Took a look at his workplace while he stopped at the intersection. Studied the orange brick. The vehicles in the parking lot. The statue for fallen officers, commemorating Officer Goodwin, who'd died in 1998. Stan would never forget that day. Hoped no one else would ever forget.

A horn sounded lightly behind him, and Stan jerked through the intersection, his eyes flicking to the rearview mirror. Not a cop. Thank goodness.

The other officers used to razz him about those things. Andrea's driving. Jamie's brush with vandalism. The time Andrea dialed 911 by accident, her two-year-old fingers hitting the emergency button on their phone. Eight-year-old Jamie meeting the officers at the door, all serious and sorry. Stan had been in uniform then. Hadn't heard the last of that for months.

The parking lot at The Depot was busy. Lots of folks out looking for thrift shop bargains on a Monday, the day the volunteers put out the new items. Stan glanced around. No Grand Am. No Hispanic teenagers playing hooky.

He walked through the front lobby, bright and loud, the doors to the stores open, clerks and customers talking, laughing. A different world.

Sheila sat at her desk, banging away at her computer keyboard, eyes focused, little earphones plugged in. Stan stepped up to the desk and waited for her to see him. She did immediately, smiling and pulling the plastic piece from her ear.

"Don't you end up typing what you're listening to?" Stan asked.

Her brow crinkled, then smoothed. "That's the point. It's a dictating machine."

"Oh." A brief laugh. "I just figured—"

"It was an iPod. I know." She smiled. "Don't think I'd get away with that." She leaned over, grabbed something behind her, came up with two videos. "Here you go. Keep them as long as you need to." She held them a moment longer, creating a slight tug of war. Her eyes studied his, and he looked down at the videos. She relinquished them.

Clayton Kratz: Can We Depend on You? and *Shroud for a Journey: The Clayton Kratz Story.* The one the college students made, the front photo of Kratz looking down at a dead horse. A photo of him and Edie on the back.

Sheila peered up at him. "Anything else I can help you with?"

He sighed, looked up. "Jerry in?"

"He is. Let me see if he's available." She picked up the phone, pressed a few buttons, told Jerry that Stan was there. Hung up and smiled again. "You can go on back. He's in his office."

Jerry met Stan at the door. "Get your times confused?" Eyes crinkling.

Stan held up the videos. "Picking up these."

Jerry nodded.

"Got an email from your friend Jim Smucker."

"Oh, good, he got in touch with you. I thought it might be interesting."

Stan jerked his chin toward the warehouse. "Everything okay back there?"

"Yup. Luis watched the place last night. Did a good job."

"Luis?"

Jerry smiled briefly. "Yeah. I figured he helped unload the materials, he might feel some ownership in them. Besides, he can use the work."

"But . . ."

Jerry bit his lip, shook his head, looking at Stan. "You up for tonight? You look a bit whipped."

Stan ground his teeth. Rolled his tongue around in his mouth. "I'll be fine. Having a day off messes up the schedule when you're working nights."

"I hear you."

"So. Tuesday night will be my last."

"That's the plan. You're welcome to help load it all on Wednesday, although after the night's work you'll probably be ready to sleep."

Probably. "Someone saw my son."

Jerry stilled. "When?"

"A couple of months ago. When he first went missing."

"But they just found out?"

"It takes a while to interview people. To find the right ones to talk to."

"And people are afraid to say much."

"Sometimes. Yes." Just like here at home, when he was investigating a robbery or a shooting or a case of fraud.

Jerry watched him. "So, what does this mean?"

"They have a new angle to pursue."

"And that's good."

"It is." He opened his mouth, breathed in.

Jerry waited.

"They think they might know where he is."

"What?"

"Just a possibility. Nothing for sure. They're going in today."

Jerry blinked. Looked at the floor, then at Stan. "I'll find someone else for tonight. You stay home."

"No!"

Jerry jerked back.

"No. I'll come. I need to come."

"All right." Jerry nodded. "All right."

Stan turned to leave.

"He's in my prayers, Stan."

Stan stopped. Glanced back over his shoulder. Didn't meet Jerry's eyes. "Thank you."

"As are you. And your wife."

Stan paused a moment longer, then walked back out to his truck.

∾

No message at home. Nothing from his cell phone. He looked at the receiver on the wall. Should he call Rose? Tell her they might find her son today?

No. Having his own hopes dashed would be hard enough. Having hers trampled would be even worse.

He put in the older video first. He couldn't help it. He *wanted* to watch the one with the college students. He *wanted* to see the kids. See what they saw when they followed Kratz's footsteps.

But he couldn't. He had to do things in order.

He perched himself on the edge of the sofa. Put in the tape. Was swept away at the sound of the four-part harmony, the video panning across a church and cemetery, to rest at Kratz's headstone.

MEMORIAL
CLAYTON H. KRATZ
NOVEMBER 5, 1896
WENT TO RUSSIA, 1920

Stan pinched the bridge of his nose. Watched the beginning of the video with a hand to his forehead, peering out from under his fingers.

The information was basically the same at first. Kratz's youth, schooling, studies. His relationship with Edie.

But then came some new images, new references. His baptism at age seventeen. Drawings he'd made of animals, a public speaker, the American eagle with the olive branch—but without the arrows. Graduating as valedictorian from his high school and speaking on "Courage and Endurance."

A man, old and shaking, speaking of his days as a child in Russia. Starving, frightened, eating anything he could catch: dogs, cats, gophers. Saying you don't ask what you're eating, you just eat—

"What are you *watching?*"

Stan jumped up, spinning around, tipping precariously over the sofa's arm, sending the remote flying.

Andrea stood in the doorway, her expression perplexed.

Stan placed a hand over his heart, closed his eyes. Leaned a hand against the wall.

"Sorry. Didn't mean to scare you."

He let out a breath.

She looked at the video. Caught the word *Mennonite*. "Oh. You thought I was Mom, huh?"

He swiped a hand across his eyes. "Yeah."

She laughed shortly, gestured at the TV. "So what is this?"

"A video." He took a few steps, picked up the remote from underneath a plant stand.

"Well, duh. About what?"

He looked at her face. Interested. Pleasant. Open. "A young Mennonite man named Clayton Kratz disappeared in Russia in 1920. He was never found."

She blinked, but didn't look away. "And you're investigating?"

He winced. "Not really. Sort of, I guess. Just . . ." He stopped.

"I came home to do laundry. Let me get a load started and I'll watch with you, okay?"

He gazed at her. Loved her. "Okay."

He stopped the video, rewound it to where he'd been when she'd arrived. Sat down and breathed deeply to bring his heart rate back to normal. A few minutes later Andrea was back, an icy Diet Coke in her hand. She curled up on the recliner, and Stan pushed play.

Clayton's old friend, Clarence Fulmer, boyhood buddy and college classmate, spoke to the interviewer. He was old. Gray. Nothing like the young men in the 1918 yearbook. Stan placed a hand over his chin. His mouth.

Another interview, this time with the hired hand from the farm where Clayton had worked during his semester off school. He spoke of Clayton's inexperience at farming and of the image of Clayton on his knees praying at the end of each day.

And suddenly, photos from Ukraine. Children, obviously starving, with bony knees and cloudy eyes. Bodies piled on carts, corpses with barely any flesh left to cover their bones. A line of men, shirtless, shoulders and ribs protruding, their eyes sunken.

Andrea sucked in a breath. "It's like photos from the Holocaust."

Stan nodded, his hand still covering the lower half of his face.

Letters, the handwriting shown as the text was read aloud.

Dear Sister and Family,

I am making a hurried investigation of conditions. If any clothing are collected at church send along my two overcoats from my trunk. These Mennonite people had been wealthy. One family that owned many horses has only two left and they will be taking us fifty miles north to look into conditions among the non-Mennonite Russians.

Dear Fulmer and Goshen friends,

> The people here tell us stories of murder and rape and robbery. They say some 12,000 horses were killed in the last battle. The Mennonites here are the farming backbone of the country, but the battle line has passed over them eighteen times and is now only 25 miles away. The whites are apparently retreating and we already hear the red cannons in the distance. My regards to all. I enjoy the work.

> Your old pal, Kratz

A nephew at a kitchen table, letters and photos spread out before him, speaking of his mother, Laura, always praying for Clayton's return. The hopes that someday the door to the summerhouse would open and Clayton would be standing there.

A man talking about the Clayton Kratz Fellowship. A memorial to Kratz, which handed out scholarships to students headed for Mennonite colleges, as well as money to help international students come to spend a year in the United States. Fostering education and community.

And again Kratz's friend Clarence. Saying with a new shine to his eyes, "He's never been out of my mind, all these years."

The video ran to the end, a scholarship recipient playing piano as the credits rolled. Stan felt rooted to the couch.

"I take it Mom doesn't know about these?"

He glanced at Andrea. "I only got them today."

"But it's not the first you've been looking into this guy."

He licked his lips. Looked at the floor. "No."

"And Mom knows?"

"Well, some of it." He grimaced.

"So, this is kind of a Duck Mission. We can do it, but we'd better not tell Mom."

He turned to her. "You okay with that?"

She shrugged. Hopped off the chair. "Why not? I'm going to switch the laundry."

"I have another video."

She looked back. Raised her eyebrows. Kept going.

Stan pushed aside the guilty feeling settling in his stomach and rewound the tape. Listened as it hummed, reached a high pitch, thumped to a stop. Replaced the tape with the newer one. The one by the Goshen College students.

Andrea came back. Sat down. "Got the next one ready?"

He pushed play and caught his breath at the sad guitar, the photo of Kratz, panning out to reveal the entire picture of him, the dead horse, the empty field. Stan leaned his elbows on his knees, his face resting in his hands. Beheld the black-and-white video of the war—bombs, soldiers, guns, trains. The footage frantic and fuzzy, that sped-up look of old movies. He listened to the narrative about the war, the Reds and Whites, the motives for fighting. The death. Starvation.

This video had more of the history of Anabaptists in Russia, a society that had moved there upon an invitation from Catherine the Great. Explained their great farming experience, their success, and their newfound wealth.

And then there it was. Halbstadt. The town where Kratz was staying when he was taken. A woman—a very old woman—talking in German about what a lovely town it was. Until the Communists came.

More photos of dead bodies. Talk of massacres. Photos of starving people. Again, reminiscent of the Holocaust. Except this happened first.

Interviews with a set of people, one of them the historian John Ruth. The John Ruth Stan couldn't find in information. His middle initial apparently an L. And of course the four college students, three guys and a girl. Talking about their expectations, their experiences, their conclusions. Their new photos compared to Orie Miller's—the photos of Kratz in Italy, Greece, Turkey.

Stan glanced at Andrea. She watched with a stony expression, her face giving nothing away as John Ruth talked about Kratz answering God's call. Saying that Kratz felt the call with the same intensity other young men felt the call from their government. That Kratz would've thought, "If they can do it for their country, I can do it for my God."

Stan considered the words. Could those things not be one and the same?

And there was the other historian. Paul Toews. Talking about Krehbiel's diary and the light it could shed on Kratz's disappearance. Giving new ideas of place, time, and motives.

But Toews continued talking. Saying how Kratz's death should be put in the context of the deaths of many, many Russian Mennonites. That while Kratz's death was tragic, one must think of what else was happening. How many other people were dying.

But that wasn't much help when you were his mother. His fiancée. His sister.

Stan's head sank lower in his hands, his eyes barely meeting the screen of the TV, where a collage of images assaulted him. Images and music and quotes. A sudden comprehension of what they were showing.

Three men, placed at the mouth of a pit. Lined up. A group of soldiers across from them. Raising their rifles. And the voice over it all:

> I think he might've felt fear, natural fear, but if he knew it was coming I think it must've flashed over his mind that . . . "people will remember me."

~

"Dad? Dad!"

He was being shaken. Waking up. What? Was something wrong? Was something happening?

He looked up into the face of his daughter, her eyes wild, her mouth tight.

"Dad, you okay?"

"What?" His voice husky.

He lay on the floor of the living room, his head aching. A high-pitched noise assaulted his ears, and he blinked. "What happened?"

"You fainted."

He felt her fingers, gently turning his head from one side to the other.

"No blood. But you're going to have a lump."

"I fainted?"

"Fell right off the couch. Thank goodness you don't have a coffee table here anymore. You'd be getting stitches about now."

"Here, help me up." He took her arm, and she led him to the sofa. "What is that shrieking?"

"Oh." She turned off the TV. "The end of the video. I thought it was more important to tend to you than stop it." A hint of a smile. Gone too soon.

He groaned, his head foggy, his stomach rebelling.

"Lie down before you keel over again." She tipped him sideways on the couch. Found him a pillow. "You gonna puke?"

"I don't know. I don't think so."

She left. Came back with a plastic wastebasket. "Just in case."

He grimaced. Closed his eyes. And just before drifting off, murmured something Andrea seemed to understand.

But he forgot it.

$\sim$

When he awoke, his first thought was that Rose couldn't see the videos. He sat up, too quickly, and lay down again. The videos were gone. As was the wastebasket and any sign that he was doing anything other than taking a normal nap.

Another thought shot through him, and he searched for

the time on the wall clock. Only three-thirty. Good. He wasn't even close to being late for work.

He sat up again, slower this time. Wondered if Rose really was home. If she'd confiscated the videos. If it were possible he'd slept through the phone's ring.

"Rose?"

Footsteps in the hallway. Not Rose. Andrea.

"Hey, Dad. I'm just heading out." She sat beside him. "You all right?"

"I haven't been getting enough sleep, is all."

"Yeah. I know." Her eyes were thoughtful. The skin tight around them. She leaned closer. Whispered, "I put the videos in Jamie's room. Under the mattress with the rest of your stuff."

He choked on a breath. "How did you know?"

"You told me."

"I did? When?"

She shook her head, grinning. "Right after you passed out. Before you crashed."

He felt the bump on his forehead.

"I meant crashed as in fell asleep. Not what you did to your head." She made a face and got up. "You might want to put some ice on that. Want me to get you some?"

Without waiting for an answer, she got up and left. Came back with a Ziploc filled with ice cubes, surrounded by a towel. She placed it against his head, and he raised a hand to hold it in place.

He grabbed her wrist as she turned to go. "Thanks, Andi."

"Sure."

He looked over her shoulder, said quietly, "Your mom home?"

"In your bedroom."

"You're not staying for supper?"

"Can't. Got practice in an hour. I have to get moving."

"Oh. Well. See you soon?"

"Yeah. Love you, Dad."

He squeezed her hand. Let her go.

When she was gone, he lay back down, knowing he needed more sleep, also knowing he wasn't likely to get any more now that he'd been awakened. He stayed there for a few minutes, until he heard Rose moving around.

"Hey."

She stopped and peered around the corner from the hallway, looking at the ice pack on his head. "What happened?"

"I fell off the couch."

She looked at him. Drew a breath. Shook her head. "I'm going out."

"Yeah? Where?"

She bit her lips together, looked at her purse. "To meet someone for coffee."

"Really? That's great. Who?"

Her eyes met his. Defiant. Then hesitant. "That lady from the college."

He stared at her. "The professor? The one who called?"

"Yes. Do you . . . do you have a problem with that?"

"No. No. Not at all. It's just . . ."

"What?"

"Nothing. I hope it goes well."

She raised an eyebrow. "Why wouldn't it?"

No possible response to that.

She left, her footsteps disappearing into the kitchen, the door clicking shut.

Stan sat back into the sofa. Surveyed the room. The clock. The lump on his head. He got up—slowly—and made his way to the kitchen. Looked on the back porch while he ate a piece of toast. No food bowl. No water dish. No cat.

His wife's Duck Mission. Except it was a cat.

The phone rang, and Stan practically jumped across the room. His head spun. "Yes?"

"Detective Windemere?" A young voice. A woman.

"This is him. He."

"My name is Petty Officer Marilyn Reed. Chief Borgman asked me to call you."

Stan groped for the wall. Leaned against it. Why wouldn't Borgman call himself?

"The chief asked me to look into some historical deck logs for you."

Stan sucked in a breath, held his spinning head. Breathed. Not the call he needed. But a call he wanted. "Did you find them? Did you find *him?*"

"I did. At least I think so. On the dates you requested we found record of two Americans traveling on the USS *Whipple* to Sebastopol. From what I can find, they were on board about five days. Does that sound right?"

"Yes. Something like that."

"There really aren't any more details than that, except to say that they were relief workers. I'm sorry I couldn't find more."

"That's all right, Petty Officer. You gave me something. I appreciate it."

"If I can do any more to help you, please let me know."

Stan laughed to himself. He could give her a whole list. "I will. Thank you."

He hung up and walked to his den. The door was shut. He opened it. Grimaced at the mess of papers on the floor. It was a wonder Rose hadn't torched the whole lot.

He got down on his knees and began picking up the piles. Strapped them all together with a big rubber band and stood looking down at them. Then went to Jamie's room and shoved them under the mattress, where they joined *When Apples Are Ripe*, the yearbooks, and, yes, the videos.

Back in the den he went online. He was not hoping for news on Jamie. He was not. He was not.

There was nothing from Jamie.

But there was an email from Paul Toews. The historian. The email read:

> Dear Mr. Windemere:
>
> I recently spent a year in Zaporizhzhia Ukraine. In research in various archives I found nothing that in any way further illumines the Kratz story. For years I presumed there was a record somewhere that would tell us what happened. That may still be so, but I am now less confident. Working in those archives one discovers how much is there and also how much is missing.
>
> After finding no information in the Zaporizhzhia Region State Archive, which was one of the logical places, I filed a formal request for Kharkiv Region State Archive to do a search of their holdings for any information. Several months later they reported back that they were unable to find any reference in their materials. Having also earlier checked in archives in Dnipropetrovsk and Kyiv I now assume that the only additional place where one might check would be in military archives in Moscow. From what little I know of those archives I think it could be a very long and frustrating search and with no guarantee of finding anything.
>
> Best wishes for your own investigation.
>
> > Fraternally,
> > Paul Toews

Stan swallowed the lump of disappointment in his throat. *I found nothing. . . .*

He went back out to the kitchen. Picked up the phone. Began dialing. Stopped. Set the receiver back on the cradle. Sat down at the table.

"Stan?"

He looked up at Rose. "Back already?"

She set her purse on the counter, the keys in the basket. "Stan, I've been gone almost two hours."

He blinked. Checked the clock. Five-thirty. "Oh."

"Did you . . . No, you didn't eat anything."

"Piece of toast."

She ignored this, grabbing a bun, filling it with turkey, lettuce, mayonnaise. Set it in front of him. "Eat."

He picked up the sandwich, "How did it go?"

She put away the rest of the food, the dirtied silverware, the buns. "Fine."

"She listened to you?"

"She listened."

"And?"

She washed her hands, dried them off on the towel hanging from the refrigerator handle. "And nothing. She listened. I listened. We said goodbye."

"And that took two hours?"

She looked at him. "The coffee was good." And she left, going back to their bedroom and closing the door.

Stan found a baggie, put his sandwich in it, and planned to take it for his midnight lunch.

Maybe he'd be hungry then.

∽

"You don't look so good, man."

"Yeah? So?" Stan glared at Luis, who stood against the building, one foot up on the bricks, his hands in his pockets.

"Don't you ever sleep?"

"Sometimes. What do you want?"

Luis pushed himself off the building. Shrugged. "Just hanging out."

"And you want to hang out *here*?"

"It's as good a place as any."

That was a laugh. "Where are all your cronies?"

"*Cronies?* Don't you mean *homies?*"

"I didn't say that."

"Yeah, but it's what you're thinking."

Stan sighed, running his hand over his face. "Look, you're the one who showed up here unannounced. I work here."

"Right. For another day. And I work here too. I watched the place last night, when you were supposed to be home sleeping."

Stan choked back words. Bared his teeth. Tried to relax. "Okay. But tonight it's my turn, so—"

"Stay off your turf?"

Stan looked at the boy—the man—his eyes dark, his face bunched like a little boy almost ready to cry.

"I'm tired, okay, Luis? I'm beat. But I'm here to work. If you want to stay, keep me company, you can. Just don't give me attitude."

Luis cranked his head to the side, looking blankly at Stan's truck. "And you won't give *me* attitude?"

Stan smothered a smile. "No. I won't."

Luis straightened his shoulders. Jutted his chin. "Well, all right then."

Stan unlocked the door. Looked back at Luis. Figured if Jerry trusted the kid with the supplies, he might as well let him in. He flipped on the lights in the warehouse. Checked all the corners, all the shadows. Peeked into Becky's office. Went into the inner office, did the same routine.

Luis followed silently, all the way out to the lobby. "You always come out here?"

Stan kept walking. "I like to know it's empty." He stopped at the Ten Thousand Villages window. "Plus I like to see what's displayed here." Still the baskets, with all of their color and weave.

"Yeah, well, most of my shopping's in this place." Luis stopped at the thrift store.

"Nothing wrong with that."

"Yeah." A half-laugh.

Stan checked behind the large potted plants, down the hallway by Choice Books. Led Luis back into the office. Said, "Shouldn't you be in bed?"

Luis smiled. "What for?"

"Don't you have school tomorrow?"

"School?" Now he did laugh. "How young do you think I am?"

Stan's neck grew hot. "I don't know. Sixteen. Seventeen."

Luis shook his head. "Nineteen. Graduated last year."

"Graduated?"

"Yeah. That surprise you?"

Unfortunately. "From Goshen High School?"

"The one and only."

Stan walked back to the warehouse, Luis following.

"So, what fills your time now?"

The lift of a shoulder. "Work when I can find it. Helping my mom with my brothers and sisters."

"How many?"

"Five."

Stan sat on a bale of clothing and rubbed the back of his neck.

Luis stood across from him. "You have kids?"

Stan looked at him, hand still resting on his neck. "Two. Boy and girl."

"How old?"

"Boy's twenty-five. Girl's nineteen."

"Where they at?"

"My daughter's at Notre Dame. Freshman. My son's . . . my son's in the Navy."

"Yeah? Where?"

Stan looked at the boy, who, by his age, really was a man. "I don't know."

Luis stared at him, interest lighting his eyes. "You mean

he's on a secret mission somewhere and can't tell you? Is he a SEAL?"

"No. No, what I mean is that he's missing. He's somewhere in Russia, somewhere . . . out there . . . but no one can find him."

Luis's mouth dropped open. "He's MIA?"

Stan nodded. Wanted to say more. Couldn't.

"Wow. That's heavy. I mean, wow."

Luis walked over, watching Stan's face. Stan looked down at his hands, where they rested on his knees.

Luis sat beside him.

He didn't need to say anything else.

August 20, 1920

Mr. Levi Mumaw
Mennonite Relief Commission for War Sufferers
Scottdale, Penna.

My dear Mr. Mumaw:

. . . Yesterday I also received your telegram giving the name of Clayton H. Kratz as the third member of Mr. Miller's party and I immediately sent passport application and letter for the State Department to Mr. Kratz at Blooming Glen, Pennsylvania. I trust he will not lose any time in making his application and that there will be no difficulty in his case, but if there should be any hold up similar to that experienced by Mr. Slagel, Mr. Kratz would do well to let you and me know immediately, and probably he would be wise to come promptly to New York to clear up the situation if that is what seems to be indicated.

We will now make definite assignment of cabin space on the PROVIDENCE for this party and the tickets and baggage tags will be sent you from this office within a few days. . . .

Yours sincerely,
Charles W. Fowle
Foreign Secretary
Near East Relief

Chapter 16
TUESDAY

"Where are your papers about Jamie?"

Stan blinked as he walked into the kitchen. The sun shined into the room, reflecting off the chrome of the sink.

"What?"

Rose was sitting at the table. The table was full of Stan's things.

"I mean, look at this." Her voice and expression were pleasant as she picked up the stack of yearbooks. "Four Goshen College *Maple Leafs*. This little red book. Two videos. An entire ream of copies. Enough to cause a large lumpy mound under a mattress. And I was wondering . . . is any of this about Jamie?"

Stan stood frozen.

"I guess I can understand. You're a detective. You detect. You try to find out things about the past. About what happened to people and who might've done the evil deeds, whatever they were." She tapped a finger on the stack of papers. "It's just . . . I'm remembering a few weeks ago when you were put on leave, and it seems to me it was because you couldn't detect anymore.

That all you could think about was your own son's disappearance. It was affecting your focus, your drive, your ability to connect the dots. Isn't that right? But you know, it's funny. You come home, where you'd have all the time in the world to use your skills to find our son, but the only missing person you have time for is someone who died ninety years ago."

"We don't know—"

"And even if he didn't die then, he would surely be dead by now. What does it say?" She picked up *When Apples Are Ripe*. Paged through. "This Clayton Kratz was born in 1896. He'd be over a hundred and ten by now. A ripe old age. And let's see . . . Jamie will be what? Twenty-six on his next birthday? Seems to me he has a little more time left than this Mennonite."

"Rose, the NIS—"

"Yes, yes, I know. The NIS has things under control. They're doing their best. Chief Borgman is leaving no stone unturned." She stood up, straightening the items, lining them up with each other, with the sides of the table, her fingers gently prodding them into order. "It just seems to me that my son's father, who left work supposedly because he couldn't concentrate on other people's cases anymore, can now think of *only* other people. *One* other person. A *Mennonite*. If you're so ready to find other mothers' missing children, it seems to me maybe, just maybe, you should go back to work. Don't you think?"

A shiver ran up Stan's spine when Rose turned her smile toward him. A smile that reached into his chest, wrenching his heart. A smile that went nowhere else in her face. Her body. Her presence.

"I'm going to work now. I'm going to work, because there's really no point in my staying home. Organizing hair appointments isn't a skill I can use to find Jamie. And while I'm gone, you need to figure out what you're going to do with those things." She gestured to the table, without looking at it. "And what you should be doing with your time. With whatever time our son . . . *our* son . . . has left."

She turned away, made a few attempts to grab the door-knob, finally took hold of it, and left. Stan stood still, listening as the garage door opened and her car pulled out into the driveway and down the street.

The house was still. The phone was silent. The hands of the wall clock ticked on and on and on. A new sound began. *Scratch, scratch.* A high-pitched squealing rasp on the back door.

Stan went over, looked out. The orange cat sat on the stoop, peering expectantly at the window. Meowed when it saw Stan's face. Stan turned around, leaned against the door. Blinked slowly at the materials covering the kitchen table. Sank down, down against the door, until he landed on the cold, unyielding floor.

~

When Rose returned at noon, she took one glance at the kitchen before setting her jaw, straightening her back, and walking back to her bedroom. Stan recognized, through a haze, that she was home. That his tailbone was shrieking its displeasure. That the table was still full of documents.

His legs, stretched out before him, seemed to belong not to him, but to some stranger who'd come in and made himself a place in the room. In the house. In Stan's life. His hands, limp on his lap, palms upward, open, waiting.

Rose returned. Stood by the table. Stacked the items in her arms. Took them down the hallway. Stan marked her passage by her footsteps. Past the living room. Past the bathroom. Stopped at his den. *Thwack.* The first thing hit the floor. *Thwack. Thwack.* Two more. A huge thump of the remaining books. And then the sound of rending paper. *Rip, flutter. Rip, flutter.* The storm of information, notes, dreams flooding his room. His space. His thoughts. *Rip, rip, rip.*

Finally, her return. Staring at him from the archway, her lips set in a tight line. Her chin raised defiantly. Her feet moving toward him, then stopping, changing direction. The beeping of the phone's buttons, her voice as she took the phone into the hallway. Up and down. Quiet. Steady. The phone resting in its cradle. His wife standing still, again in the archway.

The clock ticked on, until the doorbell rang. Rose left, the sound of the door reaching Stan, reaching somewhere into his consciousness.

"Stan?" A familiar voice. A familiar face. Roy Gardener. His friend. His chief. Kneeling beside him. Sitting beside him, sharing the door.

They sat there together. Stan, the chief, and the clock. Ticking. Ticking. The chief moving his toothpick from one side of his mouth to the other, arms held lightly across his stomach. Crossing his legs at the ankles. His gun belt pressing into Stan's waist. His hip.

After a while, Roy said, "You know, a middle-aged body's not meant to sit like this for so long. I'm not sure I'm going to be able to get up by myself."

He waited. Stan sat.

"And you know, Stan. Buddy. My butt's getting pretty sore."

Waited some more.

Finally the chief got himself up, heaving and pushing against the wall. The floor. He turned to Stan. Held out his hand. Held it in front of Stan's face until he saw it. Until he reached out and took it.

∾

It was late afternoon when Stan woke up. He rolled to the side of his bed and groaned, his body protesting. He reached back, pushed on his lower back. Remembered.

He shook his head, clearing it. Looked at the clock. Almost six-thirty. Blinked. Stood up, too quickly. Took a deep breath, rolled his neck. Walked down the hallway, stopping in the doorway of the den. Shut the door on the carnage.

Rose sat in the living room, the TV on. She stared at it, at the news, her eyes glassy. She didn't look up.

No phone calls. No messages. Why hadn't Borgman called? How long could it take an insertion team to assemble and carry out their mission?

Stan opened the refrigerator. Took out a yogurt. A bottle of water. An apple. Put them in a bag.

"Where are you going?" Rose now in the doorway.

"To work."

"I don't think so."

He looked at her. "I do."

"You're in no shape—"

"I'm going."

That bunching of her jaw again. Those eyes. The way she looked walking away.

∾

Matthew Schwartzentruber was coming out the back door of The Depot when Stan arrived. He greeted Stan, glancing briefly at Stan's face, then looking again, for a longer study.

"Late night?" Stan asked.

The Amishman nodded thoughtfully. "I came mid-afternoon. Is everything well with you?"

"Everything's fine."

"The supplies are going out tomorrow?"

Stan nodded.

"So that means you are done working here?"

"For now."

Schwartzentruber untied Katie from the hitching post. "I hope it's been a good couple of weeks for you. Working with the Mennonites."

Stan watched as Katie readied herself for the trip—shaking her head, snorting, blinking those long eyelashes. "It's been good."

Schwartzentruber climbed up into the buggy. "Then God be with you as you move on."

Stan's keys dug into his hand. He released his fist. "Thank you."

A click of the tongue, a twitch of the reins, and Katie was moving. Out of her spot and out of the parking lot. Gone.

Stan turned and unlocked the door, stopping with surprise when he saw Luis at the door to Becky's office. "Hey."

Luis's eyes widened. "What are . . . I thought . . ."

"What?"

The boy . . . man . . . whatever he was . . . stopped, his mouth open, head shaking slowly side to side.

"*What?*"

"Nothing, man, it's just those are the same clothes you had on last night."

Stan looked down. It was true. "So?"

"So nothing. That's cool."

Stan looked around the warehouse. "Where's your bike?"

"Over there." In the corner, against the wall.

"Why are you here?"

Luis shrugged, his hands in his pockets, casual. "No reason. Thought I'd keep you company. I mean, it *is* your last night."

The last night. The last night to watch the supplies. The last night anyone would have a chance to steal them. Anyone, including Luis and his buddies.

"Where are your friends tonight?"

"My friends?" An expression of surprise. "I don't know. Where they always are, I guess. Hanging out. Home. Work. The usual."

Stan studied the boy's face. Tried to read it. Impossible. "Well, come on then. I need to make rounds."

"Sure, man."

They made the usual trek, first the kitchenette for Stan's

lunch, then the office, the lobby, and the warehouse, Luis following along silently. Watching. Whistling.

Finally stopping in the warehouse, Stan turned to Luis. "Okay. What are you really doing here?"

"Nothing, man, I—"

"Luis."

"It's just—"

"*Luis*."

The boy stopped, looked around as if searching for eavesdroppers. Or witnesses. Slumped onto a packaged blanket. "Jerry called me. Asked me to come by."

"Why?"

"He thought you weren't going to show."

Stan took a few steps away, studied a recent pile of used goods in the thrift shop area. An old chair. A bookcase. A stack of tablecloths. "Why would he think that?" But he knew. Roy. Roy had called him, told him Stan was out of commission.

"I dunno. He heard you were sick or something." He looked at Stan. "Are you?"

A laugh. "No. No, I'm not sick."

A face, like he didn't believe him. *Whatever*.

Stan walked to the door, looked out. Watched for movement. Lights. Listened for anything out of the ordinary. Made sure his truck was okay.

"What're you doing?"

Stan jumped. "Don't sneak up on me like that."

"I didn't. I just walked over. Asked a question."

Stan closed the door, bumped the young man out of the way as he walked past. Looked at the stacks of supplies. "Your friends coming tonight?"

Luis looked at him, his nose wrinkled. "What? Why would they? We don't start loading till the morning."

"They don't need anything extra? Some blankets? Clothes? Food?"

Luis's look of confusion dropped, replaced with hardened eyes. "You think we're planning to steal this? These?" He gestured at the supplies. "What would we do with it?"

"Sell it. Trade it. Use it."

Luis bounced on his toes. Stepped toward Stan, stepped away. "I can't believe . . . You think I would do that?"

"Wouldn't you?"

"No! You're . . . you . . ." He strode to his bike, grabbed it, wheeled it to the door. Opened the door roughly, held it with his butt as he pulled the bike through, scraping the pedals on the doorway. The door slammed behind him.

Stan stood still, watching. Waiting. Let his head fall back and his breath escape. Oh, man. He hadn't . . . he hadn't thought. Or he'd thought too much. Too much like a policeman? Or too much like some racist idiot who should know better?

He sagged onto the blanket where Luis had been sitting. Let his head droop, his chin to his chest. What a mess. What a jerk he was.

The buzzer jolted him upright. The back door. He walked over, opened it.

Luis looked away. Bit his lip. Reached for his bike while Stan opened the door wider. "Jerry asked me to help out tonight. I'm gonna help out."

Stan shut the door as Luis parked the bike. As Luis avoided his eyes.

"You want to stay out here?" Stan asked. "I'll go inside."

"What if I make away with all of it while you're gone?"

Stan winced. "You won't."

A snort.

Stan turned to go inside.

"I know who did it." Luis's voice. Quiet.

Stan turned back to see the boy still looking at his bike. "What?"

A shrug. "Some of the stealing. La Casa, some others. Not

the bank job, the one where they kidnapped the CEO to get them into the vault. Just the smaller ones."

Stan stayed very still.

"It's who you might expect. At least some of them. You know. Members of the gangs. Some of the rougher guys. Hispanics, like me." He lifted his eyes from his bike. "But it's not for the *reasons* you might expect."

"Not drugs? Money?"

"No. Not most of it, anyway. I mean, where are you going to find a front for used refrigerators and canned food? At least one that hopes to make any money?"

Stan waited.

"They needed it, man. They're out of work, their parents are out of work. Employers are scared to hire them if they don't have papers. Employers don't want to hire them. A lot won't keep them on even if they've worked there for years." He raised his eyes to Stan's. "They *needed* it."

Stan kept his gaze steady, Luis breaking it off first. "It's not my friends. The ones you've seen. But I'm still not going to give you any names."

Stan nodded. "I know. And I don't really want them." He watched Luis. The nervous cracking of knuckles. The shifting eyes.

"You think it's okay?" Stan asked.

Luis looked at him. "What?"

"That they're stealing things?"

He shrugged. "They needed them."

Stan nodded. "I see. So it would be okay if those same guys would come here? Take things from the warehouse that are meant for other people? Things gathered by Jerry, who's been nothing but nice to you?"

Luis gripped the handlebar of his bike, his knuckles whitening. "I didn't say—"

"I know." Stan looked at him. "Do you think these guys, the

ones stealing things, have asked for help? Will their sense of pride—*machismo*—allow that?" He held a hand out. "Look how much Jerry's helped you. Don't you think he'd do his best to help others too? I mean, come on. You get angry when I think your friends are going to steal, but am I so wrong to allow that possibility? When you know there are others from your community doing just that?"

Luis shook his head, but Stan wasn't sure if he was agreeing or simply refusing to hear what he'd said.

Stan waited, wondering if the boy would have a response, but none came. He left Luis and went into the office. Walked slowly through. Thought about those boys who only wanted to feed their families. Keep their siblings and parents warm and clothed. He looked at The World. Looked at Clayton Kratz. Looked at his cell phone to make sure it was on. Ate his lunch by himself.

Felt himself slowing down. Winding down. Winding away.

He threw away his trash. Walked into the lobby, leaned his forehead against the cool glass of the Ten Thousand Villages display. Those beautiful baskets. Those colors.

Stood at the front door, watching the lights on the parking lot. The empty, dark parking lot. No laughing out there tonight. No Spanish words floating across the asphalt. No complicated handshakes. No cars. No young men.

Walked back into the office. Avoided The World. Avoided Clayton.

Found himself walking back to Clayton. Picking up the frame. Sinking to the chair. Pressing the photo against his chest. Against his heart. Rocking, rocking. Crying out. The tears streaming down his face, to his throat, wetting his collar.

He's not coming home. He's not coming home. He's not. . . .

Arms reaching around him. Holding him. Loving him.

Staying there, with him, until the tears went dry.

The idea of going to work on the farm is all right, but I don't like the idea of trying to get out of it. It's all right for those boys that are on the farm all the time, but I think this way. If our Mennonite boys have to go to camp and suffer the consequences of a little persecution, I want to suffer with them when the time comes.

—Clayton Kratz, to his sister Laura, when she suggested he come home to her farm to avoid the draft

Chapter 17
WEDNESDAY

When the morning light began creeping through the high windows, the two men sat in the warehouse. Stan rested on an old cushioned chair, his chin on his fist, his eyes puffy, blood-shot, but more focused than they'd been in days.

Luis lay on the edge of some baled clothing, playing with a yo-yo he had found in the thrift shop pile. Up, down. Up, down. Down. Wobbling. Lifeless.

Stan cleared his throat. "It's all in the wrist."

Luis grunted. "Yeah?"

"Yeah."

"Fine. You're such a hotshot, you show me." He tossed it, green and shiny, toward Stan's chair. Hit him in the chest.

Stan took it. Wrapped the string tightly around the core. Stood up. Flicked it down. Spun it around, flung it in arcs, all the while up and down, continuous motion. He finished with a snap, holding the toy in his hand.

Luis gave a bark of laughter, clapping. "You should join the circus, man."

Stan looked at him. "Maybe I will."

"Where'd you learn to do that?"

He shrugged. "When I was a kid. Needed something to do. That was before television, you know."

Luis stopped short. "It was?"

"I was joking. How old do you think I am?"

Luis narrowed his eyes. Studied him. "I'd say not a day older than sixty-five."

Stan flung the yo-yo at him, just missing his head.

"Hey, man, hey! You trying to kill me? I think I'll just give this back."

He yanked a piece of paper from his pocket. The scrap that held a phone number. The number for Stan's cell phone.

The handle of the back door rattled, and the door swung open. Jerry was unable to hide his surprise at the sight of Stan. "Good morning, gentlemen."

Luis sat up, shoving the paper back in his pocket. "Jerry."

"Everything okay here?" Looking at Stan.

"Everything's just fine."

Looking at Luis. "Fine?"

"You heard him. Everything's fine."

"Good. Good."

Luis's eyes met Stan's briefly as Jerry took stock of the room. A smile flickered on his face. Stan's lips twitched in return.

Jerry turned back to them. "The trucks should be arriving soon to begin transporting the goods to South Bend."

Stan blinked. "South Bend?"

"We made special provisions with the airport. The first leg of the trip will go from there."

"Good."

"You going to hang around? Help load your charges?" Jerry gestured at the mountains of supplies.

"Oh, maybe for a little while. As long as I can take it." He looked at Luis. "Your friends coming today?"

Luis nodded, his eyes dancing. "Yeah. As a matter of fact, they are."

"I'm glad to hear that."

"Thought you might be."

Jerry looked back and forth between the two men. "Guys?"

"What?" All innocent expressions.

"Nothing." He smiled. "Nothing at all."

$\sim$

"You're sure you're up to it?" Rose asked.

"For a little while. I'd like to see this job to the end."

Silence. "All right. Don't hurt yourself."

Stan hung up, surprised. He'd expected a complaint. An angry retort that the Mennonites should do their own hard labor. But it hadn't come.

He returned home midday. Tired, sweating, dirty. No light blinked on the answering machine. No handwritten message from his wife gave him any news about his son.

But the *Goshen News* lay open on the table. Letters to the Editor.

Dear Goshen Citizens,

Last week Rose Windemere, mother of Second Class Petty Officer Jamie Windemere, currently missing in Russia, read in this paper about a peace rally organized by Goshen College students. She responded with a Letter to the Editor, decrying the thoughtlessness she felt the students showed for those giving their lives in military service.

Lisa Klassen, a professor of peace studies at Goshen College, saw the letter and felt a need to call Rose, to see if they couldn't talk and find a way to bridge their two worlds.

We met. We talked. We listened. And we've found

a lot of commonalities between the two of us. We both have sons. We both have a strong belief in God. And we think there is a lot to learn about each other and the beliefs we each hold.

We decided to work together to share our passions. To see how together we can make peace in this world. For if we can't make peace here at home, how can we expect our children—here or abroad—to do it? We thought that as a start we would each write a paragraph to say what we might do to begin our road of shared responsibility and care for our children and our world.

I (Lisa) will continue to oppose war and violence, but I will also try to do it with a new sense of how much love, fear, and pain military families experience. I need to be aware of people like Rose, Jamie, and their families as I work toward peace in the way I feel called. I understand more deeply now that we want the same things: peace in the world, a safe place for our children, and a sense of security.

I (Rose) will respect and understand in a new way those who oppose war and military action. I ask those who think differently from me that they would remember us, along with our sons and daughters, and all who feel called to serve their country in the military. Our troops need to know we care about them, we love them, and we support them, whether or not we support the military itself.

We encourage all of you to understand that it is possible to "agree to disagree" without disrespect or malice on either part.

May God be with us, with our children, and with our world.

Signed,

Rose Windemere, mother of Second Class Petty Officer Jamie Windemere

Lisa Klassen, professor of peace studies, Goshen College

Stan dropped the paper to the table, then picked it up again, staring at his wife's name under the letter. Yes, it was really there. Rose Windemere. The same woman, who, in a fit of rage—or something—had taken his research about a young Mennonite man and shredded it to oblivion the day before.

He walked in a daze down the hallway to his den, the image of the paper storm burned onto his mind. He stopped at the door. Pushed it open.

The paper was gone. Every scrap. Every shred. Nothing occupied the wastebasket. No filled garbage bags adorned the floor.

A stack of wrinkled, smoothed-out sheets lay on his desk, by the computer. On top of it sat the yearbooks, the videos, and *When Apples Are Ripe*, in order of size. Stan went into the room, lay his hand on top of the book. Took a deep breath and shook his head.

He was slowly, surely, losing a grasp on whatever he once thought he knew about his wife.

She was gone now, probably at work, so he took a long, hot shower. He felt sorry for those who'd been working around him in his two-day-old clothes. Disgusting. He would've stayed longer, but the nights and days of sleeplessness had made him clumsy. He'd dropped at least five buckets before Jerry gently suggested—requested?—he go home.

When he emerged from his room, clean and dressed, it was long past time for Rose to come home for lunch. Stan wanted to wait for her, but could feel his strength ebbing. He foraged through the refrigerator, finding leftover sloppy joe meat and some corn. He arranged it on a plate and was warming it in the microwave when the doorbell rang.

He hoped it wasn't Roy, coming around to see if he was still the quivering mess of yesterday. If it was, he supposed his friend would be glad he gave up his lunch hour to see that things had changed overnight. He wiped his hands on a towel and walked through the living room, trying to think of a way to give Roy the thanks he deserved.

He opened the front door and froze, his stomach heaving at the sight of the two men.

Chief Borgman, his buttons shining, his uniform pressed and perfect. And the lieutenant by his side, another version of the all-around athlete. Tall, muscular, strong-jawed. A different officer from last visit, but also the same.

Stan stared at them, his head swimming, the bile rising in his throat. *The same as last time. The same as last time. The same as last time*, except for one particular thing.

Chief Borgman was smiling.

"Hello, Detective."

Stan gripped the doorjamb in one hand, the door in the other, holding himself upright, keeping himself from tumbling onto the porch or falling to his knees. His voice stuck in his throat as he focused on the chief's smile. His teeth. Straight and white and shining. Visible between his upturned lips.

"Detective Windemere, can we come in?"

But his hands held fast, his knuckles white. His arms shaking. His jaw trembling, his eyes dry, unable to blink.

"Stan?" The chief's hand on his forearm, a gentle hold, squeezing. "Stan."

He raised his eyes to the chief's. The chief's sparkling, radiant eyes.

"We found him, Stan. We found your son." The words

strange, unbelievable, inconceivable. "We found Jamie. We found him, and he's coming home."

And then Stan's muscles went slack. He was falling. Falling across the threshold, into two pairs of arms that lifted him, carrying him back into his house. Into the living room. Onto the sofa, where he sat, stunned, forever. Or at least until the laughter came. The joyous, giddy, heightened laughter of disbelief and incredulity.

Stan laughed. Into his hands. Into a pillow. At Chief Borgman. At the lieutenant. He laughed and laughed and laughed.

"Detective?"

Through the tears, Stan looked at the chief. Recognized the concern on his face. The anxious light in his eyes.

"I'm fine." His laughter tailed off, his breathing punctuated now by sharp barks of hiccups. "I'm fine. Really."

Stan caught the shared look between the two NIS agents. Laughed again.

"Is Mrs. Windemere home?"

Stan jumped up. "She's not. Oh, no. She's not here. I have to tell her. I have to call her." He ran to the phone. Punched in a number. Wrong one. Punched in another. Got the beauty salon. Another woman answered the phone.

"Is my wife there? This is Stan. Stan Windemere."

"No, I'm sorry. She's already left for home. Is there something—"

He slammed down the phone. "She's on her way. Oh. Oh, what should I tell her?" He paced the kitchen, a frantic to and fro, around the table, to the door to the garage, and back. The two men watching from the archway to the living room, eyebrows raised, uneasy smiles on their faces.

And then he heard the garage door opening. He flung open the door, running out, avoiding the front bumper of her car as she slammed on the brakes. Grabbing the handle of her locked car door, trying to open it. Pounding on the window.

"He's coming home, Rose! He's coming home! They found him!"

The pop of the door unlocking, pushing him away as it swung open.

"He's coming home, Rose." Quieter now as he looked into her eyes. "He's coming home."

And then the sting as her hand smacked his face. As she hit him again and again, on his shoulder, his chest, with her fists, her hand, her purse. "Stop it, Stan! He's not coming home! He's not! Can't you see it? He's been dead ninety years! He's not coming home!"

He opened his arms, pinning his wife, her hands, her screams against him. Against his beating heart. His real, strong, joyful heart. "*Jamie*, my love. *Jamie's* coming home. Our son. Our *son*. Our. Son."

And she stilled, quivering, trembling in his arms. Her neck stiff, regaling against the contact, arms pinned by her side. And then her purse dropped to the ground. Her face fell onto his chest. Her shoulders lost their tension. Slowly her arms rose, reaching around him, her hands clasping together against his spine.

He pressed her head to him, his other hand on her back, holding her up, sharing his strength, loving her.

And there, in the garage, between her reliable car and his newly acquired truck, they cried together. As one.

EPILOGUE

A maple leaf, golden and curled, dropped to the water and floated away, escaping the beaks of the ever-starving ducks. It wouldn't be long until the birds fled Goshen, on to whatever warmer clime they called their winter home. But until then, they would accept the scraps thrown to them by kindly strangers.

Andrea threw the bread toward the yammering beggars. Yeasty weapons bouncing off of their heads, beaks, backs. But the silly birds dove after them, snatching the prize from the mouths of others.

A single slice of bread hung limply in Jamie's right hand, his left thrust deep into his jacket pocket. His eyes gazed in the general direction of his sister and her brood, but it wasn't clear if he saw the dilemma of the ducks or his sister's wicked aim. He could've used the bread himself, his cheekbones jutting, jeans hanging loosely over skinny hips and legs.

He'd been thinner, frighteningly so, when he'd finally come home from the hospital. No desire to eat. No pleasure in mac and cheese or sloppy joes or anything else Rose could conjure up. He hadn't been given much by the Needle. Stale bread. Water. Rotting fruit.

But he'd survived.

His partner, his chief, hadn't been so lucky. Kept as a bartering chip, living in filthy conditions, he'd become ill. Given no help by his captors, he died across the room from where Jamie tried to sleep. To pray. To live.

When the insertion team found Jamie, their information proving accurate, he'd been delirious, incoherent. Sick and weak and despondent. He hadn't been allowed to see his family until he'd been thoroughly examined, inside and out. Given the all-clear. Given the ride home.

Now the bread in his hand was useless both to Jamie and the ducks, who weren't quite brazen enough to yank it from his lax fingers. Although there was a good chance he wouldn't have responded even if they had.

Stan looked at his son, a shell, a locked box of secrets and trials. And he thought of another man who had held the bread for other people's survival. Kratz had been taken, mistreated, forever stolen from those who loved him. A leader, a lover, a friend. But his life, his sacrifice—his *family's* sacrifice—had not been in vain. *Could not be* in vain. He would be remembered. Emulated. Loved.

Stan reached into the bag of bread, pulled out a slice. Tore off a corner and cupped it in the palm of his hand. He turned, reaching out, offering the bit of crust.

Rose looked at it, considered it, and took it.

And then she took his hand.

AUTHOR'S NOTE

Stan Windemere is a product of my imagination. Clayton Kratz is not. In the fall of 1920 Clayton Kratz really did head off to the Crimea to help Mennonites suffering from the effects of the Russian Civil War, and he really did disappear there, leaving family and friends to mourn him for many years. Edith Miller, his fiancée, waited for ten years before moving on, marrying another man and having children. It is said that while she had a good marriage, she never forgot Clayton, and never stopped loving him. She told a family friend that she kept his picture in a drawer and looked at it every day. Clayton's family also felt his loss, the grief affecting even those who never knew him but experienced the lingering sadness of his siblings as they waited, hoping one day to see him walking back into the family.

The details of Clayton's life and disappearance that appear in this book are all real, excepting one. Senior Chief Borgman and I were not able to find the actual ship logs detailing Clayton's passage on the USS *Whipple*, but for storytelling purposes I took the liberty of adding them in. It is entirely possible the logs exist, but we have not yet been able to locate them. Other than that, you can take a look at any of the other works cited in this book and find them exactly as noted.

Mennonite Central Committee is also real—a vibrant, growing organization, offering hope and help to sufferers the world over. Founded in 1920, when Clayton Kratz left for Russia, MCC is still active wherever it can reach, from New Orleans to Africa to Ukraine. You can learn more at www.mcc.org.

If you visit Goshen, Indiana, you can find all of the places the book describes, with one exception. Ten Thousand Villages (www.tenthousandvillages.com) has moved from The Depot to Main Street. For my purposes it worked better to leave it in its old location.

BIBLIOGRAPHY

Bender, H. S. *Goshen College Maple Leaf*. Goshen, IN: Goshen
    College, 1918.
Bender, H. S. "Kratz, Clayton." *The Mennonite Encyclopedia*.
    3rd ed., 5 vols. Scottdale, PA: Herald Press, 1957.
Clayton Kratz: Can We Depend on You? Videocassette. Directed
    by John L. Ruth. Lederach, PA: Branch Valley Produce,
    1987.
Grassmyer, A. F. *Goshen College Maple Leaf*. Goshen, IN: Goshen
    College, 1921.
Gross Harder, Geraldine. *When Apples Are Ripe*. Scottdale, PA:
    Herald Press, 1971.
Miller, Orie O. Diary, September 2, 1920–March 1, 1921. Ts.
    Orie O. Miller Collection. Mennonite Church USA
    Archives, Goshen, IN.
Mumaw, Levi. General correspondence, August 1920–December
    1920. Russian Relief. Mennonite Church USA Archives,
    Goshen, IN.
Preheim, Rich. "After 80 Years—Diary Sheds Light on MCC

Kratz's Disappearance." *OurFaith Digest*, Spring 2001. www.OurFaithDigest.com (accessed December 15, 2006).

Sharp, John E., ed. *Gathering at the Hearth: Stories Mennonites Tell*. Scottdale, PA: Herald Press, 2001.

Shoup, Vernon D., ed. *Goshen College Maple Leaf*. Goshen, IN: Goshen College, 1920.

Shroud for a Journey: The Clayton Kratz Story. Videocassette. Directed by Sidney King. Performed by Julia Kasdorf, Tim Kennel, Sidney King, Katherine Lemons, Peter Eash Scott. Urbania Productions, 2001.

Slagel, Arthur W., ed. *Goshen College Maple Leaf*. Goshen, IN: Goshen College, 1919.

Weaver, Lois, ed. *Goshen College Maple Leaf*. Goshen, IN: Goshen College, 1960.

THE AUTHOR

Judy Clemens is the author of the Stella Crown mystery series of books and a playwright, and she has written for periodicals and short-story anthologies. She graduated from Goshen College with a degree in theater and has worked at theaters in Louisville, Kentucky, and Philadelphia. Clemens was born in Harrisonburg, Virginia, grew up in Goshen, Indiana, and now lives in Ottawa, Ohio. She and her husband and their two children attend Grace Mennonite Church.

.